DON'T GIVE A DWARF

DON'T GIVE A DWARF

DWARF BOUNTY HUNTER™ BOOK TWO

MARTHA CARR
MICHAEL ANDERLE

DISRUPTIVE IMAGINATION

This book is a work of fiction. All of the characters, organizations, and events portrayed in this novel are either products of the author's imagination or are used fictitiously. Sometimes both.

Copyright © LMBPN Publishing
Cover Art by Jake @ J Caleb Design
http://jcalebdesign.com / jcalebdesign@gmail.com
Cover copyright © LMBPN Publishing
A Michael Anderle Production

LMBPN Publishing
PMB 196, 2540 South Maryland Pkwy
Las Vegas, NV 89109

Version 1.01, November 2020
ebook ISBN: 978-1-64971-289-9
Paperback ISBN: 978-1-64971-290-5

THE DON'T GIVE A DWARF TEAM

Thanks to our JIT Team:

Jackey Hankard-Brodie
Diane L. Smith
Deb Mader
Jeff Goode
Dave Hicks
James Caplan
Dorothy Lloyd
Larry Omans
Paul Westman

If I've missed anyone, please let me know!

Editor
SkyHunter Editing Team

CHAPTER ONE

"Oh, man. This is amazing!" Amanda Coulier crouched in the bow of the flat-bottom airboat as it skimmed through the Everglades and she uttered a whoop of excitement.

Johnny Walker stood in front of the boat's massive propeller at the stern, his hand on the throttle control stick as he steered the craft around the fallen logs and clumps of reeds in the swamp. "The point of huntin' is to keep quiet, kid."

"Keep quiet?" The twelve-year-old laughed. "Are you kidding me? I'd be able to hear this boat from five, maybe even eight miles away."

On either side of the girl, Johnny's coonhounds Rex and Luther leaned into the wind. Their tails wagged furiously as their ears flapped along with their jowls.

Luther barked. "Because she's a shifter, Johnny."

"Yeah, shifters have that kinda hearing." Rex cocked his head at Amanda, who grinned at him and leaned forward over the bow so her face protruded farther over the surface of the water than the dogs' did.

The dwarf grunted. "Shifter or no, this ain't a pleasure cruise."

I can't believe I didn't think about hounds and shifters makin' friends when I made those collars.

"You could've fooled me." Amanda glanced over her shoulder at him, and her enthusiastic grin only widened.

He snorted and looked away into the thick growth of trees, but not before she caught his smirk. She turned again and crouched so low at the front of the airboat that her fingers touched the hull in front of her. She didn't seem bothered in the least by the mixture of salt and freshwater that sprayed into her face.

"All right, now." Johnny reduced the throttle, and the airboat's fan kicked down a few notches before it slowed to half its previous speed. "Y'all keep an eye out for any giant creatures that don't belong here. Or purple goo."

"Purple goo?" Amanda brushed her damp hair out of her eyes but didn't have to turn to shout for him to hear her now. "You said we were out here looking for that 'gator. The big one."

He scoffed. "Big one? Kid, a fifteen-foot 'gator ain't simply 'a big one.' That kinda game's a massive win, ya hear? Gonna make us enough jerky to last the rest of the boys' lifetime. Maybe we'll have a cookout."

"Johnny, you don't bring more than three people over at a time." Rex lowered his snout toward the water, sneezed at the salty spray, and shook his head vigorously.

"And that only happened once," Luther added. His claws scrabbled along the flat deck as he darted from port to starboard and sniffed at the swamp. He returned to his former place on the other side of Amanda and sat, and his tail thumped against the metal like a drum. "Not including us, Johnny."

"We're not people," Rex added.

The girl laughed and scratched the end of the larger hound's rump. "Tell *him* that."

"Ooh, Johnny. She's good."

"Yeah, *we're* good. Good people, Johnny. You hear that?"

"Girl, don't go puttin' that kinda thinkin' in their heads." The dwarf scratched his nose, hooked his free thumb through a belt loop, and tried to look stern. "Their brains can only hold so much as it is."

"Aw, you're pullin' our tails, Johnny." Rex sidled closer to her.

Luther sniffed her water-splashed shoulder and licked the slightly salty wetness from her cheek. "We all know you don't mean it."

"Including the part about having a cookout." Amanda scratched both hounds behind the ears. "That's like a barbeque, right?"

"Hold on now." Johnny reminded himself to not cut off the throttle completely and let the boat coast to a stop in the middle of nowhere. "Don't go confusin' cookouts for barbeques, kid. Ain't the same thing."

"Okay..." With a confused laugh, she brushed it aside. "Either way, I can't see you with a group of people in your front drive sitting around, eating, and drinking and having a good time."

"Naw. Folks'd come if I spread the word."

"I don't mean they wouldn't have a good time." She smirked at him over her shoulder. "Only that you wouldn't."

"Uh-huh." He eased into slow speed and steered them away from a giant tree hanging over the water in their path and the airboat's massive fan turned slowly to redirect them. *She sure thinks she has me all figured out, don't she?*

Luther barked again and his high-pitched laughter filled the dwarf's mind. "Man, Johnny. She's got you pinned down and tied up, huh?"

Panting, Rex searched the surface of the water breaking gently at the bow. His ears flopped from side to side against his face as his head whipped enthusiastically. "Watch out, Johnny. Next, she'll start guttin' you. All your hopes and dreams spillin' out right there where everyone can see—"

"Enough with the metaphors, boys." He snapped his fingers,

and even above the loud whir of the airboat's propellers, the hounds heard it and sat instantly on their haunches. Luther uttered a low whine and licked his muzzle, but that was it.

And now the hounds are in on it too. Great.

Amanda fought back a smirk as she returned to stroking the animals' backs. "You probably only want a pair of alligator-skin boots to go with your dry sense of humor."

The dogs thrust their heads into the air and howled—both literally and with laughter only Johnny and Amanda could hear.

The dwarf snorted a laugh and shook his head as he scanned the thick underbrush and pretended to be unamused. *Damn, kid.*

"I don't make boots outta big game like a fifteen-footer. Naw, I'm fixin' to have that beautiful bastard stuffed and mounted. Then Harold's movin' out."

"Oh, so you do name the trophies in your house." She forced a laugh back.

He cleared his throat. "Occasionally."

"You should stop trying so hard to keep secrets. I heard holding secrets in is as unhealthy as holding a fart in."

Rex and Luther laughed again and their tails thumped arrhythmically on the hull.

"Oh, yeah?" he asked with a smirk. "What brilliant philosopher o' bodily functions gave you that golden nugget?"

"My—" She grimaced and her smile faded instantly before she looked out over the swamp as they cruised across it. "Doesn't matter."

Shit. And there it is. Johnny sniffed and ran his free hand over his mouth, chin, and wiry red beard. He forced himself to not look at the kid. *I'd bet my truck she was about to say her sister or one of her folks.*

"Hey, hey. Come on, pup." Luther whined and licked the girl's face. "Don't think about it."

"Yeah, like me and Luther. That's what we do. Don't like thinkin' about somethin', sniff around and the good stuff'll catch your attention sooner or—" Rex whipped his head up and leaned toward the starboard side to sniff the air furiously. "Rabbit?"

"Big, *big* rabbit." Luther ran behind Amanda to join his brother at the side of the airboat and sniffed wildly too. "Three of 'em."

"Or y'all could focus on findin' the scent we're lookin' for. The 'gator." The dwarf snapped his fingers and both hounds immediately returned to the bow to sit on either side of the girl again.

"Right, right, right." Luther's head whipped from side to side as he scanned the swamp and sniffed like coonhounds did on the trail.

Rex panted, stared directly ahead, and blinked occasionally when water splashed into his face.

Amanda wiped the mist of water on her cheek—or maybe tears, Johnny thought, although it was hard to tell—and gazed with narrowed eyes at the thick stand of trees they passed. "If we're hunting an alligator, why'd you tell us to look out for a monster with purple goo?"

He shrugged. "It's always a good idea to check your front door first before steppin' out of it to go after somebody." *And to make sure the kid I took under my wing isn't more messed-up in the head than she lets on. A young'un her age can't go through everything she's been through and be perfectly fine after like nothin' ever happened. Right?*

She turned her head slowly and raised an eyebrow. "You honestly think there's a monster in the swamp?"

"There are all kindsa monsters in the swamp, kid. It merely depends on what kind you're lookin' for."

With a shrug, the girl turned toward the front of the boat and leaned forward again between the hounds.

Good. She's deflecting. It always works for me. She'll be fine.

"Ooh! Hey, pup." Luther turned toward the girl so quickly that his snout caught her shoulder and he snorted.

"Woah." She chuckled. "Someone's excited."

"That would be all of us," Rex agreed. "We're on the boat. Johnny took us on the freakin' boat."

"Yeah, but I was gonna—"

"It was more fun when we were goin' faster," the hound interrupted.

Luther inclined his head and completely forgot what he was about to say. Instead, he barked with excitement. "Yeah! Faster! Hey, Johnny. Make us go."

"No."

"Come on, Johnny. You know how many scents you can pick up when you're speedin' like that?"

"Of course he doesn't. We're the hounds." Rex panted and his tongue lolled from his open mouth.

"Lots and lots of scents, Johnny." Luther stood and spun in a tight circle. He made Amanda laugh when his tail whipped against the back of her head and dragged her damp hair across her face. "Let's go. Pick it up. Faster!"

"It *is* way more fun," she added to their pleas. "And there was less talking. I like more speed and less talking."

Aw, now she's tryin' to play to my soft spots.

Johnny grunted and jerked his chin at the hounds. "We slowed for a reason. And you know what? You boys ain't said a thing about where that 'gator went to for at least ten minutes."

"Oh. Yeah." Luther craned his neck to look at his master and panted. "That's 'cause we lost it."

"The scent, Johnny." Rex chuckled and lowered his head to sniff a tangle of waterlogged reeds that splashed up against the hull. "We lost the scent."

"You lost it." The dwarf stared at his hounds before he released a growled sigh and ran a hand through his dark-auburn hair. "It's like y'all've never been in a damn boat before."

"Not with her."

"The pup gets top priority, Johnny." Rex's tail thumped twice on the boat, then stilled. "That's what you said."

"Not when we're out lookin' for the—" Johnny darted an exasperated glance at the draping mangrove branches overhead and reduced the throttle until the fan slowed to a low hum. The airboat lost speed rapidly and its already small wake diminished across the swamp behind them.

This was supposed to be a done deal. Grab that fifteen-footer, show the kid what good clean fun looks like, and make sure she ain't broken and simply real good at hidin' it.

He shook his head at the hounds and gestured toward the swamp around them. "Well, go on, then. Better get to findin' it."

"Yeah, yeah. Find it." Luther headed portside while Rex went starboard and both dogs thrust their snouts in the air and sniffed madly. They crossed from one side of the craft to the other while their heads raised and lowered as if to smell from all angles. Amanda was whacked occasionally on the back of her head by a wayward tail before she finally scooted forward to the tip of the bow.

Johnny watched his hounds with a raised eyebrow while he turned the throttle control stick slowly when necessary to avoid the swamp's ever-present obstacles. They approached a branch of smaller tributaries, although they weren't so small that he couldn't maneuver his airboat through them. *But I gotta know which way to turn the damn thing.*

When a glance at his new watch—an all-black field watch to avoid having to give up another timepiece in a future Willen trade—told him the five-minute mark had passed, he cleared his throat.

"Y'all forget what you were doin'?"

"No way, Johnny." Rex glanced at his master, then crossed the boat again, his nose still sniffing industriously. "We're on it."

"Yeah. Lookin' for the…for the…shit. Rex, what were we lookin' for?"

Rex snorted and stared at his brother. Luther sat immediately, panting, and his tail thumped on the deck.

Johnny rolled his eyes. "And this was turnin' out to be a damn fine day. All right. We're turnin' around."

"No, Johnny. *No...* Come on." Luther padded toward his master, saw the look in the dwarf's eyes, and backed away two steps before he sat. "The boat's the best."

"Yeah, it's the best." Rex continued to scent the air. "We'll find the 'gator, Johnny."

"The 'gator!" Luther barked and spun and his paws slid across the slick deck in his enthusiasm. "We'll get him. Sink my teeth into him, too. I will, Johnny. Just—"

"No, you won't." His brother lowered his head over the side of the boat to sniff the water. "You barely made a dent in that turtle, remember?"

"Yeah, but a 'gator—"

"Wait." Amanda raised her hand and leaned forward until Johnny thought she'd fall face-first over the bow. She sniffed a few more times before she moved her raised hand to the right and she pointed. "It went that way."

He stared at her in surprise and ignored the way his hounds whipped their heads toward him to give him eager glances. "You sure, kid?"

She sat back on her heels and turned to raise her eyebrows at him. "Did you give yourself a canine's sense of smell too when you made those talking-to-your-dogs collars?"

"No." He sniffed a little sheepishly.

"Then yeah, I'm sure."

"She said she's sure, Johnny." Luther's head snapped upward and his gaze followed a flock of ducks overhead. "Probably means she's sure."

Rex snorted and pawed at the water as a dark shape swam beneath the surface. "Don't know why she'd lie about it. Unless she really, *really* hates you."

Amanda chuckled and tried to hide it with a serious expression and a curt nod. "The 'gator went that way."

Johnny looked from one hound to the next, both of them completely oblivious to his calculating gaze. *They ain't even tryin'.*

"All right. Her first time on a hunt and we're takin' the kid's advice." He pulled on the throttle control stick and shifted it to starboard to take them in the direction of her outstretched hand.

She grinned at him, turned quickly, and slapped both hands on the deck to lean into the breeze again. "I knew I'd be good at this."

Despite his frustration with the two wildly distracted coonhounds, he smirked. *There's more to huntin' than simply pickin' up a scent. We'll see how she handles the rest of it. If she ain't tellin' us to trail a damn fox instead.*

CHAPTER TWO

Johnny steered the craft toward the smaller tributary on the right, where the tree cover thinned a little and let more light in through the thick swamp foliage. Amanda scanned the water ahead of them, her face a picture of confidence.

"Hey!" Rex stood with his tail pointing straight out behind him.

Luther did the same. "'gator!"

"Johnny, this is it. Found the trail."

Rex sniffed the air again and rumbled a low growl. "Damn, she's good, Johnny."

The dwarf expected her to turn at any moment and flash him an I-told-you-so grin, but the young shifter was as intensely focused on their quarry's trail as the hounds.

"Noses up, boys." He centered the airboat directly downstream and nodded. "Let's bring this beautiful bastard home."

They moved slowly along the waterlogged reeds for another ten minutes and all four of them listened for a 'gator's warning hiss or splash in the water. The rhythmic buzz of cicadas, birdsong, and the occasional flutter and rustle through the branches meant that they had to focus to discern what they were looking for.

"Slow down," Amanda muttered.

Johnny almost laughed. "You get somethin' else, kid?"

"Yeah. I think…"

"On the right, Johnny." Luther skittered portside and his snout pointed directly at the soggy bank. "Trail goes up there."

"That's left, dummy." Rex echoed his brother's enthusiasm and his tail wagged a fraction of an inch before it stuck out rigidly behind him. "Left, Johnny. There under the trees. It's real strong now."

The girl nodded, her eyes wide as she sniffed the air and turned her whole body to face the left-hand bank.

"All right." The dwarf killed the throttle and turned the slowing propeller to direct their course toward land. When the fan cut out, all the other sounds around them seemed so much louder than before. *There's nothin' like the buzz of the Everglades. Someone should put this on a sound loop. Show all the city folk what they're missin'.*

"Johnny, it's right there," Luther whispered with a low, barely audible whine. His paws clicked eagerly on the deck as he tried and failed to hold still. "See it?"

Rex grunted. "I see it, Luther. Shut up."

Johnny squinted at the shoreline, and sure enough, the fifteen-footer came into focus. The beast lay with its belly in the mud, concealed behind tall reeds rising from the bank in an open patch of sunlight beneath the muggy heat.

"Yeah, I see it too," he whispered. "Hold steady, boys. We're almost there."

Fortunately, he'd aimed the airboat in the right direction so it would reach the shore about twenty feet from the resting 'gator —fifteen feet of crushing jaws and powerful claws and prehistoric scales. *Fuck yes. It's about damn time.*

Amanda was breathing heavily in her excitement. "So what's the plan?" she whispered.

"As soon as we reach the bank, the boys go first." The dwarf nodded at her despite the fact that she hadn't moved her fixed gaze from the reptile. "You can join 'em if you want. But wait until we hit—"

A howl rose from downriver, high and trembling before it subsided into a growl. Half a dozen other voices joined it and the intrusion snapped the girl out of her intense concentration. She inclined her head and her eyes widened. "Shifters."

Damn. And they're close.

"Don't you mind 'em, kid. We're on the hunt, so—"

The shifters howled again, and she lurched forward along the bow.

"If you throw yourself off this boat, kid, we lose the element of—"

"I have to go." Her knuckles grew white as she grasped the edge. "Johnny, they're so close. Can you hear them?"

"Yeah, I can hear 'em. Focus."

A wild, inviting yip rose from the shifters miles downriver.

Amanda lost the final remnants of her control. She shifted and her clothes fell around the body of a small gray wolf before she leapt the last three feet over the water and landed in a squelch of mud.

"Damnit. Amanda!" Johnny hissed in frustration but she was gone and now rushed directly toward the 'gator's nest in the reeds. Mud and twigs flurried behind her as she raced past in a blur of gray.

The 'gator startled and lurched toward her. Its enormous mouth opened wide and it uttered a fierce hiss. The airboat thumped against the riverbank, and Rex and Luther bounded from the boat, baying as they closed in on their quarry.

"Amanda!" the dwarf shouted.

More howls came from the shifter pack, and she stopped

briefly to orient herself. In the next moment, the damn kid splashed into the river and slipped on the muddy bottom as she tried to reach the other side.

Rex and Luther darted toward their quarry, but not before the monster thrashed its tail violently and scrabbled toward the water after the small gray wolf who now paddled across.

"Damnit!" The dwarf snatched up his break-action rifle and slung it over his head and shoulder. He scowled and jammed the safety on the harpoon gun he'd rigged with a net and jerked it sideways toward the 'gator that now slithered down the mud toward the water.

A loud thump resulted when he pulled the trigger, and the net flew end over end before it struck his target and tangled in its claws.

"Good shot, Johnny!" Rex bayed again and scrambled along the muddy bank.

"We'll take it from here. We got this one!" Luther howled and fell halfway into the swamp before he righted himself and sprinted toward the 'gator.

The beast thrashed in the net and hissed angrily as it launched massive sprays of water around it.

"Forget the 'gator, boys." Johnny leapt off the boat and paused briefly when another chorus of howls issued through the Everglades. Downriver, Amanda kicked against a fallen tree covered in thick green growth and changed direction again to return toward the left-hand bank.

"But you got it, Johnny."

"Yeah, we can finally—"

"I said leave it." He tugged as much of the airboat as he could onto the shore, left it with a snarl, and hefted the rifle that dangled at his chest. "Follow the kid."

"Aw, man."

"That's a bigass 'gator, Johnny."

The dwarf responded with a piercing whistle and pointed as

the last traces of Amanda's gray fur vanished behind the reeds and the thick, sodden underbrush.

"Yeah, yeah. Fine."

"Get the pup."

Both hounds swung away from the thrashing reptile and headed after the shifter girl, hot on her scent.

He cast his quarry a longing glance. One gleaming yellow-brown eye flashed him a venomous look and the massive creature uttered another hiss as it tried to shake the net off. As he trudged up the slippery bank, the dwarf tightened his hold on the rifle and growled with annoyance.

I almost had him. There's no way that net will hold. And no way he won't see me comin' next time either. Big motherfucker like that gotta have some brains.

The shifter pack howled again, this time a little closer, and Johnny stormed through the muddy reeds after his hounds.

Rex and Luther darted through the growth and across water-logged mounds of earth, splashing as they ran and sniffed Amanda's trail.

"We won't let her get away, Johnny." Rex panted.

"Pup's never been out here," Luther added. "She'll get lost for sure. But we'll find her."

"Stay on her, boys." He trotted after them while he checked that his rifle had a round in the chamber. Satisfied, he swung the barrel up again with a click. *She's fast, I'll give her that. I hope we're fast enough to get her before those damn shifters do.*

Having to constantly duck under tree limbs did nothing to improve his mood but he picked up the pace. As best he could, he ignored the thick swarms of gnats clustered around his face and the dangling vines and huge leaves that slapped against his body as he moved.

"Almost there, Johnny."

"So close. And she's—" Luther barked. "She found 'em."

They raced through another thick stand of reeds and a wall of cattails rising from the swamp. When they emerged on the other side, Johnny raised his rifle and aimed it at the six wolves who stood on a dry, sunny berm.

Luther and Rex skidded to a halt, panting heavily as their tails wagged. "Found her, Johnny."

"There she is."

Amanda stood halfway between the thick cattails and the small pack of Florida shifters. She paced from one side to the other as she uttered short, excited yips.

The six wolves bared their teeth at him and the hounds. The huge, mud-splattered alpha stood slightly in front of the others and growled.

"Back away from the girl." The rifle didn't exactly aim at any of the wolves, but it wouldn't take much to swing it in any direction and aim true. "She ain't tryin' to cause trouble."

Amanda continued her almost frenetic moment. She now panted in excitement and brimmed with nervous energy.

The wolf at the back of the pack sat and licked its muzzle.

"Yeah, that one thinks you're full of shit," Rex interpreted.

Behind the alpha, a dirty-white wolf paced in a short line.

Luther grunted. "Yeah, and that one wants to rip your arm off."

The dwarf ignored the canine peanut gallery, swung the rifle's barrel slightly to the side, and nodded in that direction. "Go on now. I don't want trouble either."

The mud-splattered alpha with blazing yellow eyes glanced at Amanda, snorted, and shifted where he stood. A huge man with soaked leaves, mud, and twigs matted in his disheveled hair stood on the berm in front of his pack, all rippling abs and bulging pecs and bare-ass naked.

"Aw, come on." Johnny rolled his eyes and looked away. "No one wants to see that."

The man raised an eyebrow. "You got a thing against shifters, dwarf?"

"Naw. Merely someone else's junk in my swamp."

The other wolves growled behind their alpha and their hackles raised.

"Woah, you pissed 'em off, Johnny." Rex took two halting steps toward Amanda, his ears back against his head as he snarled.

"Yeah. They don't know it's your swamp." Luther stalked slowly to the right and glared at the wolves.

The naked man tilted his head and glanced at the hounds. "We don't take kindly to two-legs tellin' us where and when we can run."

"I don't give a rat's ass where y'all run," Johnny all but snarled and swung his rifle to aim squarely at the man's glistening chest. "As long as it ain't with the kid. You stay away from her, ya hear?"

The shifter's upper lip curled in a snarl. "Why're you stompin' 'round after a pup, huh? She ain't a dwarf. And you got enough hair on ya but you sure as shit ain't no shifter."

"She's my responsibility." He didn't bat an eyelid. "Simple as that."

After he'd scratched vigorously behind his ear and dislodged a clump of mud that splattered at his feet, the alpha studied him for a moment before he sniggered. "Big responsibility for a little guy."

"Watch it, pal."

The rest of the pack studied Amanda hungrily and some of them joined the beta in short, aggravated pacing.

Rex lowered his head and growled softly. "Say the word, Johnny."

"We'll bury 'em for you." Luther lowered his head to sniff something on the ground, then whipped it up again quickly to glare at the wolves.

"I said git." He jerked his head to gesture out of the clearing again, but his rifle didn't move from its steady aim at the alpha's chest.

The huge shifter raised a hand to settle his pack and narrowed his eyes at Johnny. "You got shit fer brains, dwarf, but the kid's got spirit. She needs a pack who can show her how to use it. How to grow more than five feet tall."

"Five-two, asshole." He grunted obdurately. "The kid ain't comin' with you."

"No. She found us all on her own." The alpha's mouth twitched and his gaze settled on the gray wolf. She stopped pacing and stared at him. "We can show her what a real wolf can be. Girl needs a family."

"She has one."

When the naked man stepped toward Amanda, Johnny fired his rifle at the ground two inches from his feet. A spray of soggy, matted reeds and mud splattered the alpha's body, and the pack snarled as one.

The dwarf regarded him calmly with an unyielding expression and the wolves growled a low chorus of displeasure. He stepped forward and aimed higher on the alpha's chest. "Don't make me say it again. I don't like repeating myself."

Ignoring everything but Amanda, the naked man inclined his head toward her and nodded. "You know where to find us, girl, whenever your master lets you off that leash. But don't let him put you in a cage too."

In the next moment, he shifted into a shaggy wolf splattered with even more mud and turned to Johnny with an angry snarl. The rest of his pack echoed the sentiment and they tensed as they snapped their jaws and growled, waiting for their alpha's command.

"Johnny, we should go." Rex glared at the shifters.

"Yeah, they're itchin' for a fight. That's what that means." Luther took a step closer to his brother.

"I know what it fuckin' means. Amanda."

She turned briefly to look at him and her tail lowered slowly.

"It's time to go."

"We'll hold 'em off if we have to, Johnny." Rex snarled again and the alpha took two warning steps forward.

"We've been in way more fights than they have."

The dwarf ignored them, his gaze fixed on the alpha. "Now, kid."

She sat on the wet ground and whined.

"Get back in the boat. We're goin' home."

With a final glance at the pack, the small gray wolf stood and turned to head toward him. He gestured behind him at the thick wall of cattails, and she trotted hesitantly through them but glanced over her shoulder multiple times.

Johnny kept his rifle trained on the pack leader as he stepped slowly backward. Rex and Luther paced in front of him and passed each other constantly as their master retreated through the reeds.

"Yeah, you think you're so scary, huh?" Luther growled. "But who's got the gun, assholes?"

The alpha snarled, bounded forward, and skidded across the slippery trampled underbrush.

"Johnny does!" The hound darted through the cattails as the pack snarled and moved forward after their alpha.

Rex glanced at Johnny who continued through the reeds. "Luther has a point—"

The dwarf's whistle cut him off and he pushed through the rustling cattails after his brother. Narrowing his eyes, Johnny directed a final warning glance at the growling pack members before only the barrel of his gun poked through the reeds. After a moment, it disappeared.

As he trudged quickly through the swamp after his dogs, the pack filled the air with long, high-pitched howls that moved rapidly away in the opposite direction. Amanda stopped and looked at him with surprisingly expressive puppy-dog eyes. He pointed at her. "The boat."

She turned slowly and trotted through the underbrush as she

sniffed easily along the trail her new family had blazed to find her.

The airboat had drifted slightly offshore from where Johnny had pulled it up as far as he could, but it was still there. *Gotta love low tide.*

Amanda boarded first, followed by the hounds, and none of them said a word.

Johnny stamped one boot onto the bow, turned to sweep his rifle across the swamp, then shoved the corner of the airboat off the bank and jumped aboard. He left the rifle strapped around his chest as he settled in the stern and turned the throttle.

The propeller whirred to life, and he shoved the control stick to make a tight turn on the river. Amanda shifted into her human form and snatched her clothes up hastily. The dwarf and both hounds turned away to give her as much privacy as possible as the airboat increased speed. Its humming fan streaked them upriver and the hull bounced slightly and skimmed the water.

When the girl finished dressing, she walked quickly toward Johnny at the stern and maintained her balance easily despite their speed. "You said I could go wherever I wanted as long as I told you."

He scowled upriver, unable to look at her. "That wasn't—"

"I told you I had to go meet them."

"It's not what I meant, kid." He finally looked at her, and his scowl softened at the sight of the angry flush that raced up her neck and into her cheeks. *I can't blame her for being who she is. But not like this.* "If you wanna find a pack, you do it on your own time. And preferably not in the swamps."

Her hair fluttered on either side of her face and she folded her arms. "Why?"

"The Everglades has far more than most folks give it credit for. But the shifters here? They play into all the stereotypes—the redneck kind." He cleared his throat. "Weird family shit."

She scoffed and shook her head.

Johnny had to look away. "And now that 'gator knows we're after him. So thanks."

"That's not my fault."

When he didn't say anything, she whirled away from him and stormed toward the bow as she swiped her hair out of her face with an angry hand. The hounds had lowered to their bellies to lie on the deck for the return trip without the game they'd come for. Neither of them said anything as she brushed past them and took her seat again and crossed her legs beneath her. This time, her shoulders were hunched and all her previous excitement over an airboat ride through the Everglades had been snuffed out.

The dwarf rubbed a hand over his mouth and beard and shook his head. *Kids. She'll get over it.*

Luther inched toward her on his belly. "It's all good, pup. We'll get that 'gator next time."

"Yeah, next time, Johnny." Rex looked at his master and panted. "Not like he's goin' anywhere. Except for maybe a new nest."

"We'll find that too."

"Johnny." Rex's tail thumped once on the deck. "Hey, lighten up. She's only a pup. Remember when Luther and I—"

He snapped his fingers and both hounds stared at him. "That's enough, boys."

I don't need two coonhounds tellin' me to go soft when she can hear every damn word of it. There's no way to come out on top in that scenario—not that I ever will with a twelve-year-old headstrong shifter goin' on twenty.

CHAPTER THREE

The second Johnny pulled the airboat up to the dock behind his cabin, Amanda stormed onto the creaking wood and trudged across the grass toward the house. Rex and Luther darted after her as he tied the boat up.

"Man, I'm hungry." Luther looked at the girl as he trotted beside her. "You hungry, pup? No 'gator jerky, but I bet Johnny's got treats in the fridge."

"Yeah, he always does." Rex caught up on the girl's other side. "You like pickles."

"Ooh, pickles. And roast beef. One time, Johnny dropped a whole package of roast beef although he was fast enough to snatch it up." Luther uttered a high-pitched giggle. "Rex almost had a roast beef and dwarf-hand sandwich."

The bounty hunter swung the strap of his rifle over his head and carried it in one hand. He ran the other vigorously through his thick head of hair as he followed them to the front of the house.

It's gonna be an awkward fuckin' afternoon now. Serves me right for thinkin' I could lay down vague ground rules. I'm outta practice.

The hounds stopped beside the front porch and their tails

wagged as they stared after Amanda who strode down the dirt drive. "Where you goin', pup?"

"Hey, the fridge is inside!"

"I'm going to Darlene's." She didn't turn to gauge Johnny's reaction, but he didn't seem to have one.

"Johnny, she said she's goin' to Darlene's." Rex spun and trotted dutifully at his master's side. "She's going."

"She's gone." Luther whined and hurried after his brother to slip through the screen door before it swung shut with a creak and a bang behind them. "Want us to bring her back?"

"No. If she wants to head off on her own, that's fine. Ain't a safer place for her around here than Darlene's." *Except for this house and I ain't keepin' her in a cage. Fuck that alpha.*

He shoved the front door open, gave the hounds five seconds to scramble inside after him, then closed it and headed to his workshop. The dogs' claws clicked across the wooden floor after his heavy footsteps.

"Hey, that means more pickles and roast beef for us, right?" Rex lowered his nose to the floor and sniffed in a wide circle.

"Or at least some cheese. Hey, Johnny. Did you feed us this morning?"

"I feed you every morning." The dwarf placed the break-action rifle on the shelf beside his worktable and retrieved the heavy-duty crossbow he'd been working on instead. "I'm workin' now, boys. If you ain't fixin' to lie down and be quiet, go on outside."

"Ooh, outside." Luther's ears pricked and he stared at his brother. "It's been forever since we were outside."

"Race ya." Rex barked once and streaked past Johnny, through the kitchen, and around to the back.

"Hey! Not fair." Luther scrambled after him. "I wasn't ready."

"You're just slow!"

The dog door clacked open and closed behind them, followed

by their twin baying howls as they set off in pursuit of some creature.

Johnny lifted the huge tackle box he used for his tools from under the worktable and thunked it noisily on the surface. *The kid will be fine at Darlene's. They'll look after her there. Or at least they know who to call if they think she's fixin' to stir up more trouble.*

"That's how people are," he grumbled and snapped the lid open. "Folks look out for each other." He found his pliers and pick set and dumped them beside the tackle box. "Keep each other away from fucking shifter packs tryin' to steal little girls."

With a grunt, he slammed his palms on the worktable and hung his head. *Pull it together, Johnny. You're doin' the best you can.*

He took a deep breath, rubbed his mouth and beard with a sniff, then selected the other tools he needed. Still scowling, he slid the hulking black crossbow toward him, turned it over, and studied the barrel before he walked to the shelf to pull down the box of bolts he'd tinkered with over the last two weeks.

You can bet your ass a crossbow does a hell of a lot more than guns goin' after some slimy goo monster. Plus a few magi-tech improvements.

The dwarf opened the box of crossbow bolts and withdrew the red one on top. With one of his long picks, he activated the device on the bolt's tip and watched the red light blink slowly. *The tracker's still a good bet.*

With a sniff of irritation, he placed it beside the crossbow and scowled again. "What the hell does an Oriceran monster think it's gonna get by blowin' resorts and gas stations up?"

"Johnny!" Rex barked furiously and burst through the dog door. "She's here, Johnny."

Luther leapt through behind his brother. His rear leg caught and tripped him into a pile of squirming hound before he scrabbled to his feet and raced into the workshop. "Let her in, Johnny. Come on."

"Who?"

"Lisa!"

"Man, oh man. Wonder what she ate today." The hounds raced to the door. "Bet it's somethin' good, Rex."

"She wouldn't look like that if she ate chips and M&Ms all day."

"Hey, I like chips. Johnny, why don't you ever let us have M&Ms?"

He pushed away from the worktable and strode to the window beside the door. "Besides the fact that I don't eat crap? You boys get into enough you ain't supposed to as it is."

"And it's chocolate, man." Rex sat at the front door and whined. "Idiot."

"Oh." Luther spun in quick circles beside his brother, who backed away and sat again two feet behind him. "Well, let her in, Johnny. Come on. I miss her. *You* miss her."

"Quiet." He snapped his fingers as he peered through the sliver of curtain over the window. Both hounds obeyed. The sky-blue Camry rolled to a halt in the drive and he tugged the curtain closed again before he returned to his workshop. "Let her be, boys."

"But Johnny. She's here."

Johnny ignored them and tried to focus on the new crossbow bolts he'd been building. The tips held empty chambers he mostly filled with explosives but could hold anything at this point. He merely didn't know what he needed yet to fight an incendiary monster that currently splattered purple goo on a rampage across Florida's waterways and shorelines.

"Johnny, she's on the porch."

"She's at the door."

The dwarf closed his eyes. *I'm not in the mood for visitors but at least it ain't Nelson about to knock on my door.*

Agent Lisa Breyer didn't knock. She simply turned the handle on the front door and let herself in.

"Hey, lady!" Luther's tail wagged furiously and caught Rex in the face as his brother joined him at the open doorway. "Bring us anything?"

"Ooh, legs." Rex licked the woman's bare leg and snorted. "Woah. Easy on the lotion, lady."

"Hey, lemme try."

Lisa chuckled and closed the door behind her before she held a hand out to each of the hounds. "Hey, boys. Good to see you too."

Hidden from view in his workshop, the dwarf rolled his eyes.

"Johnny?" She sidled around the dogs who sniffed her enthusiastically and moved slowly through the house. "Are you home? I saw both your cars outside, so I assumed—"

He snorted. "What you drove is a car. I have a truck and Sheila. And simply because they're both out front don't mean I'm inside."

Lisa rounded the corner into the workshop and smirked when she saw him tinkering at the worktable. "Right. You also have a boat."

"And two legs. Sometimes a guy merely likes to walk—" Johnny paused when he saw her, scrutinized her in silence, and finally snorted. "Where'd you find *that* getup?"

"What?" She spread her arms and looked at her outfit—Daisy Dukes with frayed hems, a washed-out tank top in green-and-brown camo, and black calf-high boots that gave her already tall form an extra two inches. The wide-brimmed cream cowboy hat slid forward over her long brown hair, and she pushed it back with a smirk. "What's wrong with my...uh, getup?"

He raised an eyebrow. "Half of you is in Florida and the other half's in Texas, and those boots won't do shit to keep your feet dry."

She smirked at him and placed her hands on her hips. "My feet are perfectly dry, thank you."

"Yeah, after rollin' up in your *car*." He shook his head and tried to hold back a chuckle as he returned his attention to the crossbow bolts and his tinkering. "You'll stick out like a sore thumb in all that."

"You don't like it?"

"That's not what I said, darlin'." *Those legs go on forever.*

Lisa tweaked the wide brim of her hat and stepped into the workshop to stand on the other side of the table. "Well, I'm trying a new look."

"So it seems."

"And I wanted to check in with you about the case."

"Uh-huh."

A little impatient now, she drummed her fingertips on the table and watched him fit new hollow tips onto half a dozen bolts. "The department's getting a little nervous about how long this one is taking you."

Unperturbed, he picked the tracker bolt up and pressed the pick into the side to turn it off again. "It's been two weeks."

"Yeah, and Johnny Walker doesn't take two weeks for monsters."

"It isn't time-sensitive until that creature strikes again." He studied the bolt tip, then tilted it forward to point it playfully at her. "Once it does, we'll be hot on its trail. I ain't seen hair or hide of it. There's no point in runnin' around like a lone—" *Don't say wolf, Johnny. Come on. Too soon.* "Like a lunatic huntin' a creature I don't understand. The next time it blows something up with that purple goo, I aim to check out what's left and get more info."

"But if it happens to pop up in front of you, you'll eliminate it, right?"

He plunked the bolt down and hooked his thumbs through his belt loops. "I thought you knew me, darlin'."

Lisa smirked and gave him a playful shrug. "I'm merely making sure."

"But that ain't likely to happen—the monster rollin' up to my front door. I gotta know what I'm dealin' with so I know what gear to bring. And that report in Nelson's little file wasn't especially informative."

"Yeah, I know."

"Quit worryin' about it. Look." Johnny went to the shelf and fiddled with one of the dials on a long black box beside his usable rifle collection. A hum of static and shriek of changing radio frequencies filled the workshop. "I built this myself."

The speakers crackled. "...have a report of a break-in on Copeland Avenue. All units in the area, please respond to dispatch..."

He turned the dial again and the box fell silent.

"You built your own police scanner." She folded her arms.

"Well, don't look *that* surprised." He patted the top of the box. "This baby taps into reports and dispatch all over the state of Florida. I had to widen the radar and it's rigged to pick up certain keywords."

"Yeah, okay."

"You know, like monster, creature, Oriceran, goo—"

"Johnny, I get it."

He sniggered and returned to the worktable. "A little time to sit back and enjoy life never hurt anyone. You should try it sometime."

"I enjoy life."

"Uh-huh. I reckon you do." He peered into his tackle box and retrieved a smaller pair of pliers to help him wriggle one of the bolts' hollow caps free. "Any news from Nelson about my daughter's case?"

Lisa tilted her chin and frowned at him. "He's doing that for you, Johnny. Why would he tell me about it?"

A crooked smile spread above his red beard. "'Cause he's head-over-heels for you, darlin'."

"Oh, come on." She rolled her eyes but paused when he flicked his gaze up to meet hers. "What? You can't be serious."

"You can't be that clueless."

Lisa scowled at him but couldn't completely hide a small smile. "No, Johnny. I haven't heard anything from Nelson beyond, 'Tell Johnny to hurry up. The department's getting antsy.'"

"All right." He inclined his head in acknowledgment. *At least she's humble about it.*

He worked silently for a moment, and Lisa exhaled a long sigh. She leaned toward the doorway out of the workshop and scanned his empty living room. "Where's Amanda?"

"Darlene's." He grunted. "As soon as I'm done with a few adjustments to this crossbow, I'll head out and pick her up."

"You let her run around here on her own?"

The dwarf detached the scope from the crossbow and peered into it. "She can handle herself." *Except when she's out on a boat, it seems.* "I thought we settled that when we brought her here."

"She's still a kid, Johnny."

"It doesn't make what she's been through any less real." He sniffed, adjusted the lens on the scope, and twisted it onto the crossbow's mount. "Runnin' around this part of town is a hell of a lot safer than where she grew up. Folks'll keep an eye on her exactly like folks kept an eye on me when I was raised."

"That was a long time ago."

"Careful."

Lisa chuckled. "I only mean nowhere is as safe as it used to be. Even out here in the Everglades, things change."

"Not that much. Not here." He took another box from the shelf and opened it to remove more bolt tips in three different weights and point sizes. His expression focused, he placed them on the worktable one by one. *If I quit talkin' about the girl, she'll change the subject all on her own.*

"What are those?"

Bingo. Johnny fought back a smile. "Upgrades."

"For a crossbow?"

"You've never used one of these, have you?" He glanced at her and lifted one of the bolt tips filled with a glowing yellow liquid. "Explosive."

"Of course it is." Lisa rolled her eyes playfully.

"I call the stuff in here Boom 3. It won't take a bastard's arm off but it will leave a hole that makes him wish he had no arm."

"And how many...uh, boom levels are there?"

"I think you can guess."

She narrowed her eyes. "Six."

"Damn straight."

"You know what? You pretend to be fed up with this whole 'return to bounty hunting' scenario, but it's hard to take seriously when a level-six bounty hunter still has six different strengths of —" She snorted. "Boom."

"Do you know how many the department had for me when I started?"

"I can't even begin to guess."

He raised a finger. "One. Only one goddamn type of explosive, and it didn't even work half the time. All the shit their so-called experts came up with was like handin' Crayola markers to Michelangelo and sayin', 'Go ahead. Do your thing but make it better than everyone else.'"

Lisa folded her arms and a smile appeared but vanished almost instantly. "That's a surprisingly cultured reference coming from you."

"You gotta know the masters if you're gonna compare yourself to one." He cleared his throat. "The department wouldn't disagree with me either."

"And they gave you the go-ahead to make your own gear and ignore theirs?"

"No. They quit tryin' to stop me when they realized I could take the best tech they had to offer and improve it ten times over. I have patents on most of this now. I ain't lettin' the feds get their greedy paws on these babies." He lifted another bolt tip, this one filled with a swirling silver liquid, and raised his eyebrows at Agent Breyer. "No offense."

"None taken. It looks like you haven't lost your touch after fifteen years."

"We all have our gifts, darlin'."

"Mm-hmm." She studied him openly from the other side of the table, and a small divot formed in her bottom lip when she bit the edge of it.

Johnny tried to ignore the speculative look in her eyes. *I didn't mean it like that, but okay.*

"Well, I'm glad to see you're ready to find this monster."

"I took the case. That's all there is to it. And I'll keep takin' 'em until Nelson brings me that goddamn file I know I haven't seen half of."

"For the sake of everyone else who's about to get Johnny Walker's help, I hope it takes him a while to find it." When he looked quickly at her with a scowl, she added, "For your sake, I hope it's sooner."

"Yup." He sniffed and returned to the bolt tips. *Real backhanded way to wish me luck.*

"My offer still stands, by the way."

He didn't look up at her as he worked, using various tools to deftly put the finishing touches on his work. "Yeah, I know." *One thing at a time, Johnny. Nice and easy.*

They fell into silence as Lisa watched him, and the cabin suddenly seemed too quiet.

Johnny looked up from his work and leaned sideways to peer into the hall. "What are those hounds up to?" He whistled shrilly. "Boys?"

Luther barked beneath the worktable. "Right here, Johnny."

The dwarf stepped back and tilted his head. The coonhounds lay side by side beneath the table and stared at him.

"Been here the whole time." Rex whined and licked his muzzle. "You didn't know?"

Frowning, he glanced at Lisa, who smiled at him. He shook his head. "I must have been real focused."

"Or distracted." Luther crawled forward on his belly and stared at his master. "You look distracted."

"You look pissed, Johnny."

"Yeah. You know what helps? Roast beef."

With a snort, he snapped his fingers and pointed to the back of the cabin. "All right. Go on, now."

"For roast beef?"

"Hey, Luther. I saw him throw an empty peanut butter jar in the trash this morning. Let's go—"

"Out."

The dogs slowly rose from beneath the table and their tails wagged expectantly despite their lowered heads. "Maybe if we're real quiet—"

"Last chance to get outside and stay outside before I lock you in the house while I go fetch the girl."

"Aw, man." Rex licked his muzzle and sniffed the floor before he trotted after Luther toward the back door. "You're coming back soon, Johnny, right? 'Cause we—"

The dog door clacked open and shut, and Luther's loud baying broke the silence. "Rex! Biggest squirrel I've ever seen! Holy shit!"

His brother bounded through the kitchen and disappeared outside.

Johnny shook his head and started to pack his tools. The tackle box went back to its place under the worktable but the crossbow, bolts, and interchangeable tips remained laid out neatly on the surface. He straightened a bolt that had rolled away from the others, then nodded toward the front door. "I gotta see a friend about a kid. You can come if you want."

"Great." Lisa jumped when both hounds bayed wildly in the back.

"Woah, watch out!" Rex shouted. "Hey, that's a raccoon, you moron."

"Get it!"

The dwarf snorted as he strode toward the front door.

She smiled curiously at him. "What?"

"Nothin'." He opened the door, held it, and gestured for her to step out ahead of him.

She inclined her head and tilted the brim of her out-of-place cowboy hat. "Mighty kind of you."

Hissing a laugh, Johnny pulled the door shut behind him and headed after her down the porch. "I hope that was a bad joke on purpose."

"Maybe."

"Well, lose the hat at least. Or the joke's on both of us."

With a frown, she removed the offending headgear, stared at it for a moment, then set it on the hood of her rented Camry before she turned to Johnny.

The dwarf was already climbing into Sheila's driver's seat.

"No...Johnny, can't we take the truck or something?"

"Feel free to walk, darlin'. I'm happy to pick you up along the road on the way back."

With a laugh, Agent Breyer rolled her eyes and ran a hand through her long dark hair as Sheila's diesel engine revved to life. She clambered into the passenger seat, which bounced wildly as she sat. "You wouldn't make me walk."

"Turn your nose up at Sheila? You bet."

He accelerated out of the dirt lot at the end of his drive and smirked when she shrieked and braced herself against the Jeep's interior.

CHAPTER FOUR

A huge cloud of dust puffed up behind the red Jeep as Johnny pulled to a stop outside Darlene's trailer-turned-diner. Lisa steadied herself on the passenger seat, then hopped out to create a much smaller puff of dust beneath her boots.

He raised an eyebrow as he studied her briefly. "It didn't take you long to get your Jeep legs."

"Jeep legs. Ha." She raked a hand through her wind-whipped hair and looked warningly at him. "I wouldn't have to get them if you drove like a normal person."

"Aw, come on, darlin'." He grinned as he turned away from her toward the raised trailer's staircase. "If I did normal, I reckon you wouldn't keep comin' around."

"Uh-huh. Except for the fact that I've technically spent the last two weeks on temporary leave, waiting to join you on this next case."

"And that there might not *be* a case. Ain't nothin' wrong with my drivin', anyway."

She snorted and followed him up the narrow staircase toward the front door.

The dim light of Darlene's under-the-radar Southern diner

and a raucous howl of laughter greeted them. Johnny frowned at the two tables pushed together in the center of the trailer, where eight locals gathered around a grinning Amanda, beers or glasses of iced tea in their hands.

The girl's smile faded when she saw him before her gaze flicked toward Agent Breyer behind him. "Lisa!"

"Hey, kid."

"Speak of the goddamn devil." Arthur raised his beer bottle toward Johnny with a snicker and his white handlebar mustache fluttered around his lips. "And his name's Johnny Walker."

"Come on, Arthur." Johnny walked along the bar and rapped the edge of it absently with his knuckles. "Y'all got way better things to talk about."

"Not us, Johnny," Tripp Bolton said on the other side of the table. He stroked his wiry black beard and chuckled. "But Amanda here's been sharin' some stories we ain't never heard before."

Another round of laughter rose from the table, and the girl stared at him as she lowered her mouth to the straw that protruded from an antique milkshake glass.

"You wrackin' up a tab for me already, kid?"

"On the house, Johnny." Darlene slid a double Johnny Walker Black neat across the bar toward him and nodded toward the combined tables and the girl entertaining the diner's regulars. "For the girl, everything might be on the house."

"Thanks, Darlene." He glanced at the whiskey and shook his head. "Ain't drinkin' right now."

"You might want to." The diner's owner chuckled and swiped loose hairs and a sheen of sweat from her forehead with her thick wrist. "I don't think they're gonna let you live this one down."

He leaned sideways against the bar. "What'd she do?"

"Hey, Johnny!" Harry Gooden shouted, his graying beard flecked with beer foam. "Sing any Katy Perry lately?"

The old-timers around the table chuckled.

"Betcha feel real nice after an aria in the shower and in those nice, tight pair o' silk briefs, eh?"

The table exploded in another round of laughter. Darlene chuckled and her chest and shoulders bounced as she wiped her grill-cook hands on her already stained apron. She tried to lose the smile on her face when he darted her sidelong glance. He turned toward Amanda. "I thought I told you to stay out of my room."

The girl stared at him and the only sound in the diner was the rattling slurp of her sucking the last of her drink through the straw. She popped the straw out of her mouth and shrugged. "They were hanging on the clothesline."

With a growl, he turned to the bar for the whiskey and swallowed the entire glass. The locals roared with laughter again and smacked their palms on the tables. Tripp leaned so far back in his chair that he almost fell over, and the old-timers lost it all over again.

"Hey, watch it." Darlene pointed at them. "You break my tables or my chairs, you're buyin' new ones. And yeah, Rick. I'm talkin' to you too."

The particularly old, lanky Rick with a bright orange hunting cap and suspenders over his long-sleeved black shirt raised his hands in surrender. His blue eyes twinkled before he snorted and he joined his laughter with the others'.

"Come on, kid." Johnny gestured toward the door. "Leave your milkshake and let's get goin'."

"It was a root beer float."

"I don't care if it was a White Russian— Wait." He pointed at Darlene. "Forget I said that."

The large woman chuckled and took the empty rocks glass. "What kinda place do you think I'm runnin' here, Johnny?"

The dwarf smirked. "The kind without rules. I know that much."

She scoffed. "Get on, now."

"Let's go." He nodded toward the door again and met Lisa's gaze. The woman stared at him and covered her mouth, trying to hide her smile.

I should have let her keep the damn hat.

Amanda rose from the table and pushed the chair in behind her. "I guess I better go."

"Yeah, girl." Arthur winked at her. "You keep a sharp eye out, ya hear? We'll be waitin' for the next story."

"Oh, I have way more."

The old-timers laughed and catcalled enthusiastically.

"Hey, Johnny. You take your showers in the mornin' or at night?" Harry called. "I wanna come by and hear that purdy voice of yours."

Johnny pointed at the man in mock warning. "You won't be able to hear it with two coonhounds on your chest."

"Naw, those dogs love me."

"You teach them to sing?"

The men chuckled and sipped their beer. He smirked and flipped them the bird, which drew another round of hardy laughs.

Grinning, the girl moved past the bar. "Thanks for the drink, Darlene."

"Any time, hon. You be good."

The dwarf remained where he was and glanced at the diner owner in exasperation before he turned toward Lisa and Amanda. Darlene chuckled and wiped the bar.

"Wow." The girl studied Agent Breyer with open interest, her eyes wide. "You look nice."

"Oh, you think so, do you?" Lisa gave Johnny a knowing glance as she slung her arm around the girl's shoulders.

A man who'd already arrived at Darlene's more than halfway into his daily inebriation sat at a booth beside the door and stroked his chin as he ogled the agent. "Yeah. *Real* nice." He reached for her Daisy Dukes and yelped when Johnny threw a salt shaker at his fingers. "Ow. What the fuck was that for?"

"Hands to yourself, Bobby," he warned in a growled tone.

Lisa turned and frowned at the drunkard who now cradled his hand and glared at the dwarf. "Johnny."

"Let's go." He nodded toward the door and the agent opened it for them and frowned over her shoulder as he stalked after her.

It banged shut behind them. "Well, that was completely unnecessary."

"I disagree." Johnny passed her on the landing and hurried down the stairs after Amanda.

"That man was wasted." She glanced at the door again and followed him down the stairs. "It's all simply fun and games."

"Yeah, until some asshole wants to play a little more and takes it too far."

"Then I'll handle it."

He stopped and turned to face her. "You didn't see him reachin' for the goods, did you?"

"The goods?"

He rolled his eyes. "Fine. Next time, I'll stay out of it. Let you play 'hot pants' all you want."

"What's going on with you?"

"I'm fine." He stormed toward the red Jeep but paused briefly when he saw Amanda leaning back against the rear door, her arms folded. "What's so funny?"

The girl wiped the smile off her face and opened the door before she clambered in and closed it moodily behind her.

Great. Teach a drunk to respect women and let a kid blow off steam without a babysitter, and I'm the asshole.

When he slumped into the driver's seat and revved Sheila's engine, he felt both pairs of eyes on him. His grasp firm on the steering wheel, he stared directly ahead and raised an eyebrow. "Go on, then. Say what you gotta say."

"I wasn't ready to leave," Amanda muttered in the back seat, her arms folded.

Lisa drummed her fingers on the armrest of the passenger-side door. "I'm wondering what you're not telling me."

"More than you imagine."

"You're in a mood, Johnny."

"What?" He looked sharply at her, and Lisa raised her eyebrows in a challenge.

The girl nodded firmly. "Definitely a mood."

It's two against one and this is the only fight I can't win.

"Well, if I'm in a mood, it's because—" He sighed and shook his head. "It doesn't matter. Forget it." He looked into the rearview mirror and met Amanda's glare. "But I'm serious, kid. No more stories about my personals. That shit stays at home."

"Your personals?"

The dwarf raised an eyebrow in the mirror, and she rolled her eyes.

"Fine." She slumped in the seat and stared through the paneless window.

"Good. We're all on the same page." He shifted Sheila into drive with a quick jerk.

Lisa's drumming fingers stopped so she could grasp the armrest instead. "And maybe you could—"

She yelped when he stepped on the gas and lurched in a tight circle. Dust and small rocks flurried from the wheels as the Jeep raced out of the dirt lot. Despite the tension, Amanda laughed as they bounced over rocks and gravel and thrust her hand out the window.

Yeah. All on the same damn page. I should be better at this by now.

CHAPTER FIVE

Amanda practically skipped beside Lisa as they climbed the stairs of Johnny's front porch.

"Oh, my God. It was so cool. We were *flying* across the water." The girl swept a hand through the air in imitation of the speeding airboat. "I wanted to go faster but we had to slow for the alligator."

"For the alligator?" The woman chuckled.

Johnny shoved the front door open with a grunt and strode inside.

"Yeah. Fifteen feet long. Biggest one in the Everglades—right, Johnny?"

"That I know of." The dwarf ran a hand through his hair and sighed heavily as he headed to the kitchen. *And now she's yakkin' away like she didn't wanna kill me on that airboat a few hours ago. Better'n holdin' a grudge, at least.*

"Well anyway, we didn't get the 'gator." The girl shoved her hands into her pockets and stuck close to the woman as they walked slowly toward the living room at the end of the hall. "I found shifters instead."

"Really?" The agent sat on the couch and studied the boar's head above the mantle.

"Yeah. Right here in the swamp. Can you believe it?" Amanda sat absently in the armchair beside the empty fireplace and crossed her legs under her to lean forward with wide eyes. "I had forgotten there were other shifters here. Who would have thought we'd simply cruise up to them in a boat."

"We didn't cruise up to them," Johnny muttered as he stepped out of the kitchen and headed toward them with three glasses of iced tea balanced in his hands. "Someone decided it was a good idea to run off and spook the 'gator."

"Yeah. Sorry, Johnny." The girl glanced briefly at the glasses he placed on the coffee table. "We can try again. But Lisa, these shifters are right here. I bet they live close by too."

The dwarf sat on the opposite side of the couch from Lisa and stared with wide eyes at the table as he absently sipped his tea.

She was supposed to cool off on that little solo trip through town.

The agent glanced at him and lifted a glass off the table. "Thanks, Joh—"

"And get this," Amanda continued. "Johnny almost fought them."

"You almost what?" The woman barely managed to not choke on her tea.

"It wasn't my first choice," he muttered. "And I'm glad we didn't have to." He looked at the girl and nodded. "They aren't what you think they are, kid."

"Maybe. Maybe not. But you don't know them, do you?"

"Nope, and I don't wanna."

Amanda snorted. "That's only because you saw a naked man in the swamp."

Lisa burst out laughing. "I don't think I'm getting all the pieces of the story."

Johnny leaned back against the couch with a sigh. "There isn't much to get. It was a close call but we got outta there."

"Yeah, but if I—"

"Count it as a good thing, kid." He ran his hands down his black jeans and nodded at her. "Those are not the kinda folks you wanna get yourself tangled up with."

"Yeah, Johnny." She smirked at him. "You said that already."

"Well, I ain't sayin' it only to hear myself talk."

Lisa snorted and focused her gaze firmly on her glass of tea to hide her smile.

"I know." The girl studied him for a moment. "But you of all people know there's more to someone than where they live or what they look like."

He looked at her in surprise before he narrowed his eyes. "Uh-huh."

The living room fell uncomfortably silent and after a moment, Amanda slapped her thighs and pushed out of the armchair. "I'm gonna take a shower. I'm still covered in swamp and everything. Lisa, you'll still be here when I'm done, right?"

"Yeah. I thought about sticking around a little longer." The woman crossed one ankle over her opposite knee and looked at the dwarf. "If it's all right with Johnny."

He snorted. "You let yourself into my house without knockin'. I'm fairly sure you ain't lookin' for my permission."

"Okay. Cool." Amanda hurried to the bathroom beside the bedrooms, then stopped. "Hey. We should take her out on the airboat."

"Oh, no." Lisa shook her head.

"No, come on. You'll love it."

"I'm not a boat kinda person, Amanda. But thanks."

"Johnny, tell her she needs to come on the boat with us."

He chuckled and rubbed his mouth before he gave the agent a sidelong glance. "I can tell her until the cows come home, kid."

"Please, Lisa. *Please.*"

"If you can say no to a face like that…" Johnny nodded toward the girl, who stared at Agent Breyer with puppy-dog eyes that rivaled even Rex and Luther's.

She rolled her eyes. "Oh, come on. That's not fair."

"Say yes. I promise you'll love it."

"How about you go take a shower and I'll think about it."

With a grin, the girl glanced from one to the other and shrugged. "That's good enough."

With that, she scampered to the bathroom and slammed the door behind her.

Johnny grimaced at the noise and threw an arm over the armrest. "I can't remember how many times I've told her not to slam the doors. It's like it goes in one ear and out the other."

Lisa chuckled and sipped her tea. "That's being twelve, I think. And thirteen. And fourteen..."

"Yeah, yeah. I know how to count." He waved her off and sniffed.

The dog door clattered behind Rex and Luther, who padded swiftly through the house toward them. "Whew. You're back!"

"Took you long enough." Rex sat beside the couch at Lisa's end and lifted a hind leg to lick the underside of it. "You would not believe what we found out there."

Luther shook himself vigorously and his ears slapped against his head. "Yeah, Johnny. Some guy put a whole stack of metal boxes in the water. Filled with all kinds of goodies. Mostly fish guts, but hey. I won't complain."

Johnny straightened in the chair and stared at his dogs. "You —" He stopped, remembered that Lisa had no idea he could hear the hounds, and shook his head at them. *These yahoos helped me set the damn crab traps.*

"What's wrong?" she asked.

He gritted his teeth and muttered, "I'm not a fan of cleaning muddy pawprints."

"What?" Rex lifted his head and turned to study the floor. "Hey. You have other hounds in here without tellin' us, Johnny?"

"Ooh, great idea." Luther circled on the thick rug in front of the fireplace and curled into a ball. "I'm gonna take a nap, and when that's done, we can show the other hounds the snacks in the water. They smelled a lot like the stuff you put in those crab traps last week."

The dwarf sighed and rubbed the bridge of his nose. *And they simply keep talking.*

"Hey, lady." Rex stuck his wet nose against Lisa's leg and made her laugh. "What'd you do to make him so upset, huh? You're not leavin', are ya?"

She scratched the hound's head with a smile. "Good to see you too, Rex."

Luther's head whipped up. "Johnny, she's not leaving. Don't let her leave. You guys haven't even—"

Johnny snapped his fingers and extended a finger toward the rug. "Go lie down, Rex."

"Yeah, but—"

"I'll spray you boys with the hose later."

"Fine." Rex trotted toward his brother and curled in the same position beside him. "But tell her she can't leave yet."

Lisa watched the dogs for a moment and the sound of the shower turning on finally issued from the bathroom. She chuckled and nodded toward the door. "Do you think she was trying to listen to our conversation?"

His gaze followed hers to the closed door and he shrugged. "I wouldn't put it past her. But I wouldn't blame her either. She's smart and simply wants to know how all the pieces fit together."

"Very true." She shifted on the couch to nestle her back into the corner of the armrest and lifted one leg onto the cushion. "But truthfully, Johnny, how is this...uh, 'shifter as a ward' working out?"

With another grimace, he leaned forward to place his glass on the coffee table and shook his head. "She's a good kid and merely needs a little direction. And the Everglades is a fine place to find that direction. We're good."

Luther raised his head again. "Fine place to feed your hounds too. Right, Johnny?"

The dwarf raised an eyebrow at the hound, and the animal lowered his head to his paws again.

Lisa shrugged. "Okay."

"What? You don't believe me?"

"No, I do. You guys obviously have a good thing going between you. Arguments included."

"Yeah, that comes with the territory."

She smiled at him. "It does. And you're doing a good thing for her—helping her out. You know, if you ever want some help or… I don't know. Insight, maybe. You have my number."

"Yep." He cleared his throat. "I can handle it."

"I know."

The living room fell silent again but a moment later, Rex jerked his head up and stared down the hall toward the workshop when the police scanner clicked on with a squeal and hiss of static. "Incoming."

The dwarf turned to listen.

"What's wrong?" the agent asked.

Luther looked up beside his brother and kicked his back legs out to stretch across the rug. "I think that's your monster, Johnny."

"All available units report to Dan's Market on Tamiami. We have a sighting, perpetrator unknown. Possibly armed but confirmed extremely dangerous. And…magical. Uh, purple… slime fired at the market building."

He bounded from the couch. "That's our monster, all right."

CHAPTER SIX

Johnny stood beside his enhanced police scanner in the workshop and checked whether the call had gone out on any other channels. "It sounds like we're goin' in with troopers."

"They should have direct contact with the department." Lisa stood beside the worktable with her arms folded. "And they're going into this all on their own?"

He snorted and switched the scanner off. The static and tinny voices cut instantly. "Local PDs have always had a thing against the feds. Do you think State Troopers are itchin' to hand jurisdiction to you too?"

"It's not like we'd go in to take a regular human case off their hands. They know about bounty hunters."

"Barely." The dwarf removed a small black bolt case from the bottom shelf and slung it onto the worktable. "And if they get all twisted about a fed on the scene, they ain't gonna be any happier when I show up."

"That's ridiculous. Normal law enforcement isn't equipped to handle magicals. Not monsters like this. They know that."

"Feel free to remind them when we get there." Johnny took the bolts he'd rigged with explosives of multiple boom levels and shoved them into the case. The one with the tracking device in the tip went in last so he could pull it out first—just in case. He slung the strap he'd fitted to the crossbow over his shoulder and whistled shrilly. "Time to go, boys."

"All right!" Rex leapt to his feet as Luther scrunched the rug trying to get a running start before he rocketed past his brother.

"Hunting twice in one day, Johnny? This is awesome!"

"We can handle purple goo, Johnny. No problem."

"We gotta be careful and stay on our toes." He pulled a small duffel bag from the bottom shelf as well and swung it over his other shoulder. "There isn't a lotta info on the monster for now, so this is mostly recon. In person. And if we happen to bring the bastard down while we're there…"

"Treats for the hounds, right?" Rex gazed at his master with wide, eager eyes and his tail wagged furiously.

"Ooh, yeah. Good idea. Incentives."

"Johnny, I understand how this works." Lisa raised an eyebrow at him. "You don't have to spell it out for me like I'm some kind of rookie."

He looked sharply at her and inclined his head. "I was talkin' to the hounds."

"What? They can't even—"

The bathroom door burst open and Amanda hurried out, her hair plastered to her shoulders in wet tangles and a thick towel wrapped around her body. "Johnny, wait. I want to come with you."

"You're still wet behind the ears, kid." He looked meaningly at her damp hair with a grin. "In more ways than one."

"Give me two minutes. Please." She jogged to her bedroom door, clutched the towel against her chest with one hand, and raised the other toward him to tell him to wait. "I'm fast."

"Sorry. This ain't that kinda huntin' trip."

"You need me."

Johnny stopped on his way to the door and gave her a sympathetic frown. "Naw, I got this."

"Oh, yeah? Like you got that 'gator scent this morning?"

They stared obdurately at each other and Lisa tried to subdue a chuckle. "No one told me about the 'gator scent."

"She was good." Luther panted.

"Yeah, real good. We wouldn't have found it if she wasn't on the boat. Come on, Johnny." Rex uttered a high-pitched whine. "We might need her."

Amanda gestured toward the hounds, silently telling Johnny he had his proof right there. His scowl only deepened, so she tried the pleading-shifter-pup eyes again. "Please, Johnny. I promise I won't run off after shifters this time. I'll stay focused and do everything you say. Hey, I can be your sidekick."

The dwarf rolled his eyes. "Damnit, I already have two coonhounds and a—" He stopped with a grimace.

"Partner?" Lisa added with a smirk.

Johnny shot her a warning glance. "Fine, kid. If you're ready by the time this gear and those hounds are loaded and Sheila's engine's purrin', you can come."

"Yes!" Amanda jumped up and down in excitement, then scrambled to keep her towel from falling. "Two minutes. I'll be fast."

The door to her bedroom slammed shut and he grimaced.

"Quit slammin' the damn doors," he muttered and marched down the hallway toward the front door.

Lisa followed swiftly and the hounds whined and stepped to either side, waiting for their master to let them out. "Are you sure that's a good idea?"

"Nope. But I ain't sure it's a bad idea either." He opened the door and the dogs raced past him but skidded to a halt in front of the door to the screened-in porch.

"Come on, Johnny."

"Hurry. Let's go. Let us out."

49

"She's a kid, Johnny," the agent said.

As soon as the screen door was unlatched, Rex shoved it open with his snout and he and his brother bounded onto the dirt to race toward the red Jeep.

"Yep. A kid who's been in more fights than most kids her age. She's been through hell and back and she still wants to tag along. It seems like a good learnin' opportunity to me."

"Well, to me, it seems more like endangering a minor."

He grunted and continued toward Sheila. Rex and Luther ran circles around the Jeep, too excited to say much of anything coherent. "I ain't endangerin' her, Lisa. I'm givin' her a chance. The kid needs to feel like she's useful and not a burden."

"Did she tell you that?"

"No." He swung the duffel bag and the bolt case into the back of the Jeep. "But I know the feelin' and I see it in her, all right? That's it."

She opened her rental and retrieved her service pistol and the shoulder holster she preferred to use. "I still don't think it's safe."

"The safest place for that kid is right beside me." They both turned when the front door slammed shut and the screen door flew open. Amanda leapt off the porch like another coonhound on two legs and raced toward them with a broad grin. He nodded at Sheila's passenger seat. "Which might be literally if you have a problem ridin' shotgun with a child endangerer."

The agent raised an eyebrow at him. "I didn't say that's what you are."

"All right, then. Get in." He climbed into the driver's seat. His door shut a second after Amanda slammed hers behind her. He grimaced. "Doors, kid."

"Right. Sorry."

Rex and Luther scrambled into the back of the Jeep and their claws clicked on the metal bed stripped of the carpeting and extra flooring to allow him to rig mounted weaponry. "This is awesome, pup."

"You're gonna love this!"

"Hunting on a case." Luther threw his head back and uttered a broken howl.

The girl laughed as Johnny started the engine and revved it a little in preparation. "Yeah. This is gonna be great."

Lisa buckled her seatbelt quickly and turned to look at Amanda with wide eyes. "You'd better strap in. There's no telling how he's gonna drive when we're after a—"

Sheila lurched forward and jerked to the side as Johnny accelerated into a tight circle in the drive. The hounds slid sideways in the back and howled with excitement. Amanda threw her head back and uttered a wild laugh before she clicked her safety belt securely. The agent shrieked and braced herself against the almost nonexistent center console and the frame of the passenger door.

"Dammit, Johnny! Can't you—"

He thrust his boot down on the gas pedal, and Sheila raced along the drive in a spray of dust and pebbles. When she squawked a protest, he smirked as they barreled down the long drive away from his cabin. "Can't I what, darlin'?"

She gritted her teeth and darted him a sidelong glance. "Drive like you're not trying to kill us."

"You're buckled up. And trust me." He patted the dashboard. "If Sheila rolls, we ain't walkin' away with so much as a scratch. I made sure of that myself."

Her heavy sigh sounded both frustrated and nervous and she brushed her fluttering hair out of her face. "Somehow, I'm not reassured."

"Your choice."

They reached the dirt frontage road moments later and the bounty hunter didn't show any signs of slowing.

"Johnny."

"Lisa."

"Slow down."

His boot pressed the accelerator.

"Johnny! It's a turn! You can't simply—"

"Watch me." With a broad grin, he jerked the wheel violently with one hand and engaged the handbrake with the other. Sheila spun and drifted sharply around the corner, and the engine roared as dirt and rocks were thrown across the dirt road and into the trees and the ditch.

The agent screamed.

He released the handbrake and stepped on the accelerator again, and the Jeep careened down the frontage road.

In the back seat, her wet hair drying quickly as it whipped around her face, Amanda stared blankly at the back of Johnny's seat with her mouth open. "Woah."

Rex and Luther bayed wildly in the back.

"Now that's what I'm talkin' about, Johnny!"

"Can't do that in an airboat. Monster, here we come!"

The girl burst out laughing.

Lisa sat rigidly in the passenger seat and breathed heavily as trees and ferns and reeds blurred past them.

Johnny glanced at her. "You can't do it, huh?"

She barely shook her head, her face pale. "I…need a minute."

"Sure. You get fifteen." He punched the power button on the dash and Iron Maiden blared incredibly loudly through the speakers.

Her eye twitched and she released a long sigh. "You are terrifying sometimes. You know that?"

The dwarf snorted and couldn't hide a smirk. "You should've seen me before retirement."

"No, I think out-of-retirement Johnny Walker is enough."

"That was insane!" Amanda shouted over the music as they hurtled down the frontage road. "How'd you learn to do that?"

"Practice, kid."

"Like in your driveway?"

"Naw, like in more getaway maneuvers than I can count." He grinned at her through the rearview mirror.

Lisa scoffed and started to roll her eyes before a surprised laugh escaped her. She ran a hand through her windblown hair and shook her head. "You're unbelievable."

"Much obliged." He winked at her, retrieved his sunglasses, and slid them on with one hand before he focused on the road again. He didn't see Agent Breyer grinning as she studied him speculatively.

CHAPTER SEVEN

Six State Trooper vehicles had cordoned the road off when the team reached Dan's Market. The officers stood behind the open doors of their vehicles, their weapons drawn and aimed at two huge tentacles that rose from the swamp on the side of the road. The appendages were twenty feet long—at least the part of them that stretched above the overhanging branches and the water-logged reeds—and waved slowly from side to side. Their purple hue was so dark it was almost black and was impossible to miss against the green, brown, and yellow of the swamp and the clear blue sky.

Sheila squealed to a stop on the asphalt, and the hounds bounded out before the dwarf had even turned the engine off.

"Woah-ho-ho, Johnny!" Rex panted and stared at the two wavering tentacles on the side of the road. "Look at the size of that."

"Calamari for life," Luther added with a sharp bark.

Half the troopers turned to study the dwarf who slid out of the red Jeep with a tall brunette in Daisy Dukes and a girl in jeans and a loose t-shirt slightly too big for her.

Johnny snapped his fingers, and both hounds sat immediately.

He rounded the back of the Jeep and retrieved his crossbow and the bag of bolts. "It certainly looks like a big one."

Lisa strapped her shoulder holster on and headed with him toward the trooper vehicles. "What the hell is that?"

"That's what I'm fixin' to find out. To me, boys."

"Yeah, yeah, Johnny." Luther was at his master's side first, quickly followed by his brother. "Then to the giant snack, right?"

"I bet it tastes better raw. Johnny, does it bleed?"

Amanda craned her neck and stared at the waving tentacles. "Woah."

One of the troopers muttered something to his fellows, none of whom moved from their positions. Their guns remained trained on the partially hidden monster as their leader left the line of vehicles to intercept the newcomers.

"It's not safe for you folks to be here," the man said and pushed up the wide brim of his hat with an uncertain frown. "Y'all need to turn around. Nothin' to see here."

"Those big-ass tentacles say somethin' different," the bounty hunter said calmly and shouldered past him.

"Sir." The officer hurried after him and put a hand on his shoulder. "I can't let you go any farther. Please turn around and—"

"Look, Super Trooper." He swung his crossbow toward the tentacles as Rex and Luther uttered low growls. "Y'all've been out here for at least fifteen minutes and that monster is still wigglin' around like it's here to stay."

"Sir, I have to ask you to—"

"I have a license." He brushed past the man again and moved toward the line of vehicles.

Rex flattened his ears against his head and barked at the trooper. "You don't know what you're gettin' into, two-legs."

"Yeah." Luther growled again. "What he said."

The dwarf whistled shrilly and the hounds left the confused man to rejoin their master.

The officer grunted, took a step after them, and broke into a jog. "That's all well and good, but a hunting license doesn't give you open season on State Trooper business."

Johnny reached the line of cars and headed toward the end to skirt it but another man stepped in his way. This one had a long dark mustache and a perpetual scowl. "Sir. You can't go in there."

"Watch me." His dogs snarled at the man, who jumped away and forced himself to aim his weapon at the tentacles again. The bounty hunter rounded the line of vehicles and moved toward the road between Dan's Market and the monster still mostly hiding in the swamp.

When the other troopers turned to stop Lisa from following him past their line, she took her badge from her back pocket and flashed it. "This is FBI jurisdiction, gentlemen. And he's with me."

"Goddammit." The leader rolled his eyes. "What the hell are the feds doing on this call?"

"What we do when there's a call about an Oriceran monster no one's identified yet. I assume dealing with that wasn't part of your training."

The man with the mustache snorted and scrutinized her with narrowed eyes, taking in the Daisy Dukes, mid-ankle boots, and camo tank top. "And it was part of yours?"

She glanced warningly at him. "Want another look at my badge?"

He shook his head and stepped back to recenter his firearm over the top of the open vehicle door behind him.

A thick, purple-tinted mist rose around the two tentacles, spilled through the reeds, and crept onto the side of the road.

"If you and Rambo over there can handle it, be our guest," he said. "But watch out for the…uh, purple slime."

"Yeah, we're aware of that. Thank you." Lisa turned and nodded for Amanda to hurry. The girl jogged toward her and together, they slipped through the line of vehicles.

"Is the girl with the FBI too?" one of the troopers called, half-joking.

"I'm with the bounty hunter." She pointed at Johnny and grinned at the officers over her shoulder.

The dwarf had stopped in the middle of the road to unzip the top of the bolt case. He drew out the red tracker bolt first, then slung the case over his shoulder and loaded the projectile into the barrel. "All right, Nessie. Let's see what you're made of."

"Nessie?" Luther stared at the tentacles and the purple mist, his tail pointing straight out behind him. "Who's Nessie?"

"The Abominable Swamp Monster, bro," Rex added and copied his brother's ready posture. "Easy."

Lisa and Amanda reached Johnny and stopped. The girl gazed at the tentacles and took a deep breath. "You're not gonna shoot it, are you?"

He lowered the crossbow and looked at her. "Did you have somethin' else in mind?"

"Yeah, I don't know. Like maybe try...talking to it first?"

"This creature been blowing up gas stations and vacation resorts, kid. There ain't no talkin' to a monster like that, no matter how magical it is."

"You don't even know what it is. How do you know it can't talk?"

"Pup has a point, Johnny," Rex said.

"Yeah. Hell, you didn't know we could talk until you proved it."

Amanda pointed at the hounds and shrugged.

"Dammit. Fine." Johnny strode forward across the road, his gaze fixed on the tentacles. "I'll try talkin' to the damn thing and if it don't talk back, we're all in."

"I'm right behind you." The girl jogged after him and he spun to face her.

"Uh-uh." He pointed at her. "Y'all stay here. If I need backup, you'll know."

"Oh, cool. You mean like you have a signal?" She raised her eyebrows and nodded. "Sweet. What's the signal?"

He merely stared at her for a moment before he looked at Lisa. "You got my back?"

"From right here in the road." She nodded and drew her service weapon.

With a grunt, he turned toward the reeds half-obscured by purple mist and marched into the swamp. Rex and Luther bounded after him.

"The signal is when you see him getting his ass kicked, pup!"

"Maybe a scream."

Johnny growled and fixed his dogs with a disgruntled glare they couldn't see behind his dark sunglasses, even if they'd bothered to look at him. "That's if, not when. Big if too."

"Yeah, of course, Johnny."

"We know that."

"Just sayin'."

The bounty hunter and his hounds disappeared through the reeds and waves of mist swirled quickly behind them.

Amanda folded her arms. "Do you think he'll be okay in there on his own?"

Lisa shrugged. "I think he thinks he'll be okay in there on his own."

"Should we go in, then?"

"Not until we get the signal." They both snorted, and the agent shook her head. "Seriously, though. We said we'd wait. Whatever he has up his sleeve, we should let him try to handle it first before we step in."

In silence, the young shifter looked from the woman to the huge, waving appendages rising from the swamp maybe fifty feet beyond the road. "But you think we'll end up stepping in."

The agent smirked. "This conversation stays between us."

"Of course."

"Yeah. It's Johnny Walker. We need to be ready for anything."

Johnny slogged through the swamp and his boots squelched in the mud and water that reached to the middle of his calves. *I should've brought waders. Stupid.*

The two hounds splashed along beside him, their heads and tails lifted high. "Damn. That's a smell for you," Luther commented.

"Like fish guts."

"Fish guts and lighter fluid."

Rex snorted and shook his head. "I don't think I wanna eat this one, Johnny."

"That's fine." He waved a hand in front of his face in an attempt to clear the purple mist. "We're goin' in for a chat, boys. Not a snack."

"You're truly gonna try talkin' to it, Johnny?"

"I said I would. The kid had a point." The mist thickened around them and they slowed.

Luther sneezed. "I can't see shit, Johnny."

"Yeah, where'd you go? Luther?"

"I'm next to Johnny."

A large ripple in the water lapped against the legs of Johnny's black jeans and he snapped his fingers. "Quiet."

"Yep. Shutting up."

"Luther, shut up."

Johnny rolled his eyes and whipped his sunglasses off to slip them into the front pocket of his button-up shirt. He took one more slow step through the water and scanned the shadows flickering across the thick mist. "We're close."

A burst of hot, noxious air blasted them and cleared the purple mist away. It curled lazily into the air around them. On the surface of the water five yards ahead, more black-purple tentacles writhed on top of one another like a nest of massive snakes flowing seamlessly in and out of the water.

"Holy octopus," Luther muttered. "That's a big one."

"Don't insult it, bro."

The dwarf cleared his throat. "Hey."

Another gust of hot air blasted from the center of the rising tentacles, where a dome of glistening flesh in the same black-purple color rose a foot above the surface. One giant lid in the dome flickered open and closed.

But no eyes. They're either underwater starin' at me or this creature is blind.

"So… if you can hear me, folks are gettin' real concerned about all the damage you've done to properties over the last couple weeks." He held the crossbow in both hands, although he didn't aim it at the monster yet. "I thought I'd try the…less likely way first and ask you in person what's up."

I sound like a fuckin' moron.

The writhing mass of appendages didn't respond to his offer for a little chat. The two twenty-foot tentacles that undulated above from the back of the creature's main body didn't stop what they were doing either.

Johnny grunted. "Otherwise, I'm gonna have to do this the old-fashioned way. Weapons and hounds, right? And if you can hear me, it might be in both our best interests for you to say somethin'. 'Cause the old-fashioned way's damn effective."

A smaller tentacle rose from the water by two feet and stretched slowly toward the bounty hunter and his hounds.

He raised the crossbow and leveled it at the appendage. "That ain't talkin'."

"Maybe that little snake-thing has a mouth," Luther suggested.

"Maybe it's the goo-shooter. Careful, Johnny."

"Yeah…" He sniffed. "I'm gonna ask you to get that thing outta my face. And I only ask once."

The small tentacle opened at the tip like the end of an elephant's trunk and the hole widened as it extended closer to him. More purple mist rose around the creature that remained mostly submerged. Without warning, the small hand-like appendage at the end of it whipped against the barrel of Johnny's crossbow, and the creature snatched the crossbow out of his hands and flung it aside. The weapon sailed six feet away and into a web of small, intertwining tree branches.

"Dammit." Johnny hissed and stared at his crossbow. *At least it ain't in the water.* "That's not the way a friendly conversation works."

The water squelched and receded from him and the hounds as the creature lifted itself from the swamp with a guttural groan. Thicker tentacles slapped at the surface to spray water, mud, and reeds in every direction. The purple mist thickened again, and he caught a glimpse of at least six golden eyes that opened as water cascaded over the enormous, bulbous body. Three much thicker tentacles oozed with the purple goo, and he grimaced.

"Okay. Good talk. Now, it's over." He waded as quickly as he could toward the tangle of tree limbs and his crossbow.

The creature groaned again and moved faster than its size implied it could.

"Johnny, watch out!" Luther shouted and barked at the dripping tentacle that swung toward his master.

The creature slapped the bounty hunter aside with a wet squelch as it rose higher, shrouded by the mist. He slipped in the mud and splashed into the water. "Keep it back, boys!"

The hounds bayed and lurched through the swamp to snarl and snap at what seemed like a hundred tentacles moving all at once.

Johnny scrambled to his feet and pushed toward the trees. With a quick twist and jerk, he freed the crossbow and swung it at the height where he thought the massive body should be. "Fuck this mist."

The weapon fired with a thud and twang and the creature roared but didn't stop.

Another tentacle swiped toward him and he ducked. The movement swirled the purple fog away, and he caught a glimpse of Rex swinging with the tentacle, his jaws clamped around black-purple flesh as his back legs scrambled for purchase.

The monster flung the hound aside. "Johnnyyyyy!" he wailed before he landed with a splash and a startled yelp.

"I got it, Johnny!" Luther shouted and whipped his head from side to side with a mouthful of one of the tiny, thin tentacles. "I'll get it for you—shit!"

A tentacle rose beneath the hound and launched him out of the water.

The dwarf snatched another bolt from the case over his shoulder, glanced at the regular black tip he hadn't exchanged with any enhanced magi-tech, and shrugged before he loaded it. Two more tentacles swung toward him, these dripping with the thick, almost luminescent purple ooze.

With a scowl of frustration, he raised the crossbow and fired. The bolt seared through one of the purple-dripping tentacles, and his quarry uttered another furious roar. A long, drawn-out hiss followed, and even with a bolt embedded in it, the oozing tentacle raised with the other to join the two still waving above the swamp.

"Stop it from spraying!" Johnny shouted.

His hounds bayed and splashed after wayward tentacles.

The bounty hunter felt for another bolt, withdrew it, and glanced at the glowing yellow-filled tip. "Okay. We'll try Boom Three."

He loaded the bolt and aimed at the thick wall of purple mist that clouded his vision again.

"Johnny, it's too slippery!"

"How the hell does it move so fast?"

"Shit. I think something bit my leg!"

He peered into the mist and tried to locate the beast's main dome or whatever shape its body was. Intent on his search, he didn't see a tentacle sneak up behind him until seconds before it wound around his torso and squeezed.

CHAPTER EIGHT

Lisa and Amanda grimaced as the hounds bayed and snarled while the purple monster hissed and bellowed in the swamps.

"Is that the signal?" the girl asked.

"Nope. Stand by, kid." The agent raised her firearm in both hands and squinted. "I can't see a thing through that crap."

"Do you think Johnny can?"

"Who knows?"

"Stop it from spraying!" The dwarf's shout rose from the swamp as two more massive, thicker tentacles snaked upward to join the first two.

Amanda stared at them and nodded slowly. "There's the purple goo."

"Yep." The woman couldn't decide what to focus on—the oozing tentacles or the thick cloud of purple mist where Johnny shouted and his hounds snarled and barked. "Those are probably—"

"Look out!" The young shifter pushed her aside as another tentacle thrust from the reeds to blast purple mist onto the road.

Before the appendage struck the place where they'd stood, it lashed like a whip and hurled Johnny Walker onto dry land and he rolled across the asphalt past his partner and ward. Rex and Luther splashed and slogged through the swamp with their tails between their legs and eyes wide. They scrambled up the slight incline to return to the road and raced toward their master.

"Johnny!"

"Hey, you good?"

Soaking wet, the bounty hunter pushed off the ground and flicked water from his hands before he drew another bolt from the case on his back. "The bastard snuck up on me."

He leveled his crossbow at the giant, slick, black-purple creature that lurked above the swamp growth.

The troopers shouted in surprise, and two of them fired a few rounds that did absolutely nothing.

Johnny snorted and stalked across the road. "Idiots."

"Wait." Amanda looked from him to Lisa. "Was that the sign?"

"I don't...think so." The agent glanced at her useless firearm and holstered it. *I guess I'll go with Light-Elf firepower if I have to.*

"All right, asshole. Tossing me around like that is where I draw the line."

The scene erupted into utter chaos as a number of things happened at once. The two appendages dripping with purple ooze thrust forward from twenty feet above them, opened three sucker-like mouths on their undersides, and launched thick streams of the goo at Dan's Market across the street. The entire building was covered in thick purple slime and the remainder dripped in a path across the road and led back to the monster.

A third oozing tentacle struck through the reeds and targeted Johnny. He fired his Boom Three explosive bolt seconds before the spray of purple gunk smacked him squarely in the face and splattered down his chest and legs. The creature bellowed.

"Aw, what the fuck." He reloaded hastily with another Boom Three and fired.

Two seconds later, the first bolt detonated. A massive explosion of fire and water rose like a mushroom cloud above the swamp and streaks of purple goo everywhere ignited like long dynamite fuses.

The creature howled and splashed into the water in a puff of purple mist but not before it hurled a broken Boom Three bolt across the street. The glowing yellow tip winked in the light, and the projectile clattered into a puddle of purple goo against the market wall.

"Shit." The dwarf whistled shrilly and turned to shove Lisa and Amanda roughly forward toward the line of State Trooper vehicles. The dogs bayed wildly and raced after him. The ordnance detonated, and the entire building erupted in a thunderous explosion. Glass, metal, and brick sprayed in every direction like shrapnel. Some rained around the establishment and pieces of debris even reached as far as the troopers. The remainder splashed into the swamp.

A fire alarm activated somewhere inside the burning building until another puddle of goo burst into flame and the force of ignition pushed the roof off the store. Then, everything was silent.

From where they stood in front of the vehicle line, Lisa and Amanda stared at the burning building and the lines of fire that raced from the explosion, across the road, and into the swamp, some of which had also caught fire.

Johnny took his wet sunglasses from his soaked shirt pocket, flipped them open, and slid them on over the purple goo that dripped down his face.

The creature bellowed in rage or pain but the sound cut off as it submerged again with a massive splash. Trees groaned and swayed at the beast's passing as it raced away from the land.

Luther half-howled and half-barked at it and bounded across the asphalt. "Yeah, and don't come back!"

"We sure showed him, huh, Johnny?"

The dwarf ignored his hounds and slung the crossbow over

his shoulder before he turned toward Lisa and Amanda. "Well. There's our recon."

The woman frowned at him. "And the burning building?"

"Unavoidable." He grunted and trudged past them, leaving thick puddles of watery purple goo in his wake.

Amanda folded her arms and nodded. "We missed the signal."

"What the actual fuck?" the mustached trooper shouted and gestured wildly toward the flames. "You were supposed to stop it, not blow the building up for it!"

With a sniff, the dwarf turned to look at the blazing structure. "Ain't anyone in there, right?"

"No, asshole. But the owner's not gonna be happy."

"Tell him to take it up with the feds." He shrugged and smacked a fist against the open vehicle door in front of him. It slammed shut before he stalked between the baffled officers toward Sheila. Rex and Luther trotted behind him.

"Don't worry about the details," Lisa muttered as she and Amanda hurried after the bounty hunter. "The Bureau will get this cleaned up and we'll give a statement with a cover story, all right?"

"No, it's not fucking all right."

"Hey. You're off the hook here. Trust me, if anyone's gonna bag that beast in the swamp, it's him. You're…" She looked over her shoulder at the devastation. "You're lucky he got here."

"The fuck?" The men stared after her and Amanda as the goo-covered Johnny climbed into the red Jeep. The man with the mustache whipped his wide-brimmed hat off his head and threw it on the ground. "Goddamn feds. All right. Call it in. Shit."

Sheila's engine roared to life before Amanda and Lisa had closed their doors behind them.

"Oh-ho, man!" Luther shook himself vigorously and sprayed water and mud all over the back of the Jeep. "That was intense."

"That was a big motherfucker, Johnny."

The dwarf glanced in the rearview mirror. "Watch it."

"Oh, 'cause of the pup? Sorry, pup."

The girl chuckled.

Lisa turned to look at her, then frowned at Johnny. "She didn't say anything."

"Yeah, it's what everyone ain't sayin'."

"And what's—" She yelped as he jerked the Jeep in a tight circle and the tires squealed before he raced down the road toward his cabin. "Okay, now you're doing that on purpose."

"Naw. Now, I'm fixin' to get home." The dwarf looked in the rearview mirror. The half-dozen vehicles and their troops remained exactly where he'd left them, while Dan's Market blazed in the background. *And those idiots are simply standing there with their dicks in their hands. Come on.*

Amanda grasped the windowless frame of her door and poked her head out to look behind them. A huge flock of herons rose from the trees deeper into the swamp. "Did you try to talk to it?"

He grunted. "If that thing could talk, kid, it was far more interested in disarmin' me than sayin' so much as a 'how d'ya do.'"

"So you blew it up instead."

"I like to keep things simple." He shrugged. "And clean. Mostly clean."

Lisa snorted. "Yeah, that doesn't mesh with your 'going after monsters' MO."

"Is it dead?" the young shifter asked and whipped her head back to frown in concern at the rearview mirror.

Luther's mouth popped open and his tongue lolled out as a thin string of drool dripped from his muzzle onto the back seat beside the girl. "No way did a little fire hurt it, Johnny."

"Made a lotta noise," Rex added, "but it knew what to do with that second explosive."

"Yeah. Ka-boom!"

"Just not ka-boom monster."

Johnny shook his head. "It ain't dead."

Lisa gaped at him. "Johnny, you blew it up."

"If a creature that sprays incendiary goo like it does could be hurt by fire, darlin', it wouldn't have lived long enough to reach that size." He gave her a sidelong glance, which she didn't catch due to his ridiculously dark sunglasses. "Like if you were allergic to strawberries and ate nothin' but strawberries your whole—"

"Yeah, I understand the analogy." With a smirk, she leaned back in her seat and rested her head against the headrest. The ends of her auburn hair whipped around her face as Sheila sped along down the twisting, turning road through the Everglades. "I'm wondering why you decided to kick rocks if it's not dead in the water. Literally."

"Eh?"

"Johnny, it's not like a few explosions generally drive you to leave the scene."

He thumped a palm lightly on the steering wheel, glanced at Amanda in the rearview mirror, then looked sharply at the agent. "How many times do I have to say it? Recon."

"We could have gone after it."

"Oh, sure. I'll drive Sheila into the swamp, no problem. 'Cause she floats."

Amanda perked up in the back seat and leaned forward. "Really?"

"No."

The girl rolled her eyes and laughed when Rex's wet snout nudged the side of her face, followed by a swift lick.

"Nope. Not you, pup."

"What?"

Luther sniffed dutifully and thrust his head over the back seat. "Whew! That's Johnny."

"Damn, Johnny. You stink!"

"Yeah, not the good kinda stink, either." Luther shook his head vigorously and splattered more water droplets and dog drool across the already stained seat. Amanda shielded her face with a playful groan. "There's good stink and bad stink, Johnny."

"Like human food, hound food, trash, carcasses, game, shit—"

"Doesn't matter whose."

Rex licked his muzzle. "That's the good stink."

"And then there's… Well, you, Johnny."

The young shifter laughed in the back seat and even slapped her hands on her thighs in mirth.

"That's about it. Right, Rex?"

"Yeah. Johnny made the bad-stink list."

Lisa turned to see two panting coonhounds leaning over the back seat and the young shifter girl almost incoherent beside them. "I don't get it. What's so funny?"

Johnny glanced in the rearview mirror and shook his head. "No clue."

"Hey, when you gonna tell her about us, Johnny?"

"Might as well. Not like she's goin' anywhere. You're confusin' the heck outta her."

With a sniff, the dwarf scraped away some of the purple goo sliding thickly down his cheek and flicked it out the Jeep window. *And if she doesn't stick around, havin' a fed out there who knows I can talk to my hounds is a liability I reckon I'll regret.*

CHAPTER NINE

The dwarf left a trail of gooey purple footprints from Sheila's driver's side door to the front door of his cabin and beyond. He strode into his workshop, squelched the whole way, and grumbled belligerently. "Dammit. I got muddy pawprints and purple shit all over my floors."

"Yep. This is the stinky stuff." Rex sniffed in a wide circle around one of the purple puddles. "Kinda fishy. Kinda...bloody?"

"No, not bloody. That's..." Luther licked a purple boot print, then yelped and raced through the house. He skidded on purple slime and tracked it through the kitchen to the back door. "Shit! Shit, shit, shit! Johnny, I'm gonna die!"

"Johnny." Rex sat and whined at his master. "Hey. Help him, will ya?"

The sounds of lapping and water sloshing over the side of the dog bowl on the back patio filtered through the cabin. Scowling at the purple mess Luther had made, Johnny hurried to the racks and slid a large plastic tote with a locking lid out from under the bottom shelf. He tried to shake the goo off his hands first, but the mess was unavoidable.

It looks like I'm gonna be playin' maid around here for a few hours after this. I shoulda rigged those hounds with opposable thumbs. Or built a cleanin' bot.

Lisa and Amanda joined him in the workshop and their noses wrinkled as they waved their hands in front of their faces.

"Oh, man." The girl tried to snort the smell away and shook her head. "It's so much worse in here."

Chuckling, Lisa stepped away from the table as he retrieved a mason jar from the tote and thunked it on the table. "Wow, Johnny. Even when you've had a few drinks, you've never smelled this boozy."

"You've never been this funny, either." He looked sharply at her and shrugged. "Sorry. I'm focused."

"Sure. No problem." She gestured toward the table with a smirk. "Focus away."

With a grunt, he stretched toward a shelf and purple goo dripped from his outstretched arm and splattered on a metal box stored below, which made him growl in irritation. He grasped a wide, thin pewter plate and plunked it on the worktable before he scraped a handful of purple goo off his chest and onto the plate.

"What are you doing?" Amanda asked, her voice thin and nasally with her fingers pinching her nostrils shut.

"Testing." He scrabbled for a lighter in the shape of a pistol from his front pocket, careful not to touch the flint with his gooey fingers, and flicked a flame to life.

The agent's eyes widened. "Johnny, wait a minute—"

The flame touched the purple goo on the plate, which instantly ignited with a whoosh and four-foot flames erupted. Rex whined and took two steps away into the hallway. Lisa and Amanda both shielded their eyes but lowered their hands and arms again slowly when the flames died down rapidly to a slow burn on the glowing, gelatinous purple puddle.

"Yep." He sniffed. "Thought so."

With a sharp bark, Luther raced through the kitchen and

slipped on a streak of goo again. "What happened? What did I miss?"

"Johnny's trying to burn the house down, Luther."

"What? Come on, Johnny. At least wait until I'm inside with the rest of you." Luther skidded to a stop in the entry to the kitchen, his eyes wide, and belched. "Oh. Ew. Good thing you didn't try to burn that one off, hey, Johnny?"

Amanda sniggered through her plugged nose.

Lisa huffed a laugh of disbelief. "We already knew it was flammable. What was the point of that? Unless I'm partnered with a pyromaniac who managed to keep it a secret from me over the last three weeks."

"Have you looked at my fireplace, darlin'?"

"Why would I—"

"I haven't used the damn thing since I bought this house."

She rolled her eyes. "Right. Because an abnormal obsession with fire would be contained to a fireplace."

"I wanted to make sure that shit would burn without any other variables."

"You mean like a building to blow up?"

Johnny looked sharply up at her and narrowed his eyes.

She chuckled and gestured impatiently. "You're the only one who knows what's in your head. I'm merely trying to get on the same page."

"I mean like other incendiary agents." He covered the pewter plate with a second from the shelf to extinguish the small flames, then gathered another glob of goo from his shoulder and scraped it off his hand into the mason jar. "Other secretions. Maybe even that purple mist it was blowin' all over the damn place."

"We couldn't see a thing," Luther added. "Tell her, Johnny."

"Yeah. Make sure she knows that fog didn't smell nearly as bad as you."

The dwarf glanced at the hounds and raised his index finger. Both sat immediately and their tails brushed the floor from side to side. The tip of Luther's tail whacked a thick purple puddle and it splattered down the hall in both directions.

"Damnmit. Now you're makin' goo angels. Outside, boys. Now."

"Yeah, yeah. We'll wash it off in the swamp." Luther skidded around the corner and collided with the cabinet under the kitchen sink before he bounded through the dog door. "Hey, Rex? Is there fire in the swamp?"

"Only if someone decides to light you up." Rex trotted after his brother and the dog door clacked shut.

With a heavy sigh, the dwarf sealed the lid on the mason jar, screwed it tightly closed, and thumped it on the table. "Now we know the only thing that bastard needs to start a fire is this shit."

"And that's the only thing we know." Lisa leaned across the table and stretched a hand toward the stacked pewter plates.

He moved quickly and slid the plates out of her reach. "Other than the fact that it likes to blow up mom-and-pop stores, gas stations, and resorts. They ain't got nothin' in common."

"You think it's merely on a rampage?" Amanda asked.

"It could be." Johnny raised his hand toward his mouth to rub it, then glanced at the purple slime and wiped his hand on his black jeans. *That didn't do shit.* "If that creature was simply pissed, it wouldn't have let me and the hounds get as close as we did. I thought maybe for a second it might have said somethin', but it decided to take my crossbow." He sniffed. "No one takes my crossbow."

The girl unplugged her nose to fold her arms. "Did you try to shoot it first?"

"Jesus." He shook his head at her. "I only shoot first when I know what the hell I'm dealin' with, kid. And I have no idea what this is or why an incendiary Oriceran monster is swimmin' through the Everglades and blowin' shit up. And if it was only a random attack 'cause it's as pissed as hell and wants to get even, it would have killed both of y'all and had some fun with those troopers."

"It waited almost three weeks between that gas station and the market," the agent said thoughtfully. "Maybe if it was a fishing shop, that'd make more sense."

"Well it weren't a fishin' gas station or a fishin' four-star resort, neither," he grumbled and spread his arms so he could examine his goo-splattered clothes and beard. "This goddamn shit's everywhere."

Lisa ignored his attitude and tapped a finger against her lips. "So what do all three places have in common?"

"Dunno." Johnny sighed. "But I need to wash the gunk off and clean. Hey, kid."

The young shifter leaned away from him with wide eyes. "Yeah…"

"Do you know how to use a mop?"

"I'm not the one who tracked this inside."

"So that's a no?"

Amanda and Lisa both stared at him in disbelief.

"Yeah, I didn't think so." Johnny moved into the hall, then turned and pointed at the table. "Don't touch anything in here. Especially that."

"What are you gonna do with it?" the agent asked.

"Take it to a guy I know. I reckon he has a better idea about this goo-tentacled monster stuff than I do."

The girl sniggered. "You have a guy for goo-tentacled-monster stuff?"

The dwarf shrugged and a thick glob of purple slime dropped to the floor with a splat. "Well, he's not really a guy. Or he hasn't always been, at least, and probably won't be again in a few hundred years. But hey. If you wanna think like a monster, you go talk to a fuckin' monster."

"I'm sorry." Lisa stared at the other side of the hall with a frown. "I'm not sure whether to focus on the 'not a guy' part or the 'monster' part."

"You can leave the focus to me, darlin'." Johnny nodded and spun smartly on his heel to squelch across the floor again toward the bathroom.

She hurried after him. "Johnny, who exactly are we taking this flammable sludge to?"

"Relax. I'm not givin' it away." The dwarf kicked his boots off and grimaced when two puddles of swamp water squished out of his socks. "We'll go have a little chat with a draksa, and maybe he'll be in a good enough mood to take a look at a sample."

"Wait, wait, wait." Amanda hurried into the hall. "What if he's not in a good enough mood?"

Lisa joined them. "And don't say, 'Then he'll try to eat us.'"

He snorted. "Come on. The smart ones don't eat folks. Mostly."

"Johnny…"

"I'm kiddin'." He looked at each of his wide-eyed women companions and shrugged. *I ain't kiddin' but whatever.* "Don't worry about it, all right? Tomorrow, we'll start the day with another hunt and go truss up a little somethin' for my draksa guy. You know, butter him up a little. Then I can guarantee he won't eat us. Happy?" He jerked the bathroom door open and stepped inside.

"Not really, but I guess we—"

The door shut swiftly, and the shower turned on almost immediately.

"Don't have many options." With a sigh, Lisa turned and studied the purple slime tracked across the entire house. Then, she looked at Amanda.

"Hey, don't look at me like that." The girl raised both hands in surrender. "The only way I'll help to clean this up is if he says please."

The woman smirked. "Do you even know where he keeps the mop?"

Amanda pursed her lips, glanced slowly around the cabin, and shrugged. "Nope."

"Okay. We'll wait."

CHAPTER TEN

Johnny threw the last of the rags into the black plastic trash bag and jerked his head away from the fishy fumes that seeped out around his hand. "Damn. It's no wonder no one knows what this monster is. No one's gettin' close enough to find out."

"Except you, Johnny." Rex looked at his master from where he lay on the area rug in the living room and thumped his tail. "And us."

"Ooh, hey." Luther padded out of the kitchen and raised his head from his floor-sniffing. "Nice trash bag, Johnny. Got any goodies in there?"

The dwarf stared at the smaller hound. "I reckon we need to get your memory checked, Luther."

"Great!" the dog sat, licked his muzzle, and focused on the trash bag filled with monster-goo rags. "Why?"

"Okay." Lisa stepped through the front door and dusted her hands off. "All the gunk's in the trunk."

He snorted. "That's what you're goin' with?"

"What? Fine. In the bed of your truck. Better?"

"It's not what I meant, but sure." He tied the trash bag closed, heaved it over his shoulder, and took it outside, barely managing to squeeze it through the front door and the screen door on the porch.

"Hey, where's he goin' with that?" Luther darted after him. "Johnny, wait up! Come on. Trash is good. Don't throw it all away."

Panting, Rex trotted after him and made no attempt to correct his brother's misconception.

Johnny slung the last bag into the bed of his truck and thumped a hand on the tailgate. "Where's Amanda?"

"Out on the dock." The screen door banged shut behind Lisa as she headed down the porch steps. "She said she wanted some fresh air."

He sniffed at his hands and jerked his head away again. "I can't blame her."

Wiping his hands on his fresh pair of jeans, he turned toward the back of the house. Amanda was seated on the dock with her legs crossed, facing the water. *Maybe now's the right time to have that other talk I been meanin' to have with her.*

As she studied Johnny's scowl, Lisa put her hands on her hips and glanced at the girl. "Is this what you guys have been doing for the last two weeks?"

"What?"

"She goes off somewhere and you hang back to stare at her?"

"She's fine." He leaned against the rear of his truck and hooked his thumbs through his belt loops. "The kid needs some space. I get it."

"Or maybe she needs something fun to do."

He snorted. "We been havin' fun all day."

"I don't mean hunting or having a few laughs and a root beer float with a group of old men who could be her…great-grandfathers. Or watching you get gooed by a swamp monster."

"Come on, darlin'. Don't tell me that wasn't fun from where you were standin'."

The agent closed her eyes but couldn't help a small smile. "Despite how much fun that was, I'm talking about normal kid stuff, Johnny. You know, with normal kids her age."

"I ain't buyin' her a damn cell phone and tellin' her to go meet new friends on FaceSpace."

"On what?"

"Damn social media. The one with all the—"

"Yeah, yeah. Don't get her a phone." Lisa chuckled. "Let's take her out."

Johnny looked warily at the half-Light Elf woman. "Like shopping?"

"Maybe. If that's what she likes to do."

"Huh." He looked at the dock and narrowed his eyes. "Well, if she does, we're stayin' away from wherever you bought your clothes."

"Wow. Okay, forget the shopping. What do you do around here for fun?"

The dwarf rubbed his mouth and wiry red beard, then shrugged. "Everything we already did today. Usually without company."

Lisa took a deep breath. "How about dinner?"

He smirked. "I'm flattered, darlin'. Truly I am. But I reckon us goin' on a date probably ain't what would make her happy."

"Oh, boy." She rolled her eyes in exasperation and they both chuckled. "I meant all three of us—"

"I know what you meant." He pushed away from the bed of his truck, winked at her as he passed her, and turned to move to the side of the house. "I got somethin' in mind. Gimme a minute."

Shaking her head, she watched him but remained in the dirt lot to give him and his ward some space.

Luther and Rex bounded after him. "So what's the plan, Johnny?"

"Yeah, where are we goin', huh?"

"More hunting? Oh, man! We're gonna make it three times in

one day?" Luther yipped excitedly and Johnny snapped his fingers.

"Hush." The dwarf took two heavy steps onto the dock and stopped. "Hey, kid."

"Hey." Amanda didn't turn to look at him but she sat a little straighter.

He cleared his throat. "Whatcha doin'?"

"Nothing." She gestured toward the end of the dock. "Obviously."

"All right." He clapped briskly. "Well, since you ain't busy, come on. Let's go."

With a sigh, she stood and turned to face him, her shoulders slumped. "Where?"

Johnny scrutinized her dejected demeanor and fought back a laugh. *Well, the mood swings are age-appropriate at least. I reckon it ain't much more than that. Hopefully.* "It's a surprise. Come on."

"Johnny, I don't honestly want to—"

"Naw, you'll want to. Trust me." He waved her forward and Amanda shuffled toward him. "You ever been to a crab boil?"

"Um…I've seen crabs boiling."

The dwarf chuckled and gave her back a few gentle pats when she stepped off the dock with him. "It ain't the same thing at all, kid. Crab boil's like one giant dinner party. I reckon you been to a few of those up north, huh?"

"Yeah. All the time." A shadow passed over the girl's face and she slowed as they walked across the grass along the side of the cabin.

Shit. Stay away from the old life in the city, Johnny. Don't be an idiot.

He cleared his throat, at a loss for what else to say.

"It's not gonna be like one of those, right?"

He glanced at her. "Do you want it to be?"

"Uh…no." Amanda chuckled and wiped her hands on her pants. "And if you're excited to go, I know it won't be."

"Uh-huh." He grinned reassuringly and nodded at Sheila. "Hop in there, kid. It ain't a house party in Manhattan but this is as fancy as it gets down here."

The young shifter paused beside the Jeep and pointed at Agent Breyer. "Is Lisa coming?"

"It was her idea."

The woman smiled. "Of course I'm coming—wait. What did he tell you?"

"Crab boil."

"Yeah, I'm coming."

Johnny whistled and the hounds raced toward him again. "Get on up, boys. We're gonna have ourselves a time."

"A crab time!" Rex leapt over the back of the Jeep and landed with a scrabble of claws on the empty floor in the back.

"We love crab, Johnny." Luther stopped behind the Jeep, crouched, and sprang up. His back foot caught on the edge of the glass-less window, and he toppled forward over the side before his head popped up over the back seat and he panted. "Crab time!"

"Shrimp time!" Rex barked as Sheila's engine roared to life.

"Food time!"

"People time!"

Luther cocked his head. "Hey, Johnny. Will there be people there?"

"Like friends?"

The dwarf glanced at them in the rearview mirror as Lisa braced herself against the passenger side door. "We'll all have a good time."

He eased Sheila forward in a tight circle to turn and smirked at the woman's tense arm pressed against the door. "Are you okay?"

"What? Yeah, I'm—ah!"

With a wide grin, he floored the gas pedal and the Jeep

hurtled down his dirt drive. Rex, Luther, and Amanda howled in the back.

CHAPTER ELEVEN

"See that place right there?" Johnny pointed down Riverside Drive at the shabby looking waterfront building in Everglades City, the front plastered with crooked signs of one-line menu items.

"City Seafood?" Amanda raised an eyebrow at him. "That's as fancy as it gets down here?"

He glanced at his watch. "It's a hell of a place to eat, kid. And it's almost seven now. Just in time."

Lisa stared at the sign in front of the restaurant. "They close at six, Johnny."

"Uh-huh."

"So you're takin' us to an after-hours crab boil inside a restaurant." The young shifter wrinkled her nose. "It's kinda disappointing."

"Don't knock the food, kid. But that ain't where we're goin'." He skipped off the sidewalk on Begonia Street and headed across to the other side.

His two companions looked at one another in confusion. "So why'd we park right next door?"

"It's the off-season." He shrugged. "Free parking in the airboat tour lot."

Luther and Rex trotted across the street beside him.

Amanda turned to look at Sheila and the two other cars nearby. "I think everywhere in this town is free parking. And I thought he liked airboats."

Lisa chuckled as they hurried after the dwarf and his hounds. "I think it's the tour part he doesn't like. Mainly the tourists. Come on."

They passed only two more streets as they followed him down Camelia St. E and in five minutes, they'd crossed the entire width of Everglades City's main street from the wide river on the west to the narrower one on the east. They turned again on the far side of Collier Avenue at Everglades Family Fishing and walked past riverfront properties lining the strand.

"Oh, okay." Amanda nodded. "These houses look more like fancy party houses."

"Maybe." Johnny turned and waltzed through the next house's yard toward the water.

"Johnny," Lisa whispered and hurried to catch up with him as the hounds bounded through the reeds.

"Hey, Rex. Get that frog?"

"Where?"

"Right there—oh! Shit. Go, go, go."

"Johnny, this is someone's property."

"Yep."

"We can't simply barge through their yard like this."

"These folks only come here November through mid-May, darlin'." He gestured at the huge, pastel-pink house with the sweeping front and back porches. "It's almost June. They ain't gonna know the difference."

"A house party where the owners aren't home?" Amanda's mouth dropped open in excitement. "Awesome."

The dwarf snorted. "This was a good idea. Y'all got a hell of a lot to learn 'bout how things work down here."

"So no house?"

"No house." He led them upriver along the railroad track at the edge of the land before it gave way to the swamp on their right. Finally, he stepped onto the dock that stretched across the narrow river at the front of someone else's property and pointed at the swamp. "Mind the 'gators. They tend to get a little excited when it starts to warm up."

Amanda grinned. "Cool."

"Jesus." Lisa stepped gingerly onto the wobbling floating dock. "He's leading us through an alligator pit."

"It might be they're somewhere else. I simply said mind 'em."

Rex and Luther returned from their sprint through multiple waterfront properties and leapt onto the dock with a scrabble of claws. They raced past Amanda and Lisa—and made the woman freeze with her arms straight out on either side—and even darted ahead of Johnny into the underbrush. "Crab time, here we come!"

"Oh, man. Oh, man. Johnny! Why'd we wait so long?"

The hounds disappeared into the thick growth without waiting for an answer and uttered a single bark each.

The dwarf stepped off the end of the narrow dock with a squelch of mud and turned to offer Lisa a hand. "It looks steadier than it is. That'll clear up."

"Uh-huh." She narrowed her eyes at him and smirked as she took his hand slowly. "This how you reel 'em in, Johnny? Scare the ladies with a warning about 'gators, then pull out the minor chivalry?"

He snorted. "Only when I bring 'em out here."

"Oh, yeah? How many women have you brought out here to a crab boil in the middle of nowhere?"

"Only you, darlin'. And the kid." Johnny turned and strode through the mud and reeds and the thick branches that hung low over the swamp. "Watch your step too. There's a path but it ain't been cleared in a couple of decades."

Lisa laughed and hurried after him, ducked under the branches, and swiped vines aside. She grimaced when some snagged her hair but moved forward without hesitation.

Amanda jumped off the dock, splashed a huge puddle of mud and water everywhere, and spattered her jeans. She turned to look at the houses along the water and smirked. "This is gonna be good."

They proceeded for another ten minutes along the alleged path Johnny seemed to know like his own back yard. Lisa couldn't see anything remotely resembling a walkway but at least she hadn't gotten any swamp water in her boots.

Finally, muted Bluegrass music and a few dozen voices could be heard somewhere ahead, followed by Rex and Luther's excited barks. "We're here!"

"Johnny, hurry up before they eat all the food."

"Hey, Rex. Check it out. Chum buckets."

"Yes!"

The dwarf pulled aside a particularly large fern and held it back until Lisa and Amanda passed through.

"Woah." The young shifter's eyes lit up as she took in the open clearing in the Everglades—a huge circle of dry land complete with tables and chairs, a rickety-looking shed with only three walls, four tall wooden tables positioned end-to-end beside the shed, and a firepit covered by a grate with another sheet of metal on top. Mason-jar lanterns hung from the shed and along thick ropes strung from the roof into the higher branches of the closest trees, and at least two dozen people milled around, talking, laughing, and drinking.

The girl folded her arms and gave him a bemused glance. "This isn't a real place, is it?"

"Well, you ain't dreamin', kid. You won't find this on a damn tour map, but for us locals, this is as real as it gets. Come on."

"Is this here all the time?" Lisa asked, her eyes wide as she followed him absently toward the tables where no one had sat to eat yet.

"'S long as the storms don't blow it away." He smirked at her. "Is this fun enough for ya?"

"Oh, yeah."

"Hey! Johnny!" A skinny man in denim overalls without a shirt under them and thick construction gloves stopped in front of the metal-covered fire and raised a hand. "Ain't seen you out here in a while."

"I ain't had the itch to the drive all the way out to experience the Everglades City."

The man snorted and stooped to pick up the huge burlap sack on top of the metal sheet. "Well, it's about damn time you showed your ugly mug 'round here. Grab a drink, yeah? I'ma dump these and start handin' shuckers out."

Johnny raised a hand in acknowledgment, and the man hoisted the burlap sack off the fire to take it toward the row of tall, sturdy wooden tables.

"Shuckers as in for oysters?" Lisa muttered.

The dwarf snorted. "You don't eat oysters in a month, don't have an R."

She wrinkled her nose and frowned at him. "You know, you were much easier to understand when we were in New York."

Johnny rubbed his nose and smirked. "This is home, darlin'. I'm only loosenin' up. Look. Clive's dumpin' crab on that table. Steamed 'em all together—either softshell or blue. I can't see from here. We let those babies cool off, and then the horde will start swarmin' like a pack of starvin'—" *Goddamnit. How many poorly timed wolf analogies are there?* "Well, you get the idea. Come on."

"Okay..." The agent seemed fixated on the dozens of crabs with fist-sized bodies that Clive tossed out of the steaming burlap sack onto the tables. He spread them out with his gloves. "Where are we going?"

"To get a drink." The bounty hunter winked at her and headed toward the small crowd—a bearable size for him—and beyond them to the open-front shed.

"Johnny." A man missing most of his teeth grinned at them and his lips folded over his empty gums. "What the hell are you doin' here, man?"

"I had to clear the place out at least once before it got too damn hot, Marvin."

The man wheezed with laughter and lifted a beer bottle toward him.

"My days. Johnny Walker." A tall woman with frizzy blonde hair pulled away from her face with a large plastic clip put a hand on her hip and regarded the dwarf with a broad grin. "Well, now it's a *real* party. Ain't it?"

"Not unless you brought your shrimp."

"Honey, when have you ever seen me without it?" The woman darted Lisa a glance and her smile faded a little. "Who's your friend, Johnny?"

"Lisa Breyer. This is Hannah Bender."

A man in full camo from head to toe who stood slightly behind the woman snorted, but he looked away and focused on his beer when Johnny glanced warningly at him. *You'd think grown-ass men would quit findin' that funny.*

Lisa smiled sweetly—mostly—at the blonde woman. "Hannah makes the best damn blackened shrimp I ever had," the dwarf told her. "She still won't tell me what she uses."

Hannah winked at him. "Family recipe, Johnny. You know there's only one way you'll ever get it outta me."

"Uh-huh." With a smirk, he moved past her toward the shed and Lisa followed quickly.

"Nice to meet you."

The woman grinned at her and batted her eyelashes. "You too, honey."

As soon as her face could no longer be seen, the agent's smile disappeared. "Honey. That one gets me."

"It's only Southern hospitality, darlin'." Johnny looked at her over his shoulder and raised an eyebrow. "Is darlin' off the table too?"

She gave him a small smile. "Not when you say it."

"Uh-huh." He led her around the front of the open shed and her eyes widened when they stepped inside.

"Wow."

"Johnny!" A huge man stood behind the slightly crooked bar built into the back of the ramshackle structure and his muscles bulged beneath his tight white undershirt. "Well, hot damn. Good to see you, brother."

"Chuck." He inclined his head and approached the fully stocked bar.

A single deep shelf ran the length of the shed's sidewalls, both of them covered with serving dishes of different sizes and colors and each holding a different home-cooked side dish. At least three different variations of mac 'n cheese, scalloped potatoes, and coleslaw were immediately visible, along with summer salad and Caesar salad. Corn cobs slathered with butter and paprika were piled on a platter beside green beans cooked with bacon. A basket of still-steaming biscuits covered in a checkered cloth filled the shed with an aroma that made Lisa's mouth water.

The self-appointed bartender bent behind the bar and emerged with a rocks glass and a bottle of Johnny Walker Black Label. He grinned at the dwarf as he poured four fingers into the glass. "Folks was startin' to worry when you didn't show up for the last...what? Three cookouts?"

He took his whiskey and sniffed. "You know I don't roll around here—"

"During tourist season. Yeah, Johnny. We all know."

The agent dragged herself away from the ridiculous spread of Southern food and joined him at the bar.

Chuck jerked his chin at her with a smile as he replaced Johnny's personal bottle behind the bar. "What can I do ya for?"

"Um...a beer, thanks."

He chuckled. "Got a preference?"

"Not really."

"Good. 'Cause I got a wide selection of one." The man reached back into a huge cooler filled with half-melted ice and beer bottles, popped the cap off one of them with the bottle opener mounted on the wall beside him, and handed her the beer. "Comes from a local brewery a few miles north. Has everything you need."

"Thanks."

Smiling, he wiped his hands on a stained rag and watched the dwarf sip his whiskey. "Thought you'd bring your woman out here to show her a good time, huh?"

Lisa choked on her beer and shook her head. "Oh, I'm not—"

"She's a friend," Johnny said calmly.

"Uh-huh." Chuck looked from one to the other. "Heard that before."

"And we brought company."

"You mean them hounds runnin' wild with the kiddies out there?" The man laughed. "Sure. Call 'em comp'ny, Johnny."

"Well, one of them kiddies came with me."

"Oh, yeah? Hadn't heard 'bout you and a kid."

"I aim to keep it that way, yeah?" The bounty hunter took a longer sip of his whiskey and rapped his knuckles against the bar. "Wide-eyed kid with brown hair and too smart for her own good comes in here—"

"Lemonade or a coke, Johnny. This ain't my first gig."

"All right." He raised his glass at Chuck and turned away from the bar. "I'll be back."

"Yeah, I know."

As they left the shed, Lisa stopped beside a massive bowl piled high with chopped corn cobs, onions, small red potatoes, clams, oysters, shrimp, and sausage. She leaned forward to smell it and widened her eyes. "What's this?"

"Low country boil. With beer. That's Florida-style, darlin'."

She looked at him and pointed at the stack of paper plates at the end of the shelf. "Can we simply help ourselves?"

"Sure. But not before we get our hands on that crab outside. All this is filler for when the blues are gone."

"Blue crab."

"Uh-huh. Come on."

Chuck snorted and shook his head as he led his cookout-naïve "friend" outside.

"Better get in here quick, Johnny," Clive muttered through a dripping mouthful of steamed blue crab. "You know they ain't gonna last."

Already, the locals had gathered at the long line of tall tables and picked crabs up from where they lay and ate them where they stood. The tables reached slightly above the middle of Johnny's chest. With a grunt, he dragged a cinder block toward him with his boot and stepped onto it. "Y'all need to fix these damn tables."

The locals who heard his half-joking mutter laughed and reached for more of the steamed crustaceans.

Lisa scanned the seasoned feast and raised both hands hesitantly. "Okay, I'm new to this."

"Oh?" The dwarf laughed. "I couldn't tell. Here." He selected a medium-sized blue crab and thunked it onto the table in front of him. "It's real simple."

"Any parts I shouldn't eat?"

He chose one for himself and ripped off a huge piece that included its head and the side of its body. An open pincer dangled from his mouth as he chewed and raised his eyebrows at the half-Light Elf.

She smirked and picked hers up. "I'll take that as a no."

"It'll grow on you, darlin'."

"Not literally, I hope."

The dwarf shrugged and took another bite, and pieces of flesh and the juice of the boil beaded on his wiry red beard.

"Here." A woman with a red bandana tied around her head tossed a lemon wedge across the table toward Lisa. "Squeeze some of that on there, hon."

Johnny grunted. "Only if you wanna ruin it."

The locals gathered around the table laughed, and Lisa bit into her first boil-and-beer-steamed blue crab. Without the lemon.

CHAPTER TWELVE

Once all the crab was finished, the locals enjoying their Everglades cookout filed into the shed to fill their plates with more food and refill their drinks. It all went incredibly fast.

Lisa joined Johnny at one of the tables, which someone had since covered with a nondescript tablecloth weighted down by mason jars. "Okay, I gotta admit, this is all very good."

"Somethin' might be wrong with you otherwise." He bit into an ear of corn and butter and seasoning dripped onto his plate and collected here and there on his beard in thick drops.

She handed him a napkin and looked away while he tried to wipe the stains from his button-down shirt. "I now see the difference between a cookout and a barbeque, at least."

"Huh. Told ya."

"Do you think we should get Amanda a plate before it's all gone? I haven't seen her since—"

Right on cue, a horde of kids ranging from ten to thirteen or fourteen burst from the tree line at the other side of the clearing, laughing and throwing handfuls of mud at each other. Amanda was with them and she laughed hysterically when a boy who looked about her age caught a splatter of swamp mud in the face.

He grimaced, wiped it off, and turned to grin at her. "Oh, yeah? That's how it is?"

She spread her arms in a teasing gesture. "Hey, if you don't know how to duck—"

His throw went lower than he wanted and struck her in the stomach with a splat. "Crap."

"You should work on your aim."

"Yeah, well you throw like a—"

Amanda cocked her head. "Like a girl?"

He rolled his eyes. "No. Not really."

"Hey, hey, pup!" Rex and Luther raced toward the kids engaged in their muddy battle. "Who threw mud at you?"

Amanda pointed at the boy who tried to wipe the sludge off his face. He looked up at her, frowned, and saw the dogs. "Wait. What are you doing?"

"Man, you didn't even invite us to play?" Rex barked and skidded to a stop between the kids. "That's rude."

The kid's eyes widened. "What—"

Rex shook himself vigorously and flung mud and water all over him and the other screaming, laughing kids. The boy groaned, and Amanda laughed until Luther stopped beside her and showered her with swamp water when he shook himself next.

"Gotcha!"

"That'll teach you!"

"Ugh." Amanda swiped the mess away from her face and shook off a thick glob of dog drool. "Good boys?"

Luther barked, then raced across the clearing. "You ca-an't catch me!"

Rex snorted. "No one's chasing him."

"Those your dogs?" the boy asked.

"Kinda."

Rex looked at her and his tail wagged. "Hey, that's sweet, pup."

"They're Johnny's." She located Johnny and Lisa seated at one of the tables and gave them a small wave. Clods of mud dripped off her arm.

The woman waved in response. He merely grunted and focused on his food.

The boy looked curiously at Amanda. "You live with Johnny Walker?"

"Only for a while, I think." Her eyes lit up and she spun toward the tree line and the edge of the swamp. "Hey. Bet I can catch more frogs than you."

"You throw mud and catch frogs?"

"Yeah." She put her hands on her hips. "Got a problem with that?"

He shrugged. "Nope." Then, he raced past her toward the water.

"Hey!"

She gained on him quickly and he laughed. "But you fell for that one!"

Amanda rolled her eyes and caught up to him as he stopped at the edge of the water. She shoved him from behind and he splashed into the swamp with a yelp. "So did you."

He looked at her, dripping with mud and water and with reeds clinging to his hair. They both began to laugh as she helped him to his feet.

Johnny drank his whiskey and watched the girl disappear into the thick trees of the swamp with Clive Brightmon's son. *Anyone else's kid, and I'd be worried about what they doin' out there on their own.*

"So no on making her a plate, then." Lisa served a shrimp shell onto her plate and bit the tail off.

"Naw, she's havin' a good time."

"You don't sound very convinced, Johnny."

"It's good for her. I reckon she ain't had much time for playin' in the muck up north. Investment-banker old man and all."

Lisa nodded. "Yeah, she looks happy."

"Yep." He licked the seasoning off his fingers and swiped his beard and mouth with a napkin. *This is what she should be doin'. Not runnin' around after shifters and Oriceran monsters.*

"You're doing a good job with her, Johnny."

The dwarf looked at her with a raised eyebrow. "I had a little practice. Once." He cleared his throat. "After twelve, though, I don't know shit about raisin' teenagers."

She laughed. "Said every parent ever."

"Johnny. Hey, Johnny." Luther's snout poked over the edge of the table on the other side of Lisa. "Tell her to hand over the scraps."

"Yeah, Johnny." Rex's tail thumped against their legs beneath the table as he sniffed through the grass. "No one's droppin' a damn thing at this party. If somethin' doesn't change soon, we're gonna keel over."

"Hey, lady." Luther pressed his nose against Lisa's elbow, and she turned with a surprised laugh.

"Hey, Luther."

"You gonna eat those shrimp shells or what?"

Johnny whistled, and both dogs sat. "Table's taken, boys."

"But Johnny. Look at her. She doesn't know how to shell."

"Yeah, she'll drop something."

Johnny snapped his fingers and pointed away from the table. "Git."

"Someone's in a mood." Luther stalked off and sniffed the ground as his brother emerged from under the table.

Rex licked his chops and poked his snout over the table toward Johnny's plate. The dwarf shot him a warning glance and shoved the paper plate toward the center of the table.

"Aw… Come on, Johnny. What's the big deal?"

He grunted, downed the rest of his whiskey, and stood from the table with his empty glass in hand. "My hounds don't eat scraps."

"Luther!" Rex barked. "He said we don't eat scraps! Get over here!"

Luther raced toward the table and sat instantly beside his brother as their master headed to the shed. "Oh man, oh man, oh man. Finally."

"Is everything okay?" Lisa called after him.

"You sit tight, darlin'. I won't be a minute." As he rounded the corner of the open shed, someone turned the music up. Some of the locals whooped and laughed as "Florida Blues" by Ricky Scaggs blared across the clearing. He shook his head and placed the empty rocks glass on the bar.

Chuck smirked and slid a freshly poured four fingers of Johnny Walker Black toward him.

"Right on time." He downed the contents, nodded at the huge man, and went to find two plates. He stopped at the half-empty bowl of blackened shrimp.

"I knew you couldn't stay away," Hannah said behind him with a coy smile.

"A spread like this? There ain't no reason to stay away." He lifted the bowl and poured the shrimp onto the plates.

Her eyes widened but she didn't try to stop him. "You miss me, Johnny?"

Licking his lips, he set the empty bowl down and picked up the plates now heaped with piles of seasoned shrimp. *Not this again.* When he turned toward her, he gave her a brief smile. "That's one hell of a loaded question, darlin'."

"I missed you."

"Well, I came back." He shrugged. "Shrimp's too damn good to pass up."

Hannah laughed and brushed her blonde hair out of her face. She watched the bounty hunter as he trudged out of the shed.

"Want another drink, Hannah?" Chuck asked from behind the bar. "Might help with the disappointment."

"You mind your own business, Chuck Hornby."

The bartender shrugged with a small smile. "You're in my bar. And the only thing brings Johnny back for seconds is fixin's and whiskey."

She stared at him and rolled her eyes. "Vodka soda, Chuck."

"Uh-huh."

Outside at the table, Rex and Luther watched their master with their tongues lolling out of their mouths. Slobber pattered onto the grass, and their tails thumped against the ground.

"Yeah, yeah, yeah." Luther whined, raised his rear end two inches, then forced it down again. "Johnny. Hey, Johnny. Who are those for?"

"Shit, Johnny. Say somethin'."

"You done good today, boys. I expect nothin' left over." He set the plates on the ground. Neither hound moved. "Go on."

"Yes!"

"You're the best, Johnny!"

The dwarf rubbed his mouth and chin. Flecks of blackened shrimp scattered across the grass as the hounds gobbled as much as they could as quickly as possible.

"Oh, shit. Spicy shrimp."

"Damn, Johnny. Just…" Rex chased the paper plate across the grass in an attempt to lick it clean.

"Where'd Lisa go to?" Johnny asked.

"Lisa? Who's Lisa?"

"I know where the shrimp is, Johnny."

Rolling his eyes, he scanned the clearing and located Agent Lisa Breyer in the huddle of a dozen locals dancing with their beers and drinks in hand. *Shit. That wasn't part of the plan.*

He walked slowly toward the randomly selected "dancefloor" beneath the strands of mason jar lanterns.

"Johnny!" She grinned at him and ran a hand through her hair. "Come on."

"Nope."

"So you're simply gonna stand there?" She inclined her head

and pouted at him across the clearing.

The dwarf folded his arms and remained where he was.

"I'll dance with you, beautiful." Marcus Neiler grinned at her and shimmied and his baggy t-shirt fluttered around his scrawny shoulders.

Lisa fought back a laugh. "What do you call that move?"

"You can call it whatever you want." He lowered his head and stepped closer and his hand inched toward her waist.

"Goddammit." Johnny trudged toward the small group of dancing locals, most of whom had already had twice as much to drink as he had. The dancers paused when they saw the dwarf who never danced at cookouts moving through their ranks toward Lisa. Some of them chuckled. No one said a thing, though, and they all focused on their drinks and dancing.

"Hands to yourself, Marcus," the bounty hunter snapped.

"What the—" The scrawny man pulled away from Lisa and stared at him with wide eyes. "Hey, man. I was only bein' chivulous and all."

"Well, go do it somewhere else."

Marcus backed away with a nervous chuckle, then seemed to get into the music and flung his lanky limbs in every direction while he banged his head like he was at a metal show.

A metal show would be a hell of a lot better than this shit.

The agent swayed from side to side with the music and frowned teasingly at him. "So that's what it takes to get you to dance, huh?"

He sniffed and stared at the locals who moved around him. "I don't dance."

"Oh, come on." She twirled and sang along, then leaned toward him with wide eyes.

Johnny stuck his thumbs through his belt loops and returned her stare.

"Nothing? Johnny, no one's that immune to this song." She laughed. "The reason for coming out here was to have fun, right?"

His expression unimpressed, the dwarf glanced at the strands of lanterns and sighed. He raised an index finger and twirled it slowly.

Lisa stopped dancing and shook her head as her shoulders sagged. "You're not even trying."

"This is the most you'll get outta me, darlin'. You wanna see this dwarf dance, take me to a Led Zeppelin tribute show. AC/DC. Rush."

She smirked and straightened. "Is that an invitation, Johnny?"

"I—" He looked at her and raised an eyebrow. "That's merely the truth."

A high-pitched laugh came from the far end near the tables, and they both turned to where Amanda stood, splattered by mud and swamp water and with reeds and leaves clinging to her soaked clothes. The girl pointed at Johnny with one hand and held herself around the middle with her other arm. She doubled over and stumbled until she fell to her knees and rocked as she continued to laugh.

Lisa chuckled, and he scowled at her. "It's a little funny, Johnny. Come on."

"That I don't dance to this?"

"That you're one of the best bounty hunters who took in a twelve-year-old kid and brought us here for a cookout in the swamp, and the best you can come up with is this." She wiped all expression from her face and stared at him with drooping eyelids as she raised an index finger and twirled it slowly.

He snorted. "It looks good when you do it."

"Oh, please."

"Hold on, Johnny." Amanda fought to catch her breath, pushed to her feet, and continued to laugh as she headed toward them.

The dancing locals took one look at the girl, and her amusement was apparently infectious. A woman whooped behind the dwarf and sloshed beer against the back of his boots as the song ended and changed to something else he didn't give a shit about.

"Seriously." The young shifter swiped wet hair away from her face and grabbed his hands. "You need an intervention."

"I don't need—"

"Great idea." Lisa grinned. "Johnny Walker should know how to dance."

"Y'all are askin' for trouble now."

"Come on." Amanda swung his arms from side to side as she bobbed to the music. "There. Now move your feet."

"I ain't movin' shit, kid. Let go of me." It sounded gruff but he smirked at the girl and she tightened her hold on his hands.

"Not until you loosen up."

He stamped one foot on the grass, then the other. "There."

Ignoring his attitude, she released him and gestured with her arms. "Now do a little spin."

"For fuck's sake."

She demonstrated, laughed, and pointed at him. "Your turn."

Johnny looked hopefully at the agent but she simply shrugged. *How the hell did I get myself into this?*

He gazed across the clearing and saw Luther and Rex at one of the tables. They had both clamped their jaws on the edge of the tablecloth and stepped back, trying to pull it off—including the plates of scraps.

"The hounds are forgettin' their manners." He pointed at the dogs, then slipped past them and headed away from all the damn dancing.

"Wait. *Johnny—*"

"Y'all wiggle your little hearts out." He tossed a hand in the air but didn't turn to look at them. *Saved by the damn hounds. You bet your ass they're gettin' extra food tonight.*

Lisa and Amanda laughed and began to dance with each other.

Rex and Luther finally pulled their intended feast off the table and three mason-jar weights fell with the uneaten food and rolled across the grass.

"Yes!"

"Ha-ha!" Luther jumped onto the tablecloth. "Now that's how it's done."

"Hey, Johnny."

"Shit." The other dog spun quickly and lowered his head. He looked from his master to the mess on the ground. "Wasn't us, Johnny."

"Yeah, we found it here." Rex sat and licked his muzzle with a whine. "Folks are gettin' wild and crazy tonight, huh? Pulling tablecloths off the tables. Johnny?"

The bounty hunter took an empty chair from an adjacent table, spun it, and sat. He folded his arms and stared at the dancers and his gaze returned every few seconds to Lisa and her long legs beneath the Daisy Dukes.

"Luther?"

"Uh-huh."

"Is that his mad face or his thinking face?"

"Looks like his happy face to me. Hey, Johnny. You hungry?"

"Maybe he has to take a shit."

Luther whipped his head toward his brother and his ears flopped against his face. "In a chair?"

"A man can simply sit in peace, can't he?" the dwarf muttered.

"Yeah, yeah. Sure, Johnny."

Rex took one tentative step toward his master, then stopped to stare at the spilled plates. "What about hounds? Huh, Johnny?"

"Right." Luther inched sideways toward the spilled food. "Could two hounds, say...eat all these goodies they didn't drag onto the floor in peace?"

He snorted and watched Lisa and Amanda dancing like crazies with a group of Everglades locals who didn't look anywhere near sane. "I ain't stoppin' you, boys."

"I knew it!"

"Johnny, you're a hell of a guy. Hell of a—ooh! Bacon!"

CHAPTER THIRTEEN

At 6:55 am the next morning, Johnny stood at the bottom of his front porch stairs and squinted down the long dirt drive to his cabin.

"What are we waiting for, Johnny?" Luther spun in two tight circles. "Come on. Let's go!"

"I said seven o'clock, boys. She ain't late yet."

Amanda opened her mouth to speak but her words were swallowed by a massive yawn that she covered halfheartedly with a limp hand. "Maybe she went back to sleep. Which sounds like a great idea."

"Go ahead and curl up, then." He nodded toward the front door. "I ain't forcin' you to tag along."

"No, I wanna come." The girl sighed and rubbed her eyes, then forced them open. "But why did it have to be so early?"

He frowned at her. "When would you rather wake up?"

"I don't know. Ten, maybe."

"Oh, sure. Sleep through half the day."

"Well, if you didn't keep us up all night—"

"The way I remember it, you were the one beggin' Daphne Harrison not to pack her speakers up before we headed out."

Amanda smirked. "Yeah. Why do people at parties always save the good music for the very end?"

"You call that good?" Johnny snorted. "You must have been at all the wrong parties, kid."

"Whatever." With a tired chuckle, she turned in a small circle and yawned again. "I'll wake up on the boat."

"If you're comin' with us, you'd better." He nodded at the cloud of dust that billowed up the drive around Lisa's rental Camry. "I need you sharp for another hunt."

"Yeah, I'm good." Ignoring the agent's approach, she lowered herself onto the grass, crossed her legs, and held her face in her hands. "I can be sharp."

"I got a water hose out back."

She looked at him with wide eyes. "You wouldn't."

"You've been with me for three weeks, kid. Did you ever hear me say I'm gonna do somethin' and then not do it?"

Rolling her eyes, she pushed to her feet and slapped her hands against her cheeks to smoosh them together. "Do not spray me with a hose."

"Then don't fall asleep."

Lisa slid out of the Camry and reached inside to retrieve two to-go coffee cups before she shut the door with her hip. "Morning."

Johnny looked quickly at the young shifter. "Do you drink coffee?"

"What?"

Lisa walked swiftly toward them wearing dark-blue jeans and a button-up plaid shirt. Her pistol swung slightly in her shoulder holster. "I'm not late, am I?"

"Nope."

She thrust one of the coffees toward him and smiled. "Thanks for last night, Johnny. That was fun."

"Woah." Luther hurried toward her to sniff excitedly at her legs and backside. "What did you guys do last night, Johnny, huh?

Usually, we can hear it when you and a lady—"

He snapped his fingers and the dog sat.

"What? What'd I say, Johnny?"

"Not in front of the pup." Rex snorted. "And you watched her drive away last night."

"I did?"

"Chased her too."

"Huh."

"Thanks." The dwarf lowered his head to sniff the coffee. "This ain't some damn fancy frilly shit, is it?"

"Nope." She studied him as she sipped her coffee. "Just black."

"Good." He took a long slurp and widened his eyes. "Your hotel serves this?"

"It's not exactly the Greenwich Hotel, Johnny." She shrugged. "I'll always take a detour for good coffee."

"'Preciate it." Taking another sip, Johnny turned toward the side of the house and looked at Amanda, who swayed on her feet. "Here, kid. Drink that. It'll put hair on your chest."

"What?"

Lisa sighed. "Johnny, it's probably not a good idea to say something like that."

"Folks around here say it all the time."

"To twelve-year-old girls?"

He glanced from one to the other and his mustache bristled. "Well if she were a boy, I'd say it would grow hair on her balls. His balls. Whatever."

"Oh, my God." Amanda took the coffee cup absently and stared after him as he headed toward the back of the house with the dogs at his side.

"Johnny." The agent hurried after him and shook her head at Amanda. "You don't have to drink that."

"I know. It smells gross." The girl took a small sip and stared at the cup. "Woah."

"Yeah, yeah. The boat." Luther jumped around Johnny as his

master untied the rope and coiled it on the dock. "Johnny, let's get on."

"We're goin' huntin'!" Rex threw his head back and howled.

"Hey, if I thought it was a good idea for Amanda to drink coffee, I would've brought three."

The dwarf looked at her and frowned. "You were all for my parentin' style last night."

"Well, last night didn't include loading an adolescent girl with high levels of caffeine and making wildly inappropriate comments about her chest."

"Oh..." He glanced off into the trees and sniffed. "You're one of those."

"One of what?"

"The 'don't say anythin' 'cause it might hurt someone's feelings' people."

She folded her arms. "It's called being considerate. Respectful."

"I ain't short on respect, darlin'." He picked up a heavy black metal trunk from a stack of them against the back of the house and carried it toward the airboat.

"But I'm very sure you don't have a"—she turned to look at Amanda, but the girl had disappeared—"clue about what goes on in a little girl's head. Especially when it centers around her body."

With a snort, he dropped the trunk on the deck and slid it toward the back, where he attached the loose nylon straps to two hooks on the stern beneath the giant propeller. "I've seen that kid fight, rip out a few bastards' vital body parts with her teeth, and shift again as naked as the day she was born. We both have."

"That's not the point."

"Naw. The point is if any young'un's at home in their skin, it's her. And I ain't fixin' to tiptoe around her because someone else tells me it's disrespectful. She can handle it."

Lisa sighed and shook her head. "You can't teach an old dwarf new tricks, huh?"

"Lyin' ain't a trick, darlin'." He stepped onto the dock and raised a finger as he passed her. "Merely a liability."

And I shouldn't have to defend myself in my damn back yard.

Rex and Luther scrambled onto the airboat as the bounty hunter took one of his many rifles off the flat railing of the back porch. "Yeah, get the gun."

"What else you bringin', Johnny? Grenades?"

"Rocket launchers?"

"Those little robot spider things?"

"Ooh, yeah. Those are cool."

Johnny ignored them and nodded at Lisa. "Ready?"

She stood at the edge of the dock and watched him stride toward the boat again. "You said we were going hunting this morning."

"Yep."

"You didn't say anything about a boat."

He rested his hand on the throttle control stick and shrugged. "It's the fastest way to get anywhere 'round here."

"Johnny, I don't—" She swallowed. "I don't do well on boats."

"That so?" He sniffed. "Take it or leave it, darlin'. Either way, we're bringin' back game and then we'll go take that draksa a little snack."

"I think I'll stay here for this one."

"It's your call. We'll be ridin' this airboat to the draksa too, by the way."

"Of course you will." Lisa ran a hand through her hair and frowned at the craft.

"How fast does it go?"

"As fast as I want her to go."

"Yeah, so let's hurry, Johnny." Luther pranced from bow to stern and yipped in excitement. "Go fast. Hunt somethin'. Man, oh man. What a day!"

Rex sat in the bow and scanned Johnny's property, panting. "Is the pup coming with us, Johnny?"

The dwarf frowned and cupped a hand around his mouth. "Amanda!"

A moment later, the back door burst open with a bang and the girl raced down the porch steps with her hand raised. "Coming!"

He nodded at the agent as Amanda raced toward the dock. "Last call, darlin'."

"We're ready to go, right?" The young shifter slowed beside Lisa, folded her arms, sighed, and lowered them again as she nodded. "Yeah, I think I'm ready to go."

"Then get on." Johnny started the airboat's engine with a sharp jerk on the ignition.

"Come on, Lisa. You'll love this," Amanda said.

"I...think I'm good."

"What?" She blew loose hair out of her face. "No, no, no. You have to come with us."

"Yeah!" Luther barked sharply.

Rex whined. "Come on, lady!"

"See? Everyone wants you on. You'll love it, I promise." She caught the woman's hand and pulled her fiercely toward the dock. "You don't have to do anything—unless you wanna try to hunt with us. I wasn't sure I'd like hunting on a boat, either, but it turned out to be awesome. You ever been on a boat like this?"

The agent chuckled nervously as she let herself be dragged down the dock. "Not in a long time."

"Ever been hunting?"

"Well, I—"

"It probably wasn't anything like with Johnny. He's got all kinds of weapons. Knows how to be sneaky too, which is a weird thing to think about when you're on a boat. Sneaky on the water. Especially with that fan. Man, it's loud!" She hopped onto the deck and spun quickly. "Come on. It's fine. Look."

When she hopped up and down several times, Johnny intervened. "Kid, that ain't helpin' none. Come on."

"Oh. Right. Sorry, Lisa." She waved the agent forward

urgently, then wiped her hands on her pants. "Please, please, please. You'll love it."

"Uh-huh." The woman looked at Johnny, who frowned at the back of the girl's head. "Amanda, are you feeling okay?"

"What? Yeah. Totally. I feel great." She exhaled a sigh and nodded. "Only...uh, is it normal to have to go to the bathroom like that after downing a whole cup of coffee? It didn't seem like that much, but whew. Went right through me, you know?"

"Oh. Yeah..." Lisa raised an eyebrow at Johnny. "I'd say that's very normal. Especially if you're not used to drinking caffeine first thing in the morning."

"I think I'll do that every day." With a grin, the shifter spun to face him and gave him a tight, jittery salute. "Got her onboard, Cap'n. Do whatever—" She stabbed her fingers one after the other like pistons at the simple airboat controls. "Whatever you do to get it going. Let's nail this...what are we hunting, again?"

He cleared his throat. "Go ahead and sit before you hurt yourself."

"Yeah, okay." She dropped to the deck and crossed her legs beneath her as he stalked toward the bow.

"A whole cup of coffee," Lisa muttered as he passed her.

"I get it. Point to Agent Breyer." He kicked fiercely against the dock to shove the airboat away.

The woman gasped and staggered as her arms flailed at her sides for balance. "I should have stayed in your yard."

"You should probably take a seat, too."

The dwarf returned to the controls, and Lisa swallowed thickly before she lowered herself to the deck on slightly trembling legs.

"Hey, lady. You stink." Luther sniffed her and nudged her arm with his snout. "Smells like fear. Rex?"

"Check her pits. Always the first place a two-leg gets scared."

"Oh, yep. That's fear."

Rex licked the side of Amanda's face as she grinned at the

water and her crossed legs jerked up and down in excitement. "And you are way too salty, pup. What did you do?"

"Ooh, lemme try." Luther joined them.

The young shifter responded with a high-pitched chuckle and rubbed both hounds' heads vigorously. "I love coffee."

"Coffee? What, did you drink it? Ha. That's nothing. One time, Johnny had this—"

Johnny cranked the throttle and the airboat's propeller whirred to life and cut all sound out as the craft increased speed along the river.

Lisa pulled her legs up to her chest and hunched over her knees.

"Relax, darlin'. These airboats are known for staying level on the water."

"We don't even have life vests," she muttered.

"Oh, my gosh." Amanda crawled toward the woman on her hands and knees as the airboat accelerated even more and raced down the river toward the thickening foliage. "Are you afraid of water?"

"I'm not—" The agent shook her head and released her legs to cross them beneath her. "I'm not afraid of the water. I've had a few bad experiences, is all."

"Yeah, I know what that's like." The girl sat beside her and grinned at the light spray blown toward them from the bow. "You know, I almost drowned."

Lisa looked quickly at her with wide eyes.

"Oh, not with Johnny. No. It was at a beach party. My parents took Claire and me to Saratoga Springs for a few weeks last summer. It's a crazy place if you know the right kinda crazy people, right?" She snorted. "And everyone there was so boring. There were only, like, two other kids there my age, and all they wanted to talk about was insider trading. Gag. So I went to the beach to look for seashells. I used to find all kinds of good stuff there. And there was this…"

As the girl babbled on, Rex and Luther slunk toward the stern, sat beside Johnny, and stared at her as she gestured wildly with both hands.

"Johnny. What's wrong with her?" Rex asked, his voice barely above a whisper in the bounty hunter's mind.

"Yeah, is she ever gonna stop talking? You should give her something."

Rex lowered his head to sniff the black metal box clipped to the stern. "You put tranquilizers in here, right?"

"Johnny, how are we supposed to hear anything when she won't stop?" Luther slumped onto his belly and his rear paws clicked against the huge fan's mount.

The dwarf sniffed and steered the craft downriver. "It'll run its course."

"I don't know, Johnny. What if she's like this forever?"

"Yeah, bring the old pup back. My ears hurt. Don't your ears hurt, Johnny?"

"Nope." He glanced at his hounds and tried to hide a smirk.

They probably would if I hadn't had two coonhounds talkin' in my head all day and night for the last three weeks.

CHAPTER FOURTEEN

Twenty minutes later, they were deep in the swamp. Johnny had eased the throttle to bring them to a moderate glide across the water. Lisa slapped a bug on her neck, then peeled her sticky hair away and pulled it into a messy bun. "It sure gets much hotter when you slow down."

"The sun's not even all the way up, darlin'. You might feel differently 'bout hangin' around down here in another week or two."

"Why's that?"

"The air right now is crisp in comparison."

"Hey, does anyone have any water?" Amanda muttered. "I could use some water."

"Yeah, you're looking a little pale. Did you eat anything before your...adventures with caffeine?" Lisa asked.

The girl frowned at her. "No."

"Does he usually not feed you breakfast?" The woman tilted her head and gave Johnny an exasperated glance over her shoulder.

"She didn't wanna eat." The dwarf grunted. "Said she was too tired."

"Not very much thinking things through happening today," she muttered and caught the water bottle he tossed at her. "By either of you. Here."

"Thanks." Amanda opened the lid and drank almost the entire bottle before she lowered it from her mouth with a sigh. "Maybe I'm not cut out for coffee."

"Ha. Wise words, kid." Lisa patted her shoulder gently and scanned the riverbank as they skimmed across the water at medium speed.

Johnny ran a hand over his hair. "Do you think you can pick yourself up to help us bag a beast, kid?"

"No problem." The young shifter grinned at him and nodded. "I'm ready."

"Good." *And I hopefully got us far enough away from those damn shifters.* "Now, we ain't lookin' for no fifteen-footer today. 'Gator probably wouldn't be a good choice anyway. What we want is somethin' nice and juicy a draksa can't say no to."

"Or a hound," Rex muttered.

"Yeah, what if we find something nice and juicy we can't say no to?"

Johnny glanced at his dogs. "We flush it out, bag it, get it on the boat, and that's it. Understand?"

"Yessir."

"Wait, we're bringing your draksa friend a live snack?" Lisa asked.

"It's the best way to the scaley bastards' hearts." He steered them around a huge tangle of dead branches and reeds that had washed up against the bank. "And their expert advice. The draksa have a soft spot for fresh meat. Even softer if they don't have to work for it."

"I can't believe I'm gonna see one up close," Amanda muttered. "In real life."

"Not until we bring it a present. So keep your eyes open and your noses up."

"Except for the lady, Johnny." Luther panted with unbridled excitement.

Rex sat to scratch vigorously behind his ear with his back leg. "I bet she can't tell the difference between a rabbit and a rhino."

Amanda laughed. "What?"

"I mean by smell."

Lisa smirked. "How about I simply keep my eyes open?"

"What?" The girl frowned at her.

"You're the one with the good nose, right?"

"See?" Rex snorted and shook his head when a large black fly landed on his ear. "Noses up doesn't apply to your girlfriend, Johnny."

The bounty hunter ignored his hound's slip of the tongue. *She's not my girlfriend—if I ever had one. But things might get a little complicated if I don't tell her about the collars.*

They skimmed around another wide bend until the river started to narrow. With a grunt, he pulled back on the throttle and let the airboat coast downstream. "We'll get off here."

Both animals stood abruptly as the craft puttered toward the swampy bank.

"Land!"

"Game!"

"Hey, look. Mud crabs."

They bounded off the deck and splashed through a few inches of swamp water before they scrambled onto dry land.

Lisa didn't stand until the hull of the airboat bumped gently against the soggy earth. "So this is the spot, huh?"

"Not really." Johnny stepped off after her and Amanda before he tied the rope around a thick tree trunk. "I can't take the boat much farther downriver. Don't wanna get stuck."

"Please tell me that's not something you generally do out here."

"Naw. It ain't." He leaned over the edge of the airboat to retrieve the coil of rope hanging above the box and slung it over his shoulder. With that in place, he unlatched the black metal box, sifted through the compartments for a handful of rounds he wanted, and grasped the rifle he'd upgraded to handle anything and hopped onto the shore. His boots landed in the mud with a splat. "But this is as good a place as any to find somethin' worth bringin' home."

At his shrill whistle, Rex and Luther darted without warning through the reeds to rejoin their master. "This is it, huh, Johnny?"

"Yeah, you gonna let us go on our own? Find somethin' juicy?"

"Ignore the vermin, boys. It's gotta be at least as big as one of y'all." The dwarf pointed ahead through the thickening trees and underbrush. "I'm right behind you."

They stared at each other.

"One..."

"Two..."

"Five! Go!" Luther darted off through the swamp, his tail sticking straight up in the air like a radar antenna and his snout pressed to the ground.

Rex snorted and sniffed in a wide arc away from his brother. "Who taught you to count?"

"Johnny did. I can count all the way to... Wait. How high, Johnny?"

The hounds moved through the trees and Johnny shook his head. He looked ahead occasionally as he loaded two glowing blue tranquilizer rounds into the chamber. *I didn't teach him how to count shit.*

"So..." Lisa jerked her boot out of a particularly stubborn mudhole and stumbled forward. "Do you set traps out here?"

"Nope."

"Do you have any particular kind of animal in mind?"

"Nope."

She stopped and looked at him. "And this is what you do all day long when you're not hunting flammable monsters."

"Yep." He smirked at her and hefted the rifle in both hands as he trudged after the dogs. "Nowhere and nothin' better than this, darlin.'"

"Totally cool, right?" Amanda's nose wrinkled when she grinned at Lisa and moved slowly after the dwarf.

"Uh-huh." As she swatted a swarm of tiny humming insects away, Liza shook her head and followed.

"Woah." Luther's head whipped up out of the reeds and he snorted. "You get that?"

Rex paused. "It was here...what? Twenty minutes ago."

"What is it?" Amanda leaned forward slightly and sniffed. "Did we find a pig?"

"Oh-ho-ho, buddy!" Luther yipped and raced through the underbrush with Rex on his heels. "I'm gonna rip it apart."

"No, you ain't!" the dwarf shouted. "We're only baggin' it, boys."

"Johnny." Amanda's outstretched fingers wiggled at her sides. "I'll listen this time. I can help."

"Why d'ya think I brought you along?"

"Really?"

"Hurry or they'll beat you to it."

The girl wasted no time before she shifted, leapt out of her clothes, and uttered a chilling howl as she loped after the hounds.

Johnny broke into a jog after them and held the rifle close.

Lisa stared at them before she bent to collect the pile of Amanda's clothes. She stacked the girl's shoes on top, looked around, and found no sign of anyone—dwarf, girl, or hound. "Okay. I'll...uh...stay right here."

"Close, close, close."

"So close, Johnny. Keep up."

"Yeah, you don't wanna miss all the—hey. Hey, pup! Slow down!"

Amanda darted through ferns and reeds and over old tree trunks covered in moss.

"Get along," Johnny grumbled and hurried toward them. "Corner him."

The dogs yipped again, raced forward, and skidded to the left when the scent changed direction. "Ha! Pup got too excited."

"She'll find us. Go! We're so fucking close."

"Hey, Luther. In there!"

Luther darted forward through a wall of ferns and Rex went wide to the other side. Johnny followed the former and brushed aside the ferns with his rifle to emerge in a small, sunny clearing. The hound bayed and startled the massive wild boar into action. With a squeal, it charged and barreled at the hound without a moment's hesitation.

Johnny held the rifle's scope to his eye and aimed.

Rex leapt out of the bushes from the other side of the clearing and echoed his brother's howl of triumph. "Gotcha now, you juicy—"

A gray streak burst through the reeds, and Amanda launched herself at the boar before Luther had a chance to respond. She snarled and pounded into the terrified animal. It squealed, snorted, and lost its footing, and its huge tusks gouged the earth as it slid to a halt. Immediately, it squirmed and regained its feet.

Johnny cocked his head. "Well, that's one way to corner a hog."

"Get it!" Rex shouted.

"I got it." Luther leapt in front of their dazed quarry and snarled. "You're not goin' anywhere, porky."

The animal charged again, this time away from Johnny.

"Come on, pup! Cut it off!"

Amanda darted in front of it and leapt at it again. They rolled across the ground in a scramble of wiry hair, tusks, gray fur, and snarling teeth.

"Nice one!" Luther raced toward them.

"Yeah, now pen it in."

The hounds spaced themselves equally around their quarry,

barked, and snapped their jaws. The young shifter closed in slowly with a low growl.

And that's my cue.

Johnny released a long, slow breath and squeezed the trigger gently.

The rifle cracked and the cornered animal screamed.

"Nice shot, Johnny!" Luther bayed again.

"Nighty-night, little piggy."

The boar thrashed its head and charged, its instincts to escape overriding the tranquilizer. It weaved and swerved, unable to move in a straight line.

"Yeah, I think one will do." The bounty hunter sniffed and headed toward the clearing. "Good work, boys. Now we—"

Amanda attacked without warning and clamped her powerful jaws around the thick hide on the animal's neck. It squealed and thrashed its head to flurry huge sprays of dirt and grass as it tried to throw the young wolf off its back.

"Amanda!" Johnny ran forward. "Goddammit. Cut it out. We got it."

She snarled, lost her hold, and rolled before she scrambled to stand and try again.

"What the hell, pup?" Rex shouted.

"Yeah, weren't you listening? He said don't rip it apart!"

The hounds raced toward both the young wolf and boar as she attacked again. This time, it knew what was coming and charged. She yelped when one of its huge tusks collided with her rear leg and catapulted her away. Again, she bounded to feet and her jaws snapped and sprayed spittle everywhere as she snarled and targeted the wild pig's throat.

Goddamn shifter instincts.

The dwarf raised the rifle again and aimed as his target turned toward him this time and attacked with an angry grunt.

Amanda raced after it, but Rex intercepted her and nipped at her face and neck with a firm snarl more in warning than in anger. "Hey, hey, hey. Chill, pup. You're takin' it too far."

Johnny squeezed the trigger, and the second tranquilizer round struck the boar in the chest. It grunted, lowered its head for impact, then finally succumbed to the two heavy cocktails racing through its blood. An odd squeal issued from it as its front legs buckled and it fell, skidded forward and stopped two inches away from his boots.

He lowered his rifle, sniffed, and looked at the hounds who paced in front of Amanda to keep her away from his juicy bargaining chip. "How bad is it?"

"Little blood, Johnny." Luther sniffed at her hind leg. "Okay, a lotta blood."

The bounty hunter knelt beside the boar and shrugged the coiled rope off his shoulder to tie first the front hooves and then the back. "Can she walk?"

"Looks like it."

"Can you walk, pup?"

Amanda responded with a low whine and limped forward past the dogs.

Rex's upper lip twitched as he watched her. "Yeah, well, I only did that 'cause you weren't listening."

When he'd finished trussing the unconscious animal, Johnny squatted and heaved it onto his shoulders, two tied limbs in each hand, and turned to head through the brush. "Let's go."

The young shifter trotted three feet behind him, her shimmering wolf's eyes focused on the boar draped across his back as she licked her muzzle.

"Better watch her, Johnny."

"Yeah, you should've fed her before we left."

He passed through the next dangling curtain of moss to where Lisa stood among the trees exactly where they'd left her. "Enjoyin' yourself?"

"Well, someone had to get her clothes."

He squinted at her, then strode past through the foliage toward the airboat. "I think you simply don't like huntin'."

"I don't have a problem with it." She turned to study the huge head that dangled away from his back. "Except maybe hunting for something like that. Look at the size of those tusks."

"Don't wanna touch, 'em, lady."

"Yeah, take it from the pup."

Lisa looked at the small gray wolf who slid past her and left a trail of blood splatter. "Amanda."

The shifter stopped and tried to sit on her haunches, but the pain in her hind leg made her whine and stand again. In the next moment, she shifted into a naked twelve-year-old with leaves and twigs in her hair and a four-inch gash down her thigh. "You didn't have to stand guard over my stuff. But thanks."

She handed the clothes to the girl and stared at her in concern. Amanda dressed quickly and grimaced when she had to stand on her injured leg to push her other foot into her pants. "What happened?"

"Pup tried to rip its throat out, lady," Luther called, although Agent Breyer only heard a sharp bark.

"Yeah, but Johnny put that piggy to sleep. Didn't ya, Johnny?"

The dwarf ignored them and sloshed carefully down the bank toward the airboat with his rifle under one arm and the trussed boar over his shoulders.

"Come on, kid." Lisa touched the girl's arm gently. "You were hurt out there, I can see. What—"

"I'm fine." The young shifter tugged her hair out from the back of her shirt collar and shrugged. "It's no big deal."

She limped barefoot after Johnny and the hounds and the leg of her jeans quickly darkened with a crimson stain.

The agent shook her head. "Well, you get points for toughing it out. I'll give you that."

The bounty hunter thumped the boar onto the deck as the

girls caught up with him. He set his rifle down and went to untie the rope from around the tree.

"So no one's gonna tell me what happened, huh?" Lisa grunted when her boot squelched into a deep mudhole and filled with dark slime and swamp water. "Oh, great."

"Lady, I already told you—"

"She can't hear you, numbnuts." Rex leapt onto the airboat after his brother. "You get into those mushrooms down by Odie's again? I keep telling you not to eat the mushrooms. They make you stupid."

"Oh, yeah…" Luther sat and lifted a leg to nibble an itch on his inner thigh. "Wait, those are mushrooms?"

"Johnny…" Lisa grunted again and tried to pull her boot out of the mud. "If you're not gonna tell me what happened —woah!"

Her foot popped free with a squelch but left her boot behind and she stumbled forward toward the edge of the boat. He clamped a hand around her wrist and pulled her up before her face could impact the hull.

She sighed and took his other hand for a boost onto the boat. "Thanks."

"I told you those boots were no good."

With a laugh, she folded her arms and raised an eyebrow. "Seriously, Johnny. I heard two gunshots and animal noises. Then Amanda follows you out of there seriously injured, and no one will tell me anything."

"It's not serious," the girl muttered and lowered herself gingerly to the deck. Rex and Luther did the same on either side of her and didn't say a word.

"Well?" Lisa cocked her head at Johnny, who stepped over the lightly snoring boar and turned on the airboat's propeller engine before he took hold of the throttle.

He looked at her with a small smirk and sniffed. "It's kinda hard to take you seriously when your feet don't match."

She glanced at one mud-globbed boot and one muddy sock in a puddle of swamp water. "You're deflecting."

"Damn straight I'm deflectin'." He jerked the throttle control stick toward him to turn the fan before he kicked the propeller into a higher gear than he probably should have. The airboat lurched away from the shore and flung twigs and leaves into the thick swampy woods as they made a tight turn on the river.

The agent steadied herself against the fan mount but pulled away hastily when she looked into the whirring blades two feet away from her face. "And you're pissed. I can tell that much at least."

"I ain't—" Johnny growled and rubbed his mouth vigorously as he glared upriver. "Kid, you have any idea what just happened?"

Amanda shrugged but didn't turn to look at him. "We went hunting?"

"We went hunting for live game, fixin' to keep it alive to haul on out to that draksa. No live game, no draksa chat. No chat, I can't discover what the fuck the creature is that splattered me with goo yesterday and blew up a damn market. Ya hear?"

"The boar's fine."

"You can't go lettin' your instincts get in the way. I know it's hard and I know you ain't got—"

She whirled where she sat and startled the hounds. "You don't know anything about being a shifter, Johnny. Don't talk to me about that."

His upper lip twitched and he cleared his throat. *The kid's gonna give me a hernia.*

"And none of that even matters." Amanda gestured sharply at the trussed boar. "We got it, didn't we?"

"Yeah, but we almost didn't. If you're gonna be out here with me, you gotta listen, follow directions, and stick to the plan."

They stared at each other, and Lisa raised her eyebrows. "Oh. The boar did that to you."

"It wouldn't have if a certain wolf hadn't tried to gut it instead of pen it in so I could tranquilize it." The dwarf pushed the throttle away again to take them around the wide bend in the river. "It didn't need two tranqs. We'll be lucky if the draksa don't pick up on a little extra flavor."

"Ha-ha. Flavor. Good one, Johnny." Luther's tail thumped against the hull. "Wait, what does tranquilizer taste like?"

Rex growled and rested his head on his forepaws. "Bad idea, bro."

Amanda scowled at him and her face flushed before she spun away again and hunched her shoulders over her outstretched legs. "Whatever."

"Uh-huh." He wrinkled his nose and ran his tongue along his top teeth. *If we keep goin' this way, I'm fixin' to run outta patience. And she'll run outta chances.*

"Johnny." Lisa took an awkward step toward him with her shoeless foot and nodded toward the girl.

"What?"

"She's trying. Not many kids in her situation would be able to bounce back the way she has. You have to give her credit for that."

With a grunt, he rubbed the side of his face and his thick red beard. "Well, shit."

I bet the kid's listenin' to every whisper and smirkin' up there. Well, now we're both embarrassed.

"You know what, though, kid?"

Amanda didn't respond.

"When I saw you leapin' into that clearin', the first thing that went through my mind was that I'd hafta keep a full-grown wolf off my hounds. That was some good aim."

"Yeah, right."

"Hey, it's true, pup." Rex raised his droopy eyelids to look at her. "You were dead-on."

"Yeah, but not dead." Luther stretched his back legs out

behind him until they splayed comically to either side. "Piggy back there hasn't kicked the bucket yet."

She wiped swamp-water spray off her face.

"Might not have gotten in that first shot if you hadn't pounced when you did," Johnny added.

The girl said nothing.

He darted the agent an exasperated glance.

She wrinkled her nose. "That was…a start."

"Yeah, well I'm tryin' too."

"You'll get there." The airboat knocked against a piece of driftwood with a thump. Lisa gasped and thrust her hand out to clutch his bicep.

He raised an eyebrow and regarded her with a smirk. "You need more time on the water, darlin'."

"Let's take it one trip at a time, huh?" She noticed his almost-smile at her and didn't release his arm as quickly as she could have. "Do you think you could slow down a little, though?"

"Nope." For fun, he cranked the throttle and with a roar from the fan blades, they hurtled even faster upriver.

CHAPTER FIFTEEN

"Go take a seat, kid." Johnny nodded toward his living room as Lisa and Amanda followed him inside. "I got somethin' that'll fix you right up. For the most part."

"It's not whiskey, is it?"

The dwarf did a double-take as she passed him and gave him a cheeky grin. "Girl, you get that outta your head. That ain't happenin' until you're at least eighteen."

"What?" Lisa laughed and gave him a reproachful glance as she followed the limping girl down the hall.

"Or unless you're lyin' on my floor with a bullet wound and need emergency surgery." he shrugged. "That changes things."

"Not by you, though, right?"

"If Doc Bruno's not in, then yeah. Why the hell not?" He jerked his bedroom door open and strode inside to root around under his bed.

The agent guided the girl gently into the living room and gave Johnny's open bedroom door another disbelieving look. "Maybe don't ask him those kinds of questions, huh? You might not like the answers."

Amanda laughed. "Are you kidding? His answers are awesome."

She cleared her throat and sat on the couch beside the young shifter. *And that's why an orphan shifter and a not-so-retired bounty hunter get along so damn well.*

"How's the leg?"

"Meh." The girl shrugged. "Kinda stings."

"Oh, yeah. I bet. Do you have any shorts?"

"Um…not like the ones you were wearing yesterday."

Lisa fought back a laugh. "I meant any kind."

"Yeah. They're a pair of Johnny's old gym shorts. Does that work?"

"His gym shorts?" Her wide-eyed gaze fixed on the boar's head over the mantle and she ran a hand through her hair and sighed. "Has he taken you to get any clothes at all?"

"No. I don't need new clothes."

"You don't need Johnny's clothes."

"It's fine. They all get dirty or ripped or…bloody, anyway." She peered at her thigh and grimaced. "Very bloody."

"All right." The dwarf moved swiftly down the hallway toward them with a huge trunk balanced on one shoulder. "I've used this more times than I can count. Anything you could think of, it's right here."

The trunk thumped loudly onto the floor and he kicked the latch up with his boot.

Amanda smirked. "More guns?"

"Very funny." He opened the hinged lid, then squatted in front of it with a grunt. "First-Aid. We have bandages, gauze, tweezers, a couple of different sizes of scalpels… Morphine. Adrenaline. Heating packs. Ice packs."

"What's in here?" The girl leaned forward to pluck a prescription bottle from the trunk and rattled the pills around.

He took it from her, studied the label, and frowned. "Somethin' I've been lookin' for. Don't you go lookin' for it neither." He slipped the bottle into his back pocket and continued to rummage through the trunk. "Coagulants. Anti-coagulants. Glue stitches—useful in a pinch. Needle and thread for the regular stuff. Alcohol. Disinfectant. Shit, that's where my mouthwash went. Piece of advice, kid? Don't let a fed go through your things when you're bleedin' out. They don't put shit back where it goes."

Lisa frowned at him. "What was that?"

"I'm talkin' 'bout Nelson a long time ago." He sniffed and tossed the gauze, bandages, tape, and Neosporin onto the couch beside her. "Do you think we'll have to sew that up?"

She folded her hands in her lap and smiled pertly at him. "You do realize I'm half-Light Elf, right?"

He draped his hands over the side of the trunk and grunted. "You can heal her completely?"

"Well, no. But it's better than Neosporin and a band-aid."

"Huh. We'd better use both, then." The dwarf drew his knife from his belt and flipped it open.

"Woah." Amanda leaned back on the couch. "What's that for?"

"Those jeans are no good after this, kid."

"Don't cut my jeans."

"I'll buy you new ones. But you ain't runnin' 'round with blood all over your pants. Not on my watch. Mud? Sure. A few holes from wear and tear? Yeah, okay. Not blood. Hold still."

She stared at the agent with wide eyes as he grasped the bottom of her pants leg and slit the denim cleanly to the gash in her thigh. He stood, snapped his blade closed, and shoved it on his belt with a nod. "Have at it. I gotta take care of that pig."

Without waiting for a reply, he trudged out of the living room toward the back door, which groaned open and swung shut with a bang behind him.

The girl snorted a laugh. "I could have put the shorts on."

Lisa shook her head and studied the four-inch wound in her thigh. "And take away his chance to feel useful with a knife?

Come on." They both laughed, and she placed her palm over the injury. "Try to relax. This will help with most of it."

"Does it hurt?"

"I don't know." She looked at the shifter's wide eyes and grinned. "Tell me about it when I'm done."

Outside, Johnny headed to the airboat for the boar. Luther and Rex raced toward him from the front of the house. "What're we gonna do with it, Johnny?"

"Hey, what if the draksa doesn't like bacon? What then?"

"I like bacon."

"Drop it, boys. Y'all ain't gettin' this one." *We almost didn't, either.* Johnny dragged the animal toward the edge of the boat, lifted it onto his shoulders again, and trudged up the dock.

"Then why is it here, Johnny?" Luther barked and turned in quick, tight circles. "That's not fair."

"Yeah, that's like…like…shit, Johnny. It's like leaving a fat ol' pig outside right in front of us and sayin' we can't touch it."

"Good analogy." With a snort, he dropped it on the ground in plain view of the kitchen's back window and snapped his fingers. Both hounds sat. "Don't move."

"Worst day ever, Johnny."

"Look at it." Rex lowered his head and stretched it toward the boar. "It's moving, Johnny. I can nip it a few times. Make it stop."

The dwarf ignored them and stepped into his shed for an iron stake, a sledgehammer, and the old chicken-wire fence he hadn't touched in three years. When he came out with his supplies, the hounds ignored his last command and trotted toward him.

"Hey, look at that, Luther." Rex's tail wagged as he sniffed at the chicken wire. "Know what that is?"

"Is it food?"

"Ha! That's what you said last time. Johnny, that's not for us again, right?"

"Wait, that's our pen?"

"Remember when you cut your mouth trying to chew through it? Man, you were a real crybaby back then."

"I was ten weeks old! So were you."

"Yeah, but I knew the difference between walls and food."

Johnny dropped the wire and pushed the stake into the ground. He hefted the sledgehammer over his shoulder with both hands and stopped when Luther stuck his snout against the stake.

"Ew. What is this, Johnny? Tastes like dirt and metal."

Rex stared at his master. "Something's wrong with him, Johnny."

"Yeah, I noticed. Inside, boys. Go on."

"But we can help, Johnny." Luther looked up at his master, saw the sledgehammer, and backed away. "You've got the opposable thumbs and all, but we—"

"Go check on the kid."

"Oh, yeah. The pup!" Luther darted up the stairs of the back porch and through the dog door.

Rex panted and stared at the stake that protruded from the ground.

"Rex."

"I only wanna see you hit it once, Johnny. Come on."

"Git."

"Aw...fine. Party-pooper." The hound trotted up the steps and stepped nimbly through the dog door. "Luther! You check the floor under the sink yet?"

"What do you think I'm doing—ooh! Crumbs."

Shaking his head, Johnny swung the sledgehammer again and pounded the stake hard to drive it over halfway into the ground. The hammer thumped on the grass four feet away, and he squatted beside the hog to untie the creature's legs and fashion a lead to slip around its neck instead.

"Damn hounds. Good for sniffin' out your hairy hide. Loyal as a hound can get. Good for the kid." He tugged on the knot around the stake and grunted. "What the fuck am I thinking? She needs friends, not talking dogs. It's a good thing a fella like you can't talk."

After erecting the chicken-wire fence around the boar that began to slowly twitch into consciousness, he headed inside to where Amanda and Lisa were still on the couch, laughing. The girl had removed the ruined jeans and now wore his old pair of gym shorts.

"Hey." They both looked at him. "Where'd you get those?"

"They were in my room."

I shoulda cleaned it out before I told her to get comfy in there.

Rubbing his beard, he walked into the living room and pointed at the girl's bandage-wrapped thigh. "All good?"

"Yeah. Did you know Light Elves could heal like that? Okay, it's…like, ninety percent, maybe. But still."

"I do now."

"The rest will heal on its own." Lisa shrugged. "She'll be fine."

Amanda snorted and pushed off the couch. "I already told you guys that."

"Where you goin'?"

"I'm starving."

"Yeah, all right. You know where the kitchen is."

She hurried across the house, her limp noticeably improved.

"Oh, hey, pup," Luther said in the kitchen. "What're you doin' in here?"

"Luther, look. The fridge."

"Oh, the fridge. Hey, hey. Grab that steak on the top shelf, huh? Johnny's been a real selfish bastard with that one."

"It's not even cooked," the girl muttered.

"The rawer the better, baby." Rex sat at her feet and panted. "Pretend to drop it on the floor. He won't know."

"Don't touch the steak!" Johnny called from the living room.

"I wasn't planning on it," she shouted in response.

"Dammit. He hears everything. Hey, Rex. Think you could chew through this collar for me?"

"If it was made outta steak, yeah."

The dwarf dropped onto the opposite side of the couch with a sigh and slung his arm over the armrest.

Lisa studied him silently for a moment. "Are you okay?"

"I'm waitin'." He closed his eyes and rested his head against the cushion. *I need a drink.*

"For the right time to go visit your draksa friend, I assume."

"Yep. We have a few hours still. This one likes to come out at high tide, so that's when we'll load up and head out."

"It sounds like you've done this before."

"It's been a while, but yeah." Johnny sniffed and crossed one boot over the opposite ankle. "Got a few pointers from the guy back in the day. It don't happen all that much but sometimes, I come across Oriceran magic I ain't seen before. This draksa's got far more know-how in certain areas. He's real smart."

"Probably because it's so old, right? I heard they live for centuries."

"Well, I don't know about all that. But anyone who settles in the Everglades is a damn genius in my book."

Lisa snorted. "Oh."

"Holy shit, Rex! Would you look at the size of that sandwich?"

"What's that you made, pup? Triple-decker?"

"That's a freakin' quadruple—hey. Mm. You keep droppin' mustard anytime you want, kid."

Amanda's laughter rang out from the kitchen. "Come on. Back off. I made this for me."

"Come on, come on. Only a little taste."

Something wet smacked onto the floor, followed by the girl whispering, "Don't tell Johnny."

"No way, pup. Are you kiddin'? He won't know a damn thing about you droppin' chunks of meat on the floor—"

"You ain't feedin' my hounds in there, are ya?" the dwarf called.

Silence followed.

"No…"

"Shit. We're made," Rex whispered.

Claws scrabbled on the floor, combined with snorts and grunts and lapping tongues.

Amanda stepped out of the kitchen with a massive sandwich piled on her plate. Lisa burst out laughing.

"Now listen here." He pointed at the girl's sandwich. "You don't need all that—"

"I skipped breakfast."

"Half of that will end up on the floor."

"Fine." She raised her chin and spun quickly on her heel. "I'll eat it outside."

"Don't you even think about goin' out there without us." Rex darted out of the kitchen and followed her. Luther went out the back through the dog door.

"Don't feed the hounds," Johnny shouted again.

Lisa chuckled as the girl shut the front door behind her. "I've heard about teenagers eating a lot, but that's a massive sandwich."

"Uh-huh." He rubbed his mouth and scowled. *Dawn didn't eat like that and wasn't merely any kid, either.*

"Do you think that's the shifter part of her?"

"If it is, I'm gonna have to double my shoppin' list every week."

"She can't eat that much."

Johnny turned his head slowly to fix her with his gaze and raised his eyebrows. "She eats that much."

"Wow."

"Yeah, I might not have thought this one all the way through."

It's not like I give a shit about the grocery bill. I'm merely less prepared for raisin' a shifter than I thought.

"Don't say that." The agent leaned back against the couch and scanned the rustic décor. "You're doing fine, Johnny. Sure, maybe she's a handful, but what kid her age isn't, right?"

"You mean all the shifter kids her age who lost their family and were trafficked across New York all in the same week before movin' in with a bounty hunter?"

She rolled her eyes but her smile was teasing. "I'm only saying she looks happy. You too are more alike than I thought."

"Oh, sure. Two peas in a fuckin' pod."

"You say that like it's a bad thing."

"Naw, it ain't. If she's happy, I reckon I'm happy too. Or I will be when we track this exploding Oriceran goo-face."

Lisa snorted a laugh.

I can fool my own damn self into thinking this'll all work out after that. Happiness ain't everything, though, is it? The girl needs someone to show her how to be who she is. I ain't sure it's me but I sure as hell can keep tryin'.

CHAPTER SIXTEEN

Two hours later, Johnny stalked across the back yard with his improved tranquilizer gun and the hounds trotted at his side. "Wait's up, boys. Time to go see a draksa about some goo."

"Hey, look at that." Luther stuck his snout against the bottom of the chicken-wire fence and sniffed madly. "Piggy's wakin' up, Johnny."

"What?"

The boar snorted and blinked at them as its hooves dug into the grass and it tried to stand.

"Huh." Johnny stepped back a few paces, aimed, and fired another round of tranquilizer into its meaty rump. It uttered a brief squeal, snorted, and slumped again.

"I thought you said it would taste funny being shot so much," Rex mused.

"We ain't the ones eatin' it." He dismantled the fence, took hold of the animal, and hefted it over his shoulders before he walked to the airboat. "If a big'un like this wakes up that fast, he needs a little more to keep him calm for a last boat ride."

"Hey, Johnny. Wait up." Amanda limped down the stairs of the back porch, her sneakers in hand. "I wanna come."

He dumped the snoozing hog onto the boat, dusted his hands off, and stopped at the end of the dock. "Sorry, kid. Not this time."

She stopped hopping on one foot and gave up trying to slip her shoes on. "What? Why?"

"You need a good lyin' down on the couch. Maybe your bed. Whatever."

"Johnny, I'm fine—"

"You got a hole in your leg and half my damn fridge in your belly. We'll be fast."

Lisa joined them at the edge of the dock, now wearing a borrowed pair of Johnny's gray rubber knee-boots. "Are we ready?"

"Johnny won't let me come with you." The girl dropped her shoes in the grass and tried to put them on that way. "He thinks I need to rest."

The agent looked at him with raised eyebrows and the corners of her mouth turned down in surprise.

He shrugged. *Yeah, I can make* one *good call.*

"I think he's right, Amanda."

"What?" The girl stepped away from her shoes and scowled at them. "Are you kidding me? I wanna see the draksa."

"It's not the first time he's visited and I'm very sure it won't be the last." Lisa put a gentle hand on the girl's shoulder. "But this time, it's best for you to stay home. Put too much strain on that leg, and you'll end up undoing the healing I helped you kickstart, right?"

Luther snorted as he and Rex padded onto the dock and headed toward the boat. "Not to mention you smell like a wounded animal."

"Draksa might try to eat you, pup," Rex added. "No can do."

"All of you?" Amanda's mouth dropped open. "I won't try to fight your friend, Johnny."

"I sure hope not. You can prove it next time. Go on." He nodded toward the cabin, then turned and took the few steps to join his hounds.

"It shouldn't take very long," Lisa added before she followed him.

Glaring at them both, Amanda folded her arms and watched the dwarf kick the airboat away from the dock before he started the engine and turned up the fan on the stern.

"Hey, if you eat that steak," Luther called, "Johnny won't be around to see you do it."

The dwarf snapped his fingers. "Hush."

Luther sat. "Just saying."

The young shifter fixed them with the death-glare mastered by pre-teens and teenagers everywhere until the airboat vanished behind the reeds. "This is so stupid."

She stalked toward the cabin, her limp more pronounced, and left her shoes in the grass.

After half an hour, Johnny had to increase the throttle to keep them moving at a decent pace downriver as the tide came in from the Gulf.

"Is this supposed to happen?" Lisa asked as she leaned cautiously over the side of the airboat, her legs crossed beneath her.

"You're gonna have to be more specific, darlin'." He took them around another wide bend before the thick trees and water-logged swamp life thinned out and the river widened.

"I mean shouldn't we go faster when you increase the speed?"

He smirked. "It's the tide and it's supposed to happen. Trust me, tryin' to move downriver at high tide is a hell of a lot easier than fighting upriver at low tide. Safer too."

"And when exactly is low tide?" She tried to keep her voice level when she looked at him but it didn't quite work.

"You ain't spent much time on the water."

"I'm a federal agent, Johnny. Not Coast Guard."

He chuckled and tugged his beard. "Unless you're fixin' to sleepwalk and head out on this airboat all on your own in the middle of the night, don't pay it no nevermind."

"What?"

"Low tide's closer to midnight, darlin'."

"Oh."

Rex raised his head as the boat leveled when the river widened into a much larger swath of open water. "Don't worry, lady. Last guy who claimed he was sleepwalking on Johnny's property got a nice big chunk taken out of his leg."

Luther laughed. "Yeah, woke him right up. Hey, Johnny. If she sleepwalks out to the boat tonight, that means she'd have to…sleepdrive?"

"Hey, good point." Rex's tail thumped on the deck. "Is that even a thing?"

The dwarf ignored them and stared ahead at a long strip of land that cut the wide river in two. He pointed briefly, took his sunglasses out of his shirt pocket, and slipped them on. "That's where we're headed."

Lisa squinted at what looked like a narrow strip of land. "It doesn't look big enough for a draksa. Even a small one."

"Not from here. Just wait."

They approached the location and the noon sunlight glinted off the water as the airboat skimmed the surface with a low hum. Johnny pulled back on the throttle to slow them and they coasted past the first half-mile of the long island before he finally steered them toward the shore.

"How long does this go—oof." The airboat thumped against the land, and she slammed a hand on the deck to keep from falling over. "Is there anything you can drive gently?"

"Good luck, lady." Luther and Rex leapt off the boat and sniffed the undergrowth.

"Yeah, you're barkin' up the wrong dwarf for that one."

"Ha. Barkin'. Good one, Rex. Hey, hey! Fox hole!"

Johnny hopped off the boat and drew the rope taut before he tied it around the base of a low-growing mangrove at the water's edge. "'Bout twenty miles. And no. Gentle ain't exactly my style, darlin'."

"Yeah, I gathered that." Lisa stood, cast the unconscious boar a wary glance, and stepped toward the edge of the boat.

Johnny offered her a hand but she ignored it and jumped onto the bank on her own. She wobbled and staggered forward into the lowest branches of the mangrove. He chuckled. "You only need your sea legs."

"Those aren't on my bucket list, Johnny." She steadied herself, turned toward him, and gestured at the narrow island. "So let's bag this flaming-goo monster sooner rather than later, okay?"

"That's the plan." He stepped aboard again to drag the unconscious boar across the boat, then hefted it over his shoulders. "Hey, grab that bag, will ya?"

She climbed halfway onto the deck to snatch the small duffel bag and slung it over her shoulder. "No gun this time?"

"I ain't showin' up armed at a draksa nest." He snorted. "Except for a knife and my hounds. And you, if it comes to it."

"I'm not a weapon, Johnny."

"Naw. Merely good to have around."

Lisa smirked at him and cocked her head. "That was an actual compliment."

"That was a fact. Take it however you want, darlin'." He trudged up the bank until the ground leveled out.

Smiling, she hurried after him, her feet and calves protected from mud and the low-hanging branches that glanced harmlessly off the rubber boots.

"Compliments, huh?" Rex laughed and uttered a yip. "You like her, Johnny."

"Oh, man. You're done for."

He focused on his path through the slowly thickening mangrove trees and tried not to snag the draksa's tranquilized snack on branches and vines. *One more pro to leavin' the kid at home. I'd never hear the end of it.*

"What are we looking for again, Johnny?"

"Yeah? What's a draksa smell like? Chicken?"

Rex snorted and looked quickly at his brother as Luther trotted along and paused here and there to sniff at thick snarls of tangled branches and fallen leaves. "It's a lizard."

"Same thing."

"I wouldn't call it either of those things," the dwarf muttered. "Better yet, don't say a damn thing when we get there."

"What was that?" Lisa called and brushed a thin branch aside as she passed before it whipped into place behind her.

"Nothin'."

She widened her eyes and strode after him. *For a guy who dishes out more explosives than words, he talks to himself a lot.*

The mangrove trees thickened the farther they moved. At the peak of high tide, the water infiltrated the island, spilled in through smaller tributaries, and filled the narrow trenches made by hundreds of high-tide overflows. Mosquitos, gnats, and cicadas hummed and droned everywhere. Combined with the muggy heat and the blazing sun overhead that cut through the mangrove branches, the effect was a damp, lulling, buzzing trance.

Lisa sighed and wiped a sheen of sweat from her forehead. "We couldn't have parked the boat farther down this way?"

The dwarf snorted. "You don't park a boat—"

"Johnny, I smell something." Luther turned in a tight circle and sniffed furiously at a small puddle of muddy water. "Ooh. Shiny."

"What's wrong?" Lisa asked.

Johnny turned to peer into the puddle, where a glint of silver reflected the light when Luther retreated. "Yeah, we're close."

"What is it, Johnny?" Rex shouldered his brother out of the way to sniff the puddle.

"Because of some mud?" Lisa asked.

"A scale," he muttered. *I might as well answer 'em both.*

He led them through the thickest part of the mangroves and ignored her hisses of surprise and stifled exclamations of "Ow," or "Let go," as the branches snagged her hair and clothes. When he saw the brighter light on the other side of the stand, he hunkered down beneath the mangroves' branches and slid the hog off his shoulders with a thump.

Lisa half-squatted, half-crawled toward him. "What are we waiting for?"

"Shh." He pointed up ahead to where the trees thinned.

Wind rustled through the trees and died out again. When the next breeze kicked up in the opposite direction, she widened her eyes at the mound of silver scales that rose from the swampy ground twenty yards away. "That's not wind."

"Nope. The draksa is takin' a catnap." He fixed his gaze on the creature's slowly heaving sides. The silver scales winked in the light that spilled through the taller trees and vines above the clearing. Johnny slipped the rope over the boar's head and dropped it.

The hounds circled their master in their hiding place. Rex stretched his neck around Johnny to sniff the boar's wiry-haired flesh. "Throw it in, Johnny."

"Yeah, come on. If we don't get to eat it, give it away already."

The dwarf flicked the boar's ear and tried to wake it. "Hold steady until the hog makes a run for it. Flush it out that way if you have to."

Lisa frowned at him. "You want me to chase a pig through the swamp without a gun?"

He gave her a sidelong glance and pointed at Rex. "The hounds."

"Okay, I don't get it," she whispered. "People don't lay plans out for their—"

"Shh." He raised a hand to silence her and flicked the boar's ear again with his other hand.

"Wakey, wakey. Eggs and bakey." Luther pawed at the boar's rump.

"Ha. Yeah, and you're the bakey, little pig." Rex nudged the hog's head with his snout.

Johnny snapped his fingers quickly in the boar's ear, and the creature uttered a groggy snort.

The draksa's long inhale paused before the exhale began and sent a flutter of hot air and leaves skittering toward the thick mangroves.

"Smell it now?" Luther whispered.

"Get up. Dead pig walkin' here." Rex growled quietly and the boar snorted again.

Its eyes opened and nostrils flared as its senses—including the smell of two hounds, a dwarf, and a massive draksa—surged into its awareness.

Johnny leapt away from the captive, caught Lisa by the arm, and jerked her back beneath the mangroves with him. It squealed and its legs scrambled across the dirt and leaf-strewn ground. Mud and soggy brush sprayed up beneath its hooves.

"Get along, boys," the dwarf shouted, then lurched toward the boar and clapped his hands. "Yah!"

The hog's eyes rolled in its head as it gained its feet and screamed in panic.

"Go, go, go!" Luther leapt after it and darted aside when the animal swung its tusks. It veered away from him but Rex snarled at it on the other side.

"Not this way, dummy." Both hounds bayed and snapped their jaws at the terrified animal.

The boar kicked up another spray of leaves and muck and darted through the mangrove trees.

"Yeah, you better hope that draksa gets you before we do!" Luther howled with excitement.

Both hounds raced after the boar and sloshed through the muck and warm, stagnant water that filled the center of the clearing like a recently emptied damn.

A sharp burst of air cut through the clearing, followed by a flash of glittering silver scales from the swampy water in the center.

The draksa rose from his sleeping place, unfurled an incredibly long neck from the mountain of scales, and raised his huge reptilian head to the underside of the tree branches shading him overhead.

"Woah, woah!" Rex skidded to a halt and his front legs kicked wildly at the swampy muck to stop himself.

"You're a goner now!" Too excited by the chase, Luther didn't see the mighty head and his neck coiling to strike. He gained on the hog and it lurched to the side when the head cast a massive shadow across the terrified animal.

In the next moment, the reptile struck.

"Luther!" Rex barked.

The sinewy neck covered in blindly glinting scales contracted, and the draksa's snout descended and his jaws clamped around the boar. Muddy water splashed around it, the animal squealed, and Luther dropped to his belly with a yelp and slid forward in the muck. "Holy shit!"

The creature raised his head with a wet crunch. Swamp water and a diluted stream of blood sloshed from his mouth and splattered against Luther's face. With a noisy gulp, he swallowed his barely chewed snack and rumbled with satisfaction. A shudder rippled through his scales from the tip of his head and down his long, sinewy neck and body. The clearing filled with a sound like rustling leaves and a rattlesnake's rattle. Light glinted harshly off the rippling scales as he rumbled a long sigh.

Johnny emerged from the thick mangrove stand and straightened. He walked three yards toward the shuddering draksa and folded his arms. "Well done, boys."

CHAPTER SEVENTEEN

"You dumb shit," Rex muttered as he trotted toward his brother. "That creature almost got an extra snack for free."

His brother jumped to his feet. "You see the size of it? Holy lizard, bro. Moves faster than a 'gator."

"Yeah, good thing you know how to get down on your belly. Idiot." Rex snorted as the hounds trotted to their master's side.

The draksa rumbled again and coiled his long neck on top of his thick, slithering body that remained halfway submerged in the high-tide pool in its clearing.

"Johnny," Lisa whispered from beneath the mangroves. "Johnny, get back here. It's about to—"

In a silver blur, the creature thrust its head across the clearing toward him and it stopped three feet from his face. Large, luminous silver eyes the size of the dwarf's fist focused on him. The reptile snorted through huge nostrils in his glittering snout, plastered his beard against his chest, and ruffled his hair. The dwarf stood his ground.

"Ahh..." The draksa tilted its head. "You always bring me the best treats, Johnny. It's been a while."

"I reckon neither of us has changed that much in the last

twenty years." He lowered his head. "Good thing I still know what you like."

"Indeed." The creature withdrew his head on his snakelike neck and peered around him at Lisa, who still crouched beneath the mangroves and stared at it with wide eyes. "And you brought a friend."

"Hey, what about us?" Luther yipped.

"Johnny, tell the lizard we're not more snacks, huh? We're friends."

The bounty hunter snapped his fingers and focused his gaze on the massive silver head that glittered as it swayed from side to side. The hounds sat. *I told them not to call it a lizard.*

"Come on out, darlin'."

"Yes, do," the draksa rumbled. "I don't bite—intelligent humanoids, at least." A lilting chuckle rose from his throat followed by a hiss, and a few final drops of boar's blood spilled through his scaley lips when he grinned.

Lisa crawled slowly out from under the mangroves and hitched the duffle bag higher on her shoulder as she straightened. "Does he always look at your friends like that?"

"Dunno. I've always come solo before."

"Won't you introduce us, Johnny?" The creature studied her with disconcerting curiosity.

Johnny cleared his throat. "Lisa Breyer. Sevol."

The draksa rumbled with laughter. "What a pleasure. Johnny's been hiding his friends from me for decades. I'm delighted to make your acquaintance, elf."

She started to correct him with a mumbled clarification of half-elf, then thought better of it. "Yeah. Nice to meet you too."

"Give it here, darlin'." The dwarf held his hand out and she looked briefly at him but immediately returned her attention to Sevol who glittered a mere ten feet in front of her.

"What?"

"Bag."

"Oh." She took a halting sidestep toward the dwarf and dropped the nylon strap absently into his hand.

"Another riddle you cannot solve on your own, Johnny?" Sevol fixed his huge silver eyes on him. "I do love a good mystery."

"A mystery to me, sure." He unzipped the duffle bag with a quick jerk and rummaged around inside. "But I'm puttin' all my bets on your giant magical brain one more time."

"After such an easy snack, I'm more than happy to oblige." The draksa's slow, hot breath drew in and out through huge slitted nostrils as he waited.

Johnny finally retrieved the mason jar of purple goo and dropped the bag with a thud. He held the jar up and wiggled it. "Ever seen this before?"

Sevol tilted his head almost a hundred and eighty degrees and focused on the jar. "Yes. Where did you acquire it?"

"Off my shirt after some Oriceran creature unleashed it from giant tentacles."

The draksa chuckled. "Whatever did you do to upset it so much?"

He tossed the goo-filled mason jar up and down. "Nothin'. I tried to talk to it, but I reckon it ain't smart enough for a civil conversation. It tried to disarm me and targeted a store instead."

"Oh, it is most certainly intelligent enough for civil conversation." Sevol retracted his massive head and coiled his neck on top of his body before he lowered his chin onto the mountain of scales beneath him. "Do not underestimate a Logree, Johnny."

"Uh-huh. Do you mind tellin' me what that is, exactly?"

The draksa purred. "Logree. Oriceran, of course. A distant cousin to the Kraken and you are not the first to assume a lack of sentience. I imagine you won't be the last. Quite dangerous and volatile when they feel threatened. And I do mean on both an emotional and incendiary level."

Johnny snorted. "I noticed."

"The Logree is quite a useful variable within certain habitats on Oriceran." Sevol closed his eyes slowly and exhaled. "Think of them as an intelligent embodiment of naturally occurring forest fires. Logree are responsible for clearing away dead growth, renewing an area in a natural way to allow room and resources for new budding life to emerge."

"That's actually cool," Lisa muttered with a shrug.

"But we ain't on Oriceran, darlin'. And neither is the Logree. Any idea what it's doin' on Earth?"

The draksa's scales rippled again in pleasure as it slid its head under a patch of sunlight that flickered through the branches overhead. "What are any of us doing on Earth, Johnny?"

With a sigh, he looked at Lisa and gestured toward the huge, dragon-like creature. "This one's been around so long, he's passed the speakin' and thinkin' stage and moved onto magical philosophy. Gotta love evolution, right?"

She frowned at him and glanced at the draksa. "I guess…"

"All right, Sevol. How 'bout you bring that big 'ol thinkbox of yours outta the clouds and help me out. I ain't seen one of these things before. Got any ideas why a new Oriceran creature decided to cross through worlds and play Smokey the Bear's pyro cousin on manmade structures?"

"It is an excellent question, Johnny. Alas, I do not have an answer."

Luther whipped his head up from where he'd been sniffing Johnny's boots and his ears flopped against his face. "Ha. He said alas. Who says alas?"

"Big lizards, apparently. Hey, Johnny—"

"Not now." The dwarf folded his arms and tapped the jar of goo against a bicep. "So how do I get rid of it?"

"Ah. Another case, is it? Johnny Walker has finally pulled himself out of despair?"

Lisa snorted and looked away quickly to hide a smile.

"Naw, bein' dragged into a case I can't solve is the despair part. I was happy in retirement." Sevol rumbled with laughter and he rolled his eyes. "This Logree's havin' a time terrorizin' Florida, and I aim to stop it. I simply gotta nail down what works 'cause bullets and bolts ain't doin' shit."

The draksa snorted and raised his snout toward the sun. "Well, you certainly would not be successful fighting a Logree with fire."

"Yeah, I learned that yesterday."

"How would one combat a fire, Johnny?"

Come on. It's been twenty years, and he still can't answer a damn question with a straight-up answer.

"You spray it with water."

Lisa shook her head. "The Logree's been hiding in the Everglades, Johnny. It doesn't look like water is much of a deterrent."

"It is not," Sevol replied flatly. "But perhaps water in a more stable form."

The bounty hunter's lips twitched in a smirk of realization. "You mean like ice?"

"Not like ice, Johnny. Of ice. I have no doubt you possess the means with which to garner aid from one of them. Assuming, of course, you have not burned all your bridges in retirement."

He snorted. "Don't worry, big guy. You're the only creature in both worlds who gets live snacks delivered to their front door by me."

"How flattering."

"Thanks for the tip, Sevol."

"Thank you for the snack, Johnny. Do come see me again before the next twenty years have run their course."

"Yeah, we'll see. But don't hold your breath."

"Not even underwater, Johnny."

Picking up the duffel bag, he stowed the jar of goo in it, zipped it, and slung the strap over his shoulder. "Time to go, boys."

"Wait, that's it?" Rex looked from his master to the already snoozing draksa. "We did all that work for a five-minute conversation?"

"Johnny. Hey." Luther backed away from the draksa, panting. "How long is its body, Johnny? Like when it's not in a pile?"

"Oh, yeah. Does it have legs?"

"Where's its butt?"

The dwarf stooped beneath the mangrove trees and retrieved the rope to wind it around his arm and shoulder as he walked. The hounds hurried after him, and Lisa cast Sevol a final awed glance before she scrambled through the low-hanging branches.

"Okay, you obviously had an aha moment back there," she muttered and stopped when the branches he'd pushed aside swung in front of her. "But I get this feeling it went right over my head."

"Ice, Lisa. We need an endless supply of ice."

"Yeah, that's where I thought you were heading with this. Thanks." She nodded at him as he held the last of the particularly thickly growing mangrove branches out of the way for her. "So you want to go find a Crystal now?"

"Look at you. Puttin' all the pieces together yourself."

"Johnny, it was hard enough to get you to accept having me as your partner."

"It ain't happened yet, darlin'."

She bit her lip and forced herself to ignore that. *It happened, all right. And he knows it.*

"I'm still having a little trouble seeing you teamed with a Crystal and asking them to help us defeat that Logree."

He stopped on the other side of the thick mangroves and his boots squelched in the mud when he turned. "I ain't buildin' a whole team if that's what you're worryin' about. No Crystals on the case. I'm gonna ask real nicely for some portable magic and take that with us."

"Oh, right." She laughed, but it died quickly when she saw his face. "You're serious."

"Sure am."

"That's a big favor to ask of someone. To give you a piece of their magic."

"Uh-huh. But I know one Crystal in particular on Marco Island who owes me a favor. Or five."

"Please tell me we're driving to Marco Island."

Johnny smirked and strode ahead through the swampy undergrowth without a word.

CHAPTER EIGHTEEN

They made a quick stop at the cabin to switch out the duffel bag for the explosive disks he strapped to his ammo belt and to trade the airboat for Sheila. Plus, he wanted to check on the kid.

He found Amanda curled on the couch beneath the quilt she'd taken off his bed. His eye twitched when he saw it. *Damn. I told her not to go through my shit, but how the hell can I be mad about this? Either she misses me or she broke the rules to get even.*

Johnny left her sleeping on the couch and walked quietly down the hall to let himself out through the front door. He whistled sharply, and both hounds came running around the side of the house from the back.

"We're ready, Johnny!"

"Yeah, more adventures. We gonna hunt a Crystal too now?"

"Naw, you boys are gonna stay here. Keep an eye on Amanda. Be good company if she wakes up."

"Yeah, sure, Johnny." Rex sat to scratch behind his ear. "We're all over it. Pup won't get into any trouble while we're on watch."

"What he said." Luther's mouth opened repeatedly and his jaws didn't entirely close as something crunched between his teeth. "Ow. Shit, that's sharp—ow!"

"Luther," he snapped and raised his index finger. The hound sat. "What the hell's in your mouth?"

"Nothing." The dog's jaws opened again and he lowered his head toward the ground. He licked the grass until a section of the chicken wire fence coated in drool toppled onto the grass.

The dwarf stared at it, snorted, and folded his arms.

"Oh, shit!" Rex trotted toward his brother and sniffed the piece of fence quickly. "You did it. How stupid do you have to be to keep trying to eat it? We're three, man. Grow up."

"I might be stupid, Rex..." Luther licked his muzzle, then bared his teeth and uttered a low growl. "But my teeth are way sharper than when we were pups."

"Give me that." Johnny snatched it off the ground and shook it at Luther. "Leave the fence alone, hear? I ain't cleanin' bloody shit off my floors."

The hound cocked his head. "Why? Somethin' wrong with your butt?"

"Get inside and watch the kid," he snapped and pointed at the house.

"You got it, Johnny."

"Yeah. Count on us. We can do anything. Climb trees. Swim. Chase stuff. We don't have to feed the pup, do we?"

"No, but she can feed us."

The dog door clacked open and shut behind them, and he turned toward Sheila. He looked at the chewed, twisted metal in his hand before he threw it into the bushes beside the drive. *Somethin' is seriously wrong with one of my hounds.*

Lisa was already seated in the Jeep when Johnny reached it and opened the driver's door. He paused when he saw her, then snorted and climbed in. "Already making yourself right at home, huh?"

"Sorry, should I have asked Sheila's permission first?"

He sniffed and cranked the keys in the ignition. "You're hilarious."

"And I don't think you're as prickly about your personal space as you want everyone to think."

"Uh-huh. Just like you ain't as bothered by my drivin' as you say you are." He jerked the shift into reverse and lowered his head to look at her as he raised an eyebrow over the rims of his sunglasses.

She braced herself against the door. "Okay, fine. Forget I said anything. But please don't—"

Johnny floored the accelerator and Sheila lurched at top speed in reverse, bumped along the dirt drive, and threw up thick clouds of dust around the hood of the car.

"Johnny!" Lisa shrieked. "Are you insane? Turn around!"

The dwarf grinned and looked in the rearview mirror, his hand draped casually over the steering wheel.

"Fine. You're prickly. I don't care. Now please, turn around and drive like you have a brain!"

Sheila went over a small ditch at the end of the drive before he jerked on the steering wheel and spun a reverse doughnut out onto the frontage road with a roar of the engine and a spray of dirt from the wheels. He switched from reverse to drive and they hurtled down the road toward Everglades City.

"Jesus Christ." Lisa removed her hand from where it clutched the armrest on the door and licked her lips. "You can't do shit like that, Johnny. I don't know what—" She looked up at him and his raised eyebrow again. "Don't say it. I know. I already watched you."

"I'm only lookin' for a little faith, darlin'."

"That you won't roll this Jeep into the swamp and drown us both? Sure. I'll work on that. But you gotta give me somethin' to work with."

He reached into the front pocket of his button-down shirt and pulled out a five-count pack of gum, thrust it in front of her, and smirked as he stared at the road. "Juicy Fruit?"

"That's not what I meant." Lisa scowled at him and when he

didn't lower his hand, she rolled her eyes. "That's my favorite kind."

"Huh. Go figure."

Lisa snatched a stick out of the pack, ripped the wrapper open, and crammed the gum angrily into her mouth, breathing heavily through her nose. By the time he was chewing his, she was laughing.

"Okay, so who is this Crystal who owes you a favor. Or five?"

"Half-Crystal, really." He sniffed and took the exit coming up on their right. "But the magic's the same, right?"

She stared at him and waited for the explanation she knew was coming.

"'Bout seventeen years ago, I was on a case in Miami. Goin' after a Kilomea with way too many daddy issues and a back-room gambling ring under his thumb. Met the Crystal halfway through and couldn't exactly turn my back when I realized what was goin' on."

"What was going on?"

"The Crystal had a gamblin' problem and owed more money than is acceptable to bring up in conversation."

"Right. But we're not simply having a conversation." Lisa folded her arms. "You're telling me about a contact that'll help us with this case."

"The exact amount don't matter, darlin'. A lotta zeros."

"Okay. Does this half-Crystal have a name?"

"You bet." *I ain't spillin' those beans until I got no other option.*

Lisa studied his profile as he drove them down Everglades City's main street and narrowed her eyes. "You're being ridiculously vague, especially for someone who likes to have all the details."

Johnny sighed. "You'll have a clearer picture when we get there, all right? Let's leave it at that."

Ten minutes later, they pulled into the parking lot of a nondescript one-story building—a small strip mall that had been purchased, gutted on the inside, and turned into a single establishment.

She shut the Jeep door behind her and stared at the flickering neon light over the steel door. "Dark Moon?"

"Yep."

"Johnny, a strip club's one of those places you go to on your time."

He stepped around Sheila, whipped his sunglasses off, and raised an eyebrow at her. "You're chock-full of wit today, ain't ya? We're here to see the owner."

"Oh. Your mysterious half-Crystal contact owns a strip club. You know, you said he owes you a favor, but it looks very much like this guy has something hanging over your head instead. Is there anything your partner needs to know before we head into such a...respectable establishment?"

The dwarf grasped the door handle and pulled it open with a quick jerk. "Yeah. Don't touch the couches."

"O, jeez." She rolled her eyes and stepped through the open door. Johnny turned to scan the parking lot before he slipped inside after her.

Guns N' Roses played over the sound system and two girls danced on different stages in the center of the club.

The bounty hunter glanced around and squinted at the dark corners in the rounded booths and the red light that cast its glow over everything. *Someone could spend all day here and never notice time passin'. No cover charge helps.*

There were six patrons in Dark Moon at 2:00 pm. Four of them sat in the armchairs around the stages, spaced far enough apart that they couldn't see each other as they all stared at the dancers. A fifth stood at the back, engaged in animated conversation with one of the strippers. The last guy sat at the bar, his head hanging and his shoulders hunched as he stared into his drink.

It ain't the worst place to be.

They headed directly to the bar and a tall woman in a

miniskirt and a cropped tank top grinned at Johnny. She studied him speculatively and tossed her short black hair out of her eyes. "Hey, there. What can I get you?"

He rapped his knuckles on the bar. "I'm lookin' for Logan."

"Oh, yeah?" The bartender bit her lip. "You have an appointment?"

"Not today, sweetheart. Go tell him Johnny Walker's waitin' at the bar, huh?" He winked at her and nodded toward the room off the bar into the back.

"Yeah, okay." With a smirk, the woman gave Lisa the same intent study and jerked her chin at the tall brunette. "You want a drink, honey?"

"No thanks." The agent smiled and waited for the bartender to disappear into the back. "An appointment?"

"This ain't the only joint Logan owns."

"More strip clubs?"

"Naw, only this one. But a real high-end nightclub in Miami and maybe an apartment building. Or condos." He shrugged. "We're lucky we chose the right place on the first attempt."

"Uh-huh." She turned to glance at the dancers on the stages, then shook her head and faced the bar again. "It's a weird combination of businesses to run."

"Hey, different strokes, right?" He rubbed his mouth and beard and stared at the door through which the bartender had disappeared. *So this is what that Crystal wanted all the money for. I can't say it wasn't put to good use. Unless it's as empty as this after five o'clock.*

The bartender walked slowly behind the bar again and returned Johnny's wink. "She'll only be a minute."

"That's fine." The dwarf glanced at his watch.

Lisa frowned teasingly at him. "You look nervous."

"I ain't nervous. Only—"

"Well, I'll be damned. Johnny Walker." A gorgeous woman with thick blonde curls stood in the doorway to the back, her arm draped against the doorframe. She studied him and grinned. "You have any idea how long I've been waiting for you to find me again."

"It's been a while."

"Too long, Johnny." The woman slunk out of the doorway, stepped slowly around that end of the bar, and trailed her fingertips behind her along every bar stool in line. When she reached the dwarf—and stood at least eight inches taller than him in bright yellow stilettos and her striped mini skirt in black, pink, and neon-orange—she trailed manicured fingers through his hair and leaned toward him.

Johnny turned his head slightly toward the counter. It wasn't enough to be an insult like jerking away from her would have been, but her soft, bright red lips landed on the corner of his mouth instead of dead-center.

She chuckled. "You're so bad."

"I agree." Lisa leaned sideways on the bar and gave him a pert smile. "Especially at introductions."

The dwarf cleared his throat. "Well, just—"

"Oh, of course." The woman's fingers danced along the back of his neck as she stepped behind him toward Lisa. "Jordan Palmer."

She ran her right hand over his upper back, played with the hair at the nape of his neck, and extended her left toward Lisa. Her hand dangled limply from her wrist like she expected the agent to drop to her knees and kiss the gaudy cubic Zirconium ring that flashed on her finger under the club's musty red light. "And you are?"

"Agent Lisa Breyer." She grasped the tips of Jordan's long-nailed fingers and gave them a little jiggle. "FBI."

"Oh…" The woman raised her eyebrows and stepped between Lisa and Johnny with a conspiratorial smile. "You work for the feds now, baby?"

"Baby." Lisa lifted her elbow onto the bar and clasped her hands to stare at Johnny. "How cute."

The dwarf hunched his shoulders over the counter. "I work for myself, darlin'. You know that. Sometimes, the Bureau foots the bill."

Lisa chuckled and glanced at the liquor bottles stacked along the back shelf behind the bar. *Unbelievable.*

"Well, I don't know." Jordan ran both hands up his back until her fingers dangled over his shoulders before she leaned closer to mutter beside his ear. "You've been gone for so long, I'm not sure what to think anymore."

Finally, he moved and lifted Jordan's hand gently off his shoulder as he slipped out from under her touch and turned to step beside Lisa. He patted the back of that hand, then released it. "For now, think of this visit as an evenin' of the scales, huh?"

"You came here to get even with me?" Jordan's laugh was a delicate tinkle above the next song for the next two dancers—something by Jewel. "So this is about Miami again, huh?"

The agent nodded slowly with an understanding smirk. "You're the half-Crystal."

The woman spread her arms with a tiny shrug. "With an incredible illusion, don't you think?"

Lisa pursed her lips and glanced at Johnny. "You couldn't turn your back when you realized what was going on, huh?" He rubbed his mouth and grunted. "Or more like you couldn't turn down the chance to help a woman in trouble."

He stepped aside and returned her look.

"That ain't got nothin' to do with it. I simply got a big heart."

"Which I warmed up a time or two," Jordan added in a sultry purr. "Didn't I, Johnny?" She lifted a finger slowly to her mouth and bit the tip, smiling the whole time and quite shamelessly undressing him with her wide eyes.

Not only undressing him, Lisa thought. *She's reliving the whole damn thing.*

Johnny sniffed and ran his tongue along the inside of his cheek. *It's women like this one gonna drag me on down to an early grave.*

"I need a favor, Jordan."

"Oh." The woman grinned and leaned against the bar, propped both elbows on it, and lifted one stilettoed foot to slide it up and down the wall beneath the bar top. "I can't wait to hear it."

He ignored her finger twirling slowly in a tight lock of her blonde curls and hooked his thumbs through his belt loops. "Ever heard of a Logree?"

"Can't say I have, Johnny. Sounds like fun, though."

"Oh, boy…" With a wry chuckle, Lisa plastered a grin on her face and raised her eyebrows at Johnny. "So much fun."

The dwarf cleared his throat again and looked at the almost six-foot-tall woman making eyes at him the same way she had seventeen years before. "I was hopin' I could get a little magic from ya. Crystal magic."

"Sure." Jordan bit her lip and her shoulders wiggled as she inclined her head toward the other end of the bar. "We can go into the back and I'll give you whatever you want. Free drinks for your FBI friend while she waits."

Lisa laughed sharply. "Hey, that's so sweet."

"Uh-huh." He slid his hand into his back pocket and removed a small sample-sized glass jar nestled in the magically reinforced metal net he'd made for occasions like this. *I didn't think I'd be puttin' her magic in it, but it is what it is.*

He thumped the metal-wrapped receptacle on the bar and nodded once at Jordan. "Here's good."

Her smile faded. "Fine."

Johnny stared at her as he unscrewed the lid of the jar and slid it toward her. The woman glanced around her club, turned her back toward the patrons and the stages, and lowered her hand in front of her thigh beneath the overhanging lip of the bar. A soft, blue-white light illuminated in her palm and she raised a conjured blade made entirely of ice.

"Don't look so surprised, sweetheart," she murmured and smirked at Lisa. "It's very simple."

"Right. I'm sure anyone could do it."

The dwarf gave her a warning glance. *The last thing I need is for these two to be at each other's throats for no goddamn reason.*

Jordan lifted the razor-sharp ice-blade, drew a lock of blonde curls forward from the back of her head, and quickly sliced about three inches off. When it separated from her body, it lost its illusion and was now studded with tiny, glittering particles of ice. She dropped it into the jar and dusted her fingers off, and the ice-blade in her hand disappeared. "Are you sure that'll be enough to remember me by?"

He responded with a noncommittal grunt as he screwed the lid on tightly. "I remember you just fine, darlin'. And it looks like you're doin' well for yourself these days."

"Well, I had a little help."

The bounty hunter pocketed the jar again and nodded. "Stay outta trouble, ya hear?"

"That's a little hard to do when you come waltzing into my club." She tossed her head and her curls bounced over her shoulders. "You come back for a little trouble any time you want, Johnny."

"Uh-huh." With a sniff, he turned without so much as a glance at the dancers who slid up and down the poles in the center of their stages and strode to the hallway leading to Dark Moon's front door.

Lisa smiled with glaringly fake sweetness at Jordan and wiggled her fingers. "Toodles."

The half-Crystal smirked and drummed her fingers on the bar. "You too, honey."

CHAPTER NINETEEN

Lisa caught up with the dwarf in the parking lot and finally released the rest of the laughter she'd held back in the club. "That was…an experience."

Johnny jerked Sheila's driver's open door and climbed inside. He removed the reinforced jar from his back pocket and settled it into the compartment in the center console with a thump.

After she shut her door behind her and buckled her seatbelt immediately, Lisa turned halfway in the passenger seat to smirk at him. "Warmed your heart up a time or two?"

"It was one night." He cranked the engine and the Jeep rumbled to life. "Before I got her out of that mess with the gambling ring."

"And which one did she owe you a favor for? The one night or you saving a Crystal damsel in distress?"

"Don't think about it too hard, darlin'." He shifted into drive and surprisingly, drew out of the parking lot like a sane person this time.

The agent leaned back in her seat and shrugged. "I'm merely trying to get an accurate timeline on the whole story."

"Well, that road ain't gonna lead you toward the bigger picture. Trust me."

"Yep." She draped her arm over the glass-less window and the warm, humid air streamed beneath her hand as they increased speed through Everglades City. *So one-night stands don't mean anything until Johnny Walker needs a favor. And then it's merely leverage.*

She snorted and gazed out the window as he darted her a sidelong glance.

"So you have a jar of Logree goo and a jar of half-Crystal hair," she asked, rather than pursue her previous curiosity any further. "Now what?"

"We weaponize it. The hair, not the goo."

"Yeah, I realized that much." She pulled her hand in through the window and ran it through her wind-blown hair instead. "Let me guess. You made a machine that'll do that for you too."

"I wish." Johnny took his sunglasses from his pocket and deftly slid them on one-handed. "I rig explosives, upgrade my weapons, and occasionally build a device or two when it's called for. But I don't do science."

She laughed. "Oh, of course not. What does that even mean?"

"Look, darlin'. I can put the boom juice in any shell casing or bolt tip or grenade and call it a job well done." He patted his belt where the explosive disks hung beside his knife. "But I don't make the juice, understand? That comes from a guy who specializes in concentrated-magic formulas. I reckon he'll be happy enough with a custom order like this one."

"And this contact is a man, right?"

"Very funny." He scratched his eyebrow and stared straight ahead down the road. "He's a gnome."

"Wow. A gnome scientist in a secret lab somewhere who can turn Crystal hair into Johnny Walker's newest explosive."

The dwarf chuckled and shook his head slowly. "Not quite."

They drove to Marco Island and stopped along the way at a

gas station with a deli inside for a couple of Po' boys. When Lisa tried to save the rest of hers for later, he shook his head and pointed at the trash can outside the building. "Eat it now or toss it, darlin'."

"What? I'm gonna eat the rest of it later—"

"If that's your top priority, feel free to hang out inside and I'll call past for you when I'm done."

She raised her eyebrows in surprise and lifted the to-go bag. "Are you serious?"

"Don't I look serious?"

"I don't know, Johnny." She heaved a massive sigh that ended in a chuckle of disbelief. "You have three expressions. Pissed, smartass, and everything else."

"Eat it or dump it. But we need to move."

"Why?" She dropped the to-go bag in the garbage can and stalked across the parking lot toward Sheila. "Did you make an appointment with the guy or something?"

"No. But his store closes in a few hours, and then it can get tricky to find him without crossin' a few personal boundaries."

"His store."

"Scientist, tinkerer, jeweler, gnome… It's all the same."

They pulled up in front of Wallace Fine Jewelers at 4:15 pm. Johnny snatched up the jar of Crystal hair, leapt out of the Jeep, and almost skipped toward the front door.

"Wow." The agent nodded in appreciation as she scanned the storefront. "I've heard good things about this place."

He looked doubtfully at her. "You know about a gnome's conversion lab frontin' as a private local jeweler in Marco Island?"

"Okay, when you put it like that, yeah. It sounds unlikely. I heard two women at my hotel talking about new jewelry they got, okay?"

"Oh, nice. Recommendation by eavesdropping."

She snorted and shook her head as he opened the door and

gestured for her to step inside first. A bell dinged softly and they entered a brightly lit lobby filled with glass display cases lined in gold. The left one showcased men's and women's watches, plus a few older pocket watch timepieces and a grandfather clock in the corner. A hatstand beside those held several designer handbags dangling from their straps. The right wall's shelves were lined with designer sunglasses, bola ties, and bulky jewelry pieces inlaid with turquoise and copper.

The center display case in the back boasted an impressive selection of gemstones, cut and uncut, and three different lines of diamond jewelry collections. All of it sparkled in dazzling brilliance beneath the glass and the bright overhead lights.

"This is a ton of collateral if something in a hidden lab goes wrong," Lisa muttered.

"Naw. Wallace knows what he's doing."

A door into the back opened and the gnome slipped out, only his balding head visible behind the back counter. "Welcome to Wallace Fine Jewelers, where we wear our dreams on our—" He stepped onto the raised platform behind the counter and froze. "Johnny."

"Wallace."

The agent tilted her head and fought back a laugh. "Wear your dreams on your what, exactly?"

"Sleeves." The gnome rubbed the top of his head, ruffled what little white hair was left, and chuckled. "It seems like a ridiculous slogan, I know, but the tourists go bonkers for shit like that. Who are you?"

"Agent Lisa Breyer," the dwarf answered quickly. "Bounty Hunter Department."

"I'm Johnny's partner." She extended a hand over the display case and grinned at Wallace.

The gnome chuckled again and gave her hand a brief but surprisingly firm shake. "Is that so?"

"No," Johnny said quickly

"Yep," Lisa said at the same time. "For almost a month now."

"Well, I'll be damned. I thought you got out, Johnny."

The dwarf turned to stare at her. "I did."

"And now he's back. Special circumstances and everything. You know how it goes."

"Ha. Well not really, but okay. You lose your touch comin' out of retirement?"

He grunted and set the jar on the glass countertop with a clink. "I need some custom work done."

"Hey, look at that." The gnome leaned over the counter to peer into the jar. "Crystal?"

"He's good," Lisa muttered.

"Listen, Agent Breyer. I've been doin' this a long time. Almost as long as Johnny if we don't count the fifteen years he—"

"Yeah, yeah. Moving on." He drummed the fingers of both hands on the glass counter and Wallace looked at him with wide eyes. "Please."

"How do you want it?"

"Shootable. Preferably liquid."

"Do you have the right injection vehicle?"

The bounty hunter spread his arms expansively. "Does a catfish bite?"

Wallace chuckled. "Yeah, okay. Come on back."

He snatched the small jar up, leapt off the platform behind the counter, and hurried toward the door into the back. "Your FBI friend knows to keep this to herself, right?"

"Yeah," Lisa answered. "I'm fairly sure she gets it."

"Good. What happens behind Wallace Fine Jewelers stays behind Wallace Fine Jewelers and we all get what we want out of it." He held the door open for them, and Johnny nodded with a small smile as he passed through into the back room.

She paused when she stepped inside and folded her arms. "Huh. It's amazing that you can even fit all this behind Wallace Fine Jewelers."

"Thank you." The store owner shut the door briskly behind him and strutted into the room, his arms pumping at his sides. "It took a little finesse to get this set up exactly the way I wanted, but we've been up and running for... What do you think, Johnny? Forty-five years?"

"Somethin' like that."

"And business has been boomin'. Literally for you, huh, Johnny?" Wallace chuckled and swept his arm out toward the maze of huge machines that filled the back room.

Pistons pumped up and down. Liquids in every color bubbled in beakers clamped over open burners. Gas and goo raced through clear plastic tubes that connected one machine to the next, and the occasional burst of purple or green steam puffed from the contraptions in the far rear.

At least a dozen gnomes scurried between the machines to twist knobs and dials, crank levers, or measure ingredients. None of them spoke to the visitors and each worked beside their colleagues with a mutual understanding of the process. Focused on their work, they didn't even bother to look at their boss and his two guests where they stood in front of the door.

"Yes, indeedy." Wallace slapped his belly with a sigh. "Front and back, I might add. No shortage of high-paying customers wanting to wear their dreams on their sleeves. And no shortage of magicals in Florida wanting a little science added to their spells, either. Sorry, Johnny. You're not the only one but you'll always be my first."

The bounty hunter snorted. "What more could a dwarf want?"

"Grover! Hey, hey. Hold on." The gnome flashed the jar of Crystal hair at a worker with blue-tinted hair and huge goggles magnifying his eyes by at least ten times. "Melt it. Custom order for Johnny."

Grover looked at him with his enlarged eyes and took the jar slowly. "Johnny who?"

"Johnny who— Were you born last century? No. Quit actin'

like it." Wallace slapped his employee's shoulder and turned to gesture toward Johnny and Lisa.

"Oh, that Johnny." The gnome grinned and pulled his goggles up onto his wide forehead. "How ya doin', man? Last I heard, you were rollin' around in the swamps with not a care in the world."

"I was." Johnny jerked his chin at him and hooked his thumbs through his belt loops. "But you know me. I can't keep my fingers outta the pie for long."

"Right. Fifteen years is your limit, huh?"

Wallace darted his employee a warning glance. "And you have fifteen seconds to get started on this order."

"Yeah, yeah. Sure." Grover raised the jar toward the bounty hunter and nodded. "Gimme an hour, Johnny. You know how it goes."

"Sure do."

Shaking his head, the proprietor returned to his customers and scoffed as he pointed toward the lab with his thumb. "It's so easy to get lost in the work. Everything that used to be in his head—*zip*. Gets pushed right out."

"He still knows how to get it done, right?"

The gnome scoffed and placed his hands on his hips. "He'd better. I'm the one who taught him and there are no lapses in my brain, Johnny. Don't you worry about that."

"'Preciate it, Wallace."

"Hey, anything for you." He smacked Johnny's shoulder with the back of his hand, completely oblivious to the disgruntled frown the dwarf darted at him in return. "Crystal hair, huh? How'd you get your hands on that?"

"I asked real nice."

Wallace snorted. "Oh, yeah? Like that time the witch from Cape Coral gave you her—" He glanced at Lisa, saw her raised eyebrow, and cleared her throat. "You know what? Never mind."

"We'll be back in an hour."

"Oh, sure." The gnome waved them off and they turned

toward the door. "We'll have it ready for you, Johnny." He rested both hands on his hips and surveyed his magic-converting lab. "Ah… Like a well-oiled—Jackson! Hey! How many times have I told you not to disconnect the induction lines when they're still — Stop. Just stop, man. I'll do it myself."

Johnny let the door to the back room fall shut behind him and the rumbling whir and hiss of moving mechanical parts cut off instantly. "So we have an hour to kill."

"Not enough time to drive home." Lisa peered over the top of a display case filled with sapphire rings and shrugged. "So what do you do when you're waiting for custom orders?"

"Around here? Settle for a drink and pretend I am home."

"What?"

"Come on. An hour's long enough."

CHAPTER TWENTY

Johnny parked the Jeep in the surprisingly full lot outside a two-story tavern and grill with an upper and lower deck boasting incredible views of the water.

"All right." Lisa forced back a smirk as she studied the restaurant and shut the Jeep door. "Maybe you do have good taste."

"In what?"

"Showing a girl from up north around Florida. Not that I have anything against Darlene and her trailer. But this is nice, Johnny."

"Well, it ain't a date either." He strode across the parking lot and past the front door of the restaurant.

"Um…unless you use a back door and a secret password, Johnny, the front door's right—"

"Naw, we ain't goin' in there." He shook his head and moved quickly down the sidewalk.

"We're not?"

"We're hittin' Leroy's joint." He pointed up the street.

She cast a longing glance at the clean and very appealing waterfront restaurant before she hurried to catch up with him. "You could've said that before I went on and on about a place we're not going to."

"It ain't ever a smart move to interrupt a passionate display like that."

The agent snorted. "That wasn't passion. That was appreciation."

"Trust me, darlin'. You'll appreciate this one just fine."

The small shack positioned lower and closer to the water didn't seem to have a name—merely a crooked sign painted on a sun-weathered two-by-four that read, *Seafood*. Two rusted metal tables with two chairs each stood on the dock behind the shack, completely unoccupied.

"This is Leroy's?" she muttered.

"Damn straight."

"Why didn't we simply park here?"

"Because Seafront Tavern is for tourists. Just because it's off-season don't mean they ain't still arrivin' in droves."

The agent closed her eyes and wrinkled her nose. "So you park in the lots of tourist establishments. That'll show 'em, Johnny. Keep up the good work."

He ignored her and trudged down the sloping drive toward the shack.

"I don't think it's open," she muttered.

"That's the point." The bounty hunter stopped in front of the narrow ledge beneath the order hatch, which was closed. He knocked three times on the wooden slat serving as the window. "Leroy! I know what you're hidin' in there, man. Open up and give me what's mine."

Lisa folded her arms and frowned warily at the weathered shack. *Great. We're not here for drinks.*

A muffled thump and shuffle issued from behind the window before the wooden slats slid aside to reveal a wrinkled old man wearing rimless glasses and a straw hat with so many holes, it was little more than a straw sieve on his bald head. "Johnny boy! Now I knew that were you knockin'. How you doin'?"

"I'm fine, Leroy."

"So watcha doin' here, eh?" The proprietor wheezed with breathless laughter.

"I was in the area."

"Oh, sure. You come all the way here to be in the area for me and mine, don'tcha? Hee-hee. You want the usual, then?"

"Only reason I'm here." Johnny folded his arms and smirked.

"Yar. Hold yer pants up, boy." The old man grunted and hefted something behind the narrow window. The inside of the tiny building was completely dark, and he stared at the dwarf the whole time as a yellow light flashed behind him and the sound of pouring liquid trickled out of the shack. "There. Take it. No one else touches it. You know that."

"Thanks. And a beer."

"Ha!" Leroy snapped his fingers with another flash of yellow light and an unmarked bottle appeared in his hands. "Fer the lady. Hee-hee." He cracked the bottlecap with a hiss and handed him the beer as well. "And the chips?"

"You ever heard me say no?"

"Never! Ye're as predictable as the tide, Johnny boy. Get on and put yer pups up. Speakin' of...where them hounds at?"

"It's only me and the lady." He took a sip of his Johnny Walker Black he knew Leroy kept in the stocked bar behind the window.

"She ain't no dog, Johnny. That's fer damn sure. Hee-hee." The old man slid the wooden slat closed with a bang, then shuffled and thumped around in his shack.

The dwarf turned with the whiskey and beer bottle in hand and offered Lisa her drink. "You heard the man. Best get on and put our pups up."

She frowned at the shack and took the beer absently. "I think I know how the concierge in Manhattan felt."

He snorted a laugh and headed past the shack toward the dock and the two empty tables. "You get used to it. Or at least good at pickin' out what you can understand and screw the rest."

"This is your place in Marco Island, huh?" The agent followed him and took a long swig of beer. "A crumbling seafood shack run by a wizard no one can understand?"

"Not no one, darlin'. Only those of us who know where to find a good view and the best damn pickle chips three towns over."

She stopped in front of a metal chair that didn't look like it could support its weight much longer, let alone hers. "Pick what?"

Johnny chuckled. "Yankees. Have a seat."

He pulled a chair from the other table toward him with his boot, thumped both legs on top of it, and leaned back.

Her chair groaned when she sat but fortunately didn't collapse. "Well, at least it's not a bad view."

"Yeah, except for those damn tourists yuckin' it up next door." The dwarf shook his head and sipped his whiskey. "Folks like that should stick to Miami and the Keys. Leave the Everglades to those who know what to do with 'em."

She didn't know what to say to that, so she lifted the bottle to her lips and stared out at the water that stretched seemingly forever in front of them. "I bet the sunsets here are amazing."

"You bet right." He sighed with contentment. "I could stay here until then. But by the time that sun glows red on the water, I'll be back home fixin that Crystal magic to half a dozen crossbow bolts, at least."

"Another time, then. Maybe."

"That'd be fine."

Another window banged open at the back of the shack, followed by Leroy's high-pitched cackle and another burst of yellow light. A tin plate lined with white paper streaked out of the window and dropped onto the center of their table. "I don't wanna see no fish food in that trough, Johnny boy. Don't make me move my boots more'n I like, ya hear?"

The window banged shut again before he could even consider giving the old wizard a reply.

He chuckled and pointed at the basket. "Pickle chips."

"Oh. Fried pickles. Yeah, I've had those."

"Naw, you ain't. These're Leroy's."

"There can't be much variety with fried pickles, Johnny. Pickle, breading, fryer." She shrugged.

"You go on and try 'em, darlin'. See how quickly you eat your words."

Lisa scoffed and reached for a handful of the sliced and fried pickles, then dropped them and shook her hand. "Dammit. Those are hot."

"Yep."

"Don't laugh." She leaned back in her chair and frowned teasingly at him. "Why did you order pickles from a seafood shack anyway?"

"The seafood part's for the tourists. It ain't real."

"The food?"

"Leroy makes a fine livin' off sellin' imitation crab and...I don't know. Tofu clams or some shit."

The agent burst out laughing. "No way."

"It's true. The man's allergic to shellfish. And anything that swims, to be honest. We take care of our own down here, darlin', and the rest of the world can piss off."

"Hmm." She picked a pickle chip up carefully and blew on it. "It makes me rethink every trip I took to Miami as a kid."

"Naw. Miami's a whole different beast."

She bit into the fried pickle and froze. "Holy shit."

"Uh-huh."

"This is amazing."

"Uh-huh."

"What does he do to these things?"

"He ain't gonna tell you even if you asked." Johnny chuckled and leaned forward to help himself to a handful.

An airboat with the driver seated on a high chair at the stern and a group of six women in their forties with drinks in hand hummed down the shoreline toward Leroy's dock. The passengers shrieked with laughter until the boat reached it. Then, their voices fell into hushed murmurs and giggles as they all stared at Johnny Walker and his whiskey.

A redhead grinned flirtingly at him and raised a hand to wiggle her fingers in greeting. "Hey, there."

The others laughed and the woman seated beside her slapped her friend's hand down. "What are you doing?"

"We're on vacation, Emily. I can do whatever I want."

"She means whoever she wants," the brunette behind her whispered way too loudly. The group burst into girlish giggles and turned in their chairs to continue to stare at him as the airboat skimmed past.

Lisa chuckled and sipped her beer. "I'd ask if they were friends of yours but they kind of threw themselves under the bus."

"Well, there's your answer, then." He scowled at the back of the airboat.

"Honestly, I'm amazed you don't know every woman in Florida."

Johnny snorted. "Interestin' idea. Come on, that'd be impossible."

"Would it, though?" With a smirk, she turned toward him. "You live far longer than most of them. It keeps a fresh cycle turning through every…what? Fifteen years?"

"Now you're simply lookin' to pick a fight." He took a handful of pickle chips and crammed them in his mouth. Flecks of fried breading and juice dropped into his beard.

"I'm messing with you, Johnny. Not fighting. That's what partners do."

"Uh-huh." He wiped his mouth and the top of his beard with the back of a hand. "Well, I don't kiss and tell."

"No, the women do all that for you." She hid her smile with another sip of beer.

"Listen, darlin'. I ain't givin' specifics 'cause there ain't nothin' worth bringin' up."

"Even that gaggle of winos who left their husbands and teenage kids for a week to tour the Everglades?"

He lowered his head toward her and fixed her with a bland glance over the tops of his sunglasses. "Let's say I don't discriminate. Unless they're tourists."

"Ha! So you've been with your fair share of Light Elves too, then?"

Johnny chuckled and shifted into a more comfortable position to stare out across the glimmering water. "Not yet."

Lisa gaped at him for a moment but looked away quickly toward the swamp. *If I didn't know better, I'd say that was a come-on. But Johnny Walker doesn't hit on women. It's the other way around. Unless it's not, sometimes.*

She darted him another sidelong glance and folded her arms before she took another sip of whatever unlabeled beer Leroy the wizard had given her. "Well good luck with that."

"Thanks."

CHAPTER TWENTY-ONE

When their hour on Leroy's dock was up, they returned to Sheila in the Seafront Tavern parking lot—but not before Johnny took two twenties from his wallet and slid them in the small tin pail hanging from the side of Leroy's shack.

Wallace's jewelry store was already closed for the evening when they pulled up out front, although the marquee was still lit as well as the display cases inside.

"We're not too late, are we?"

"Naw. He's expectin' us now." A security camera blinked at them under the awning, and he removed his sunglasses to stare into it.

The gnome bustled into the lobby from the back room with an eager grin to unlock the door quickly. "You are one punctual bastard, Johnny."

"Grover said an hour and we both know you run a tight ship."

"Ha! If you ever see me steppin' on a real ship, you'll know I've lost my mind and my days are numbered." Wallace nodded toward the back of the lobby and they followed him through the rear door into the lab.

"Johnny!" Grover waved from a raised mesh platform on

wheels he'd rolled beside one of the pumping machines. "Perfect timing."

"No problems, I'm guessin'?"

Wallace's assistant stepped backward down the steps and pushed his goggles onto his forehead again. "Piece of cake. Exactly like everything else you send us."

"That's why I take it to the professionals."

Grover snatched a silver metal case up from the floor and hurried toward them with a broad grin. "Exactly like you wanted. It's all—"

"I'll take that, thank you." His boss whisked the case out of his hand and nodded toward the machine. "Don't leave that boiler unattended, man. Come on."

"Right, right." Grover trudged toward the rolling stairs up to the platform and tossed a hand in the air. "Good to see ya, Johnny."

"You too."

Wallace winked at the dwarf and clicked the latches on the case before he opened it to display a dozen small vials filled with glowing white-blue liquid. "There you are, Johnny. Melted, replicated, stabilized. Shootable."

The bounty hunter peered into the open case and nodded. "I wouldn't expect anything else."

"See, that's why I love it when you come around." The gnome chuckled and shut the case before he handed it to him. "You're an easy customer to satisfy, Johnny."

"Only when the services are worth my time and money. And you still know how to deliver."

"Damn right I do." Wallace jerked quickly on the hem of his sports jacket and nodded. "I'll send you the bill. Same place?"

"Yep."

"Great. It's good to see you working again. Not like you asked for an opinion, but I'll give it anyway."

"Uh-huh."

He nodded at Lisa. "And with a partner this time. You make sure he stays outta trouble."

She smirked at the bounty hunter and shook her head. "It's more like getting into trouble with him and helping to clean up afterward."

"Ha!" The gnome clapped and howled with laughter. "Oh, man! You found a good one, Johnny. Yessir. Don't let this one get away."

"It's harder than it looks," the dwarf muttered. He held the silver case of Crystal-magic fluid carefully at his side.

Lisa grinned at him. "Yeah, you can't seem to get rid of me, can you?"

Wallace glanced from one to the other with a knowing smile. "Well, I won't hold you up any longer. And we have a few more—"

Something clanked loudly and violently in the back, followed by an explosion of purple gas, sparks, and bolts. Two other gnomes spun from their work at the machines in the front and darted toward the smoking contraption as they waved their hands frantically and shouted.

"Turn it off, Billy!"

"Pressure valve, man! How do you not know where the goddamn pressure valve is?"

"Shut the centrifuge down!"

"Fuck." Wallace gritted his teeth and waved dismissively at Johnny as his employees darted around the lab to crank levers and gears to protect the rest of the equipment. "You...you go on. I'll send you the bill. It might be the only funds I have coming in if that damn zipperhead breaks something expensive."

"Like that machine?" the dwarf asked.

"It's all expensive. Good luck, Johnny. Lisa, nice to meet— Jesus, Billy! What the hell were you—"

Another explosion wracked the lab from a second machine.

Two gnomes were thrown back by the blast and bellowed in anger before they impacted with the wall.

"That's our cue, darlin'." Johnny turned to the door into the lobby.

"Do they need help?" The agent followed him but peered constantly over her shoulder to watch the chaos.

"Naw. If a gnome don't ask for help, the last thing you wanna do is step in where you ain't wanted."

"Okay..." She ducked a damaged bar of metal that hurtled toward her from a smaller explosion near the front. It clanged against the wall beside the door as he opened it. "Yeah, we should go."

When the door swung closed behind them, the sound of shouting gnomes and angrily hissing machines cut off immediately. The lobby wasn't entirely silent, however.

The crunch and tinkle of something moving on broken glass issued from their right beside the display of men and women's watches. Lisa drew her firearm from her shoulder holster and held it down in front of her with both hands as she scanned the trail of shattered glass and spilled jewelry.

Johnny dropped the metal case with a thud, jerked his knife off his belt, and flicked it open in one swift movement. The rustling along the wall stopped. "Bad idea."

A closely shaved head rose slowly above the other side of a display case, followed by wide, red-rimmed eyes and a gaping mouth. The man—probably in his late twenties—registered both the knife and the gun. "Shit!"

He scrambled away from the mess he'd made when he destroyed the display cases and a handful of gold and diamond-encrusted watches dangled from his fist.

"That too," the bounty hunter snapped as he raced around the other display cases to cut the man off from the front door.

"Man..." The thief stared at the knife, then glanced at the door and raised both fists in a loose, sloppy fighting stance. "I don't…I don't wanna have to hurt you, man."

"You won't."

Without responding, he hurled the handful of watches at Johnny and darted across the shattered glass toward the door.

The dwarf ducked the jewelry, snagged a designer purse with a thick chain of silver links off the stand, and raced after him. In almost slow motion, his quarry stumbled over his own feet with a cry before he barreled into him from behind and brought him down in a solid tackle.

"Fucking get off me, man! I didn't do anything!" The young man kicked his legs weakly as Johnny pressed his full weight onto his back.

"That's not what it looks like, pal."

"Aw, fuck. My legs, man. You're hurting me—"

"I ain't on your legs, shithead. Shut up." The bounty hunter flipped his knife closed, thrust it into his belt, then grasped his captive's wrists and pulled them roughly behind his back. He knelt on his arms to pin him down and ripped one side of the purse chain from the leather. "You got no business tryin' to steal from—"

Without warning, the prisoner stabbed a broken shard of glass into his captor's thigh and sliced both the dwarf's flesh and his own hand. He grunted and lost his balance and the thief squirmed out from under his knees and scrambled to his feet. The man hissed and his injured palm dripped blood across the floor.

Johnny growled and leapt off the floor as he ripped the other side of the purse chain out of its expensive stitching.

"FBI! Freeze!" Lisa shouted and raised her gun.

"Fuck, fuck, fuck…" The man raced to the door. Before she could fire a warning shot, the bounty hunter whipped the heavy chain and cracked it across the back of the thief's head.

His target cried out, lurched forward, and yelled again when he rammed him sideways with a shoulder. Both of them fell against the center display case beside the door, shattered the glass, and broke the shelves where the gemstones nestled in shiny little boxes.

"Woah, man! Hey!" His quarry shrieked when the dwarf grasped the back of his jacket and hauled him off the broken case. "What gives? This isn't your—"

Johnny's fist connected with his face and he fell on the glass-strewn floor.

Lisa stepped forward, her weapon still raised. "Johnny—"

"I got it." The bounty hunter knelt on the prisoner's back again and jerked the man's flailing arms together even harder.

The thief screamed. "You're gonna break my arm, asshole! I only need—"

"Stop runnin' your mouth." With a growl, he wound the purse chain around his prisoner's wrists and pulled it tight, eliciting another shriek. Satisfied, he tied it off with a tight knot and shoved the man's face against the floor. "It might not be my store but I'm here. You chose the wrong day and the wrong shop."

He slid his hand into the man's pockets and pulled out two more watches, a pair of quarter-carat diamond earrings, and a thick bracelet of silver links.

"Aw, come on, man. I only need a little—"

"You need to shut up before I crack your skull open." He set the jewelry on the broken shelf of the display case beside them and went through his prisoner's pockets again. "You break in here and take the least expensive stuff? What, did you think Wallace wouldn't miss a few lower-end pieces?"

"Who the fuck is Wallace?" the thief shouted again when Johnny pressed his cheek harder against the floor as he pushed to his feet.

"You're not very good at this, are you?"

The man squirmed on the ground and bucked against the very effective purse chain. He sniffed and scratched his wrist vigorously with the opposite hand. "I only needed a little, man. You don't need to bring the fucking feds into this."

"Watch it," Lisa said and stepped toward them over broken glass. "Keep an eye on him. I'll call it in."

"Naw, don't bother." The dwarf pulled his cell phone out and scrolled through his contacts until he found the gnome's number. "We'll let Wallace take care of this idiot."

"Man, come on." The prisoner coughed and squirmed. "You already took the jewelry. Let me go. I didn't do anything."

Johnny typed a text to Wallace: *Sorry about the display cases. Put it on my bill. Bag of trash in your shop needs to be taken out.*

He sent it, shoved his phone into his pocket, and nudged the thief's ribs with the toe of his boot. "You stabbed me. That ain't nothin', asshole."

"I can't go to jail, man. Come on. I won't last two days in there. Hey! Hey, where you goin'?"

The bounty hunter tugged the shard of glass out of his thigh and tossed it on the floor, then strode to the back counter to retrieve the case of Crystal-magic formula. Lisa trained her gun on the thief until her partner marched past them both and shoved the front door open. The bell jingled. "Maybe Wallace will give you enough time to rethink your choices."

"Dammit! Come on!" The thief wriggled furiously to escape. He panted and scratched his wrists and for some reason, seemed unable to stand.

Lisa stepped outside and the front door closed behind her with another jingle as she holstered her weapon. "He'll probably get up and walk out, Johnny."

"Naw. Wallace will come pick him up in a minute."

"He's busy with the lab—"

"Did you see that bastard's eyes?" He eased the case through the open window onto Sheila's back seat and jerked the driver's door open.

"Wallace's?"

"No. The wannabe thief."

She climbed into the passenger seat and strapped her seatbelt on. "What about his eyes?"

"Red. Watery. Sunken. The guy couldn't keep his balance even to escape, and he was scratchin' himself through the damn chains." Sheila's engine roared to life.

"What? Do you think he's sick or something?"

He slipped his sunglasses on and shifted into reverse. "That's probably what he calls it. Have you ever seen a junkie jonesin' for a fix?"

"Shit, Johnny."

"Some of 'em will break into anythin' they can get their hands on."

"So why didn't you call the local PD?"

Sheila jerked when he shifted into drive but fortunately, he pulled out of the parking lot and onto the adjacent road at a sane speed. "I don't need a pat on the back, darlin'. Wallace will deal with the guy. He's been down that road and made it out on the other side. And if that idiot shows his face 'round here after that, he's stupid enough to go to jail the next time."

CHAPTER TWENTY-TWO

They headed away from Marco Island and toward the cabin but at the halfway mark, Johnny turned off the freeway down a side street and pulled over at a gas station.

Lisa glanced at the gas gauge on the dashboard. The tank was still over three-quarters full.

"You want anythin'?" He nodded toward the gas station and closed the door.

"No, I'm good."

He gave Sheila's hood a little thump, turned toward the gas station, and disappeared inside.

Two other cars pulled up at the pump—a beat-up, rusted blue station wagon and what looked like an older model of the bounty hunter's truck. Lisa leaned back in the seat and drummed her fingers on the door's armrest.

The dwarf returned two minutes later with a bottle of water and nothing else. He scrambled into the driver's seat and offered her the water. "Thirsty?"

She raised an eyebrow at him. "No. That's all you stopped for?"

"Uh-huh." He placed the water in the cup holder and started the engine.

"Okay, what's going on?"

"In a minute." He pulled slowly out of the gas station and didn't move his head when he glanced in the rearview mirror through his dark sunglasses.

Lisa looked at the speedometer and folded her arms. "You're going at the speed limit."

"Yep."

"Johnny—"

"We're being tailed." He draped one hand over the steering wheel and hung the other through the glass-less window and patted the door casually. "That station wagon looks like it came out of the junkyard."

The agent looked in the side mirror and raised her eyebrows. Sure enough, the rusted station wagon rolled along the freeway about six car-lengths behind them. "Do you know who it is?"

Johnny grunted non-committaly. "It could be anyone. But that POS has been on our asses since we left Jordan's club. There were three of 'em in Marco Island."

"And now there are only two."

He sniffed and nodded.

Lisa pressed her head back against the headrest and peered into the mirror again. "Did that have anything to do with you parking in the restaurant lot?"

"Maybe."

"So what's the plan?"

"I got it." The bounty hunter pressed a little harder on the accelerator to bring the Jeep a little above the speed limit, then turned the radio on. Pantera blared through the speakers, and Lisa jerked her head away from the grind and squeal of heavy metal.

"Oh, yeah. Scare them off with loud music. Good plan."

"It works sometimes." He darted her a sidelong glance behind his glasses and smirked. "Music ain't for them, though."

Before she could ask what the hell the music was for, he made a sharp right turn onto an unmarked dirt road. She braced herself against the door and gritted her teeth as Sheila fishtailed across the dirt and kicked up a spray of pebbles and dust. *Here we go.*

The rusted station wagon slowed like any law-abiding citizen before it made the turn. The driver had even put the blinker on.

Johnny snorted. "They're tryin'."

"Or they merely happen to have the same map around town." Lisa gave him a challenging look. "Are you sure they're following us on purpose?"

"I am now."

They barreled down the dirt road that lanced through the thick growth on either side and blocked the sight of the station wagon behind them with a thick cloud of dust. The agent clutched the armrest of the door and stared straight ahead. *If anyone else comes driving the other way toward us, one of us will go off the side.*

The dwarf coaxed the Jeep to a faster speed and the speakers pumped a dizzyingly fast guitar riff seconds before they reached the end of the road. Sheila skidded to a stop when he braked sharply and parked, but he didn't turn the engine or the music off.

In front of them, the road ended in a wide dirt lot exactly like his, although the ramshackle shack with a drooping roof on one side wasn't his cabin. Even the door on the screened-in porch hung crookedly on its hinges. A dozen bright-pink plastic flamingoes dotted the patches of dry grass that still attempted to grow in front of the shack.

He glanced in the rearview mirror again and grimaced as the station wagon bounced along at a normal speed through the dissipating cloud of dust. "All right. Time to get out."

"Yeah, I'm not sure getting into a standoff outside an abandoned shack in the middle of nowhere is the best idea you've had."

Johnny finally turned the engine off and slid out of the Jeep without taking anything with him. Lisa turned in her seat to look at the station wagon, which was closing on them fast, then sighed and opened her door.

"Stand right there." He pointed at the grass on the other side of the shack's dangling screen door. "A little more to the side."

She took one step sideways. "Are you gonna tell me the plan? 'Cause you must have one."

The bounty hunter didn't have the chance to answer, even if he'd intended to.

The station wagon slid to a stop beside Sheila and both front doors opened at the same time. Two huge men in jeans and button-downs stepped out of the vehicle and looked very much like the Everglades locals they'd pretended to be for the last few hours. Except, of course, for the semi-automatic rifles nestled in each of their hands.

"Howdy, boys." Johnny hooked his thumbs through his belt loops—conveniently close to his knife on one side and the row of explosive disks hooked on his belt.

Lisa steadied her hand and didn't draw her weapon although she was tempted.

"It looks like y'all took a wrong turn," the dwarf said casually.

"Nope." The station wagon's driver smacked his lips and lifted his weapon enough to aim it at Johnny's boots. "We're exactly where we wanna be, asshole."

"We came to deliver a message," the other said with a grunt. He tossed his mop of heavy brown curls out of his eyes and swatted at the mosquitos that flitted around his head.

"Huh. Well, I ain't seen y'all before."

"We've seen you," the driver said. "So has the man we're working for. He knows what you're up to, dwarf. And he says you better drop it before things get worse for you. Because they will."

The bounty hunter sniffed and glanced at the man's weapon. "Who y'all workin' for?"

"None of your fucking business asshole." The accomplice raised his weapon to aim it at him.

His partner gave him a warning glance. "All you need to know is he has a huge chunk of Florida in his pocket. Real powerful guy."

"Sure." He jerked his chin up. "That's why he sent two thugs in a hulk of metal scraps to come talk to me instead. I reckon I could pull his name up with three guesses. What d'ya say?"

"You don't know everyone in Florida, asshole."

The second man sneered. "But we know you. And all your friends you paid visits to today. So back the fuck off and let the big boys handle it."

"You're getting in the way." The driver raised his eyebrows and swung his weapon to aim at Johnny's chest while he studied Lisa with a smirk.

She frowned at the bounty hunter, who didn't look at her. *He doesn't simply stand there and take threats like this. What the hell?*

"All right, fellas." He sniffed and nodded. "Tell your boss I don't like being followed. So if he wants to chat, let him schedule a meeting. In person."

"You don't leave it well enough alone, you won't be doing shit in person—"

Johnny uttered a piercing whistle.

The telltale click of a weapon issued from the darkness of the shack before the door to the screened-in porch flew open with a bang and a shriek. A hunched old Wood Elf stormed out with a sawn-off shotgun in both hands, his wrinkled eyes wide as he fired a round of buckshot at the side of the road. The flamingo closest to the edge of the dirt drive exploded. "Plenty more where that came from, buckos!"

"Shit! What are you doing, you crazy old—"

The resident cocked the shotgun again and fired at the station wagon. A series of holes peppered the hood and sprayed the dirt around it. The accomplice got a round of buckshot in the foot and howled.

"Aw, fuck! My fucking foot! I'll fucking kill you—"

Another shot followed, the elf's expression calm and determined.

The station wagon's still-hot engine hissed when the next shot drilled more holes through the hood.

"Get the fuck in the car!" The driver darted around the open door and threw himself behind the wheel.

"Fucking elf." His partner limped around the open passenger door and pointed at Johnny. "You stay the fuck away from those properties—"

The old-timer readied his weapon again as he continued to walk forward. "Mine too, ya bastards!"

"Go, go, go!" The passenger door slammed shut as the engine sputtered and growled. The driver stepped on the accelerator with the vehicle in reverse, then spun with a spray of dirt and hurtled down the road while steam billowed from beneath the hood.

The Wood Elf fired another shot for good measure and the vehicle's back windshield exploded. "Yar! Go fuck yerselves and yer sissy pea-shooters! Come back 'gain, I'll make y'all eat this here lead!"

A huge dust cloud rumbled down the road before the fleeing vehicle disappeared.

Johnny burst out laughing. Lisa, who hadn't moved an inch since the Wood Elf burst out of the shack, turned slowly to look at the dwarf with wide eyes. "That was your plan?"

"It works like a charm, don't it?" The elf swung the shotgun down at his side and his hunched shoulders relaxed as he winked at her.

"Every damn time." The dwarf ran a hand through his hair before he stepped forward to shake the old-timer's hand. "You haven't lost your touch at all, Ronnie."

The elf responded with a high-pitched, whistling giggle and took the proffered hand. "Ain't nothin' on two worlds gon' make me lose aim with this'n, Johnny. I thought my days of hearin' yer damn music blarin' through my head was over."

"Not yet."

Ronnie turned toward Lisa with a wrinkled grin. "Sorry fer scarin' ya, darlin'. That there look on yer face says ya don' know if'n ya wanna run fer the hills or slap someone." He raised his hands with a chuckle. "'Slong as it ain't me."

"No." She managed a shaky laugh. "No running or hitting. Not now, anyway."

Johnny snorted. "Ronnie's been scarin' off all the wrong kinda folks think they are smart enough to tail me for a long time. Or make threats."

"Goin' on what? Fifty years?" The elf nodded with another wheezing giggle. "Gets 'em every time. Even when ya ain't workin', Johnny, ya know I got yer back. And you got mine, eh?"

"Damn straight." He patted the old Wood Elf on the shoulder. "But I am workin' again. At least for now."

"Ya don't say." Ronnie nodded toward Lisa, his blue eyes glinting. "Looks like ya got yerself a pardner too."

She grinned. "Yes, he does. Lisa Breyer."

"Good ta see you, sweetheart." He drew in a long breath, leaned back despite his hunched shoulders, then whistled. "Feels damn good, Johnny. Damn good. Hey, ye're stoppin' back on by to help me set those new traps 'gain, ain'tcha?"

"I need a few more days, then I'm all yours."

"Good. I'll spread the word 'bout them good-for-nothin's, mind. Grapevine'll pick up on someone tailin' Johnny Walker in yer own neck 'o the woods. They ain't gon' find ya."

"'Preciate it."

"Yar. We take care of our own." Ronnie winked at Lisa again.

The dwarf nodded, then pointed at Sheila. "We better get on."

"Sure. Get on and do whatcha do." Ronnie turned to return to his shack, chuckling. "Turn that shit you call music down where I can't hear it 'gain, huh? I about broke my back jumpin' up when I heard ya."

"Uh-huh." Johnny shook his head and climbed into Sheila's driver seat. The screen door creaked and slapped shut and the elf disappeared.

Lisa looked at the buckshot in the dirt and the obliterated pink shreds of the single flamingo casualty. "I certainly didn't expect that."

"What can I say, darlin'?" The bounty hunter smirked at her as she took her place in the passenger seat and closed the door. "We're full of surprises down here."

"Including the grapevine, I'm guessing." She strapped herself in quickly as he started the engine, made a slow turn around Ronnie's front yard, and barely avoided the other flamingos. "Is that some kind of Everglades network?"

He snorted and straightened the vehicle to proceed down the dirt road. "You bet. It might surprise you what pops up when folks put their heads together. 'Specially down here."

"Oh, yeah. I'm already surprised." A huge heron took flight from the swamp on their right, flapped a few times, and glided slowly over the road as the Jeep raced toward the freeway. "Any idea what those idiots with semi-automatics were talking about?"

Johnny shrugged. "Again, It could be anyone."

"Not if you've been retired for the last fifteen years."

"Yeah. It's a little strange to have folks target me like that right after I get back into the game."

"They said they know what you're up to and want you to stop. Present tense." Lisa brushed her hair out of her eyes and let the rest of it whip around her head in the wind. "Like they're talking about this Logree case. Unless there's something else you're doing that someone wants you to stop."

"There might be. It don't make sense that city thugs like that would try to keep us from stoppin' an Oriceran creature terrorizin' storefronts and resorts." He cleared his throat. "Reckon whoever they're workin' for will send someone else after this little bruhaha."

"You don't look too concerned about it."

"That's 'cause I ain't. Whoever they are, let 'em come after me again if they're dumb enough to try it. There are a lotta locals down here keepin' an eye out now. Many eyes."

Lisa laughed and shook her head. "A Wood Elf with a sawn-off."

"Yeah, that's somethin', ain't it?"

CHAPTER TWENTY-THREE

As Sheila pulled into the front drive of Johnny's cabin, Rex and Luther raced around from the back, barking wildly and sliding in the dirt. "Johnny! Johnny, you're back!"

"Good thing, Johnny. You gotta come see this."

He turned the engine off and slid out of the Jeep. "All right now, boys. Settle down."

"Johnny, we tried to stop her."

"Yeah, we tried hard. Told her to back off and get lost." Rex pranced around his master's feet and barked again. "But she made us an offer we couldn't refuse."

"Steak, Johnny." Luther yipped and sniffed the ground as the dwarf headed for the front door. "Couple of real juicy ones. Dropped 'em right in the dirt and called us good hounds."

"We couldn't say no, Johnny. It wasn't our fault."

"Yeah, and the pup said it was cool, so—"

The dwarf stopped and stared at his hounds. *There's someone in my damn house.*

"What's wrong?" Lisa asked as she came up behind him.

"No one fucking feeds my hounds."

"What?"

"I should've added emergency phone calls to the damn collars." He stormed up the porch steps and threw the screen door open.

"We did our best, Johnny." The dogs raced up after him.

"Yeah, but she's real smart. Knew exactly how to get to us."

He reached under the tin mailbox mounted on the siding at the front door and jerked the pistol he'd taped there free. "I'll handle it."

"Johnny, what's going on?" Lisa shoved the screen door open again before it could smack closed in her face and Johnny stormed into his house, leaving the front door wide open.

Turning the pistol's safety off, he checked the magazine, shoved it in again, and marched down the hall. "Amanda!"

When he reached the living room, he leveled the pistol at the woman seated on his couch beside the young shifter. "Get the fuck outta my house."

"Hey!" Amanda leapt to her feet and the woman in a maroon t-shirt tucked into tight jeans and a glitzy belt stood slowly beside her. "What are you doing?"

"I never gave you an invitation," he all but snarled at the stranger. "You'd best be on your way."

"Johnny, I told her to come inside." The girl glanced at her visitor, who simply stared at him with a raised eyebrow and a smirk. "Put your gun down, okay? She's only here to talk."

"Oh, yeah, Johnny." Luther sat at his master's side. "Lady's from that shifter pack."

Rex whined and sat on the dwarf's other side. "Probably should have mentioned that part."

Goddamn shifters.

Lisa stopped six feet behind him and watched the stranger in his living room warily.

"There's nothin' to talk about." The dwarf glanced at Amanda. "Except for how you're doin' exactly the opposite of everythin' I say."

"You're gettin' your panties all in a bunch over nothin'," the woman drawled. "It was only a little chat."

"Don't matter if it was a fuckin' wave, lady. You're trespassin'."

"I stopped here to talk to Amanda." She folded her arms. "In person. See if she'd fit in with our pack seein' as now she lives in the Everglades and all. Lone wolves don't last that long, do they?"

"Longer'n you're fixin' to last if you don't get on back to whatever hole you crawled out of." He thumbed the hammer of his pistol back.

Amanda stepped toward him. "Johnny, don't."

"I ain't talkin' to you." He stepped into the living room, his weapon still leveled at the pack ambassador's chest, and nodded down the hall toward the front. "Out. My hounds have your scent now. They don't forget. If I have to, I'll track you and your whole pack of backwoods dogs to every one of your meetups and send a different kinda message."

"You're not makin' a very good case for yourself," the shifter woman said, although she stepped around the coffee table and headed toward the hallway. "Keepin' a girl locked up like this. You know how kids are. Squeeze 'em too tightly, and they'll turn against you simply for a breath of fresh air."

The dwarf turned and trailed the woman with his weapon as she walked casually down the hall. "I see you here again, you ain't walkin' out."

"See you around, Amanda."

Rex and Luther growled after the visitor, their ears pressed flat against their heads. "Won't fool us twice, lady."

"Yeah, no matter how many steaks you drop."

"Hey, where was she keeping them?"

The woman studied Lisa with a smirk as she passed. "You got a little somethin' there on your cheek, sweetie."

"Get out before he shoots you."

Chuckling, the shifter took her sweet time to stroll down the hallway.

Johnny didn't lower his pistol until the screen door slammed shut behind her and she disappeared through the high row of reeds growing along the road.

"I can't believe you did that," Amanda muttered.

He lowered the pistol's hammer, then turned slowly to face her with a scowl. "I'm doin' what has to be done, kid. Can't exactly say the same for you right now, can I?"

"Johnny, it was only a talk—"

"In my house."

"It's my house too right now, isn't it?" The girl glanced at Lisa in disbelief. "You're making way too big a deal out of this. I wasn't part of any pack in New York. I couldn't even shift if we weren't out on a camping trip in the middle of nowhere. And this is the middle of nowhere."

"Don't mean it's safe."

"But it might be! This could be a real chance for me, Johnny— to run with a pack and learn more about what I can do. Controlling my instincts like you said."

"Save it, kid." He thumped the pistol onto the side table next to the couch and shook his head. "You broke the rules—"

"I'm trying to learn who I am! Abby said they could help me do that."

"Oh, you know her name now, do ya? Don't say it again."

"Johnny—"

"I brought you here with me to keep you safe." He pointed roughly at her. "Not so you can sign up with the first redneck troop of slobbering inbred shifters that gives you the time of day. That's the end of it."

Amanda scowled at him and folded her arms. "You're the last person I expected to stereotype someone."

"Ain't a stereotype with those, kid."

"I'm not your kid." She stormed past him and bumped her shoulder against his before she rushed down the hall.

Rex and Luther leapt to their feet and raced after her. "Come on, pup. It's not so bad."

"Yeah, you'll find a pack someday. A good one."

"Hey, where are you goin'?"

She said nothing to the hounds as she burst through the screened-in porch. Luther followed her, and Rex doubled halfway back toward Johnny. "We'll talk some sense into her, Johnny. No problem."

"Stay with her." The bounty hunter nodded toward the door, and Rex scrabbled down the hall before he nudged the screen door open again with his snout. Then, he trudged into his workshop and pulled one metal box after another off the shelves and thunked them onto the worktable.

Lisa leaned against the doorway into the workshop, her hands clasped behind her back. "You should go after her, Johnny."

"Nope."

"She might be angry but she still needs you."

"Naw, what she needs is some time and space to cool off. We both do."

"And you don't think she's gonna cool off looking for that shifter pack that gave her an open invitation?"

"The hounds will keep an eye on her."

"They're dogs, Johnny—"

"Watch it." He clanged another box on the table, then heaved a sigh and scratched under his nose. "Sorry."

"I'm not the one who needs to hear it."

He looked slowly at her. "You think I'm wrong?"

"Not on principle." Lisa shrugged. "But I wouldn't say holding a gun to her guest and harping at the kid about what she's doing wrong is the best way to handle something like this."

"Huh." Johnny grunted. "She'll work it out. And when she gets back from wherever she went off to— Shit. I'm tryin' to stay on this goddamn case and that kid's too smart and stubborn for her own good. Mine too."

"So what are you gonna do about it?"

"The kid's my responsibility. I chose to take her in and I aim to keep that promise to her. I can't keep shuckin' her off onto someone else to keep an eye on her while I'm workin' and I can't keep her with me every step of the way, either. She ain't a bounty hunter."

"Very true." The agent stepped into the workshop and tilted her head to regard him with a firm expression. "You'll have to talk to her about all this eventually. Preferably without firearms and yelling. It might help to come up with a plan for when she does come back."

"A plan." Johnny sniffed and shoved one of the metal boxes away from him across the worktable. "I need a drink."

He stormed into the kitchen and she remained where she was, listening to the bang of cabinets opening and shutting and the splash of whiskey into a glass. A moment later, he returned with a rocks glass with double his usual four fingers, took a long swig, then stopped and stared at her. "Shit. You want somethin'?"

"Nope."

"All right. Let's get to work."

Once he'd retrieved Wallace's metal case from the back of the Jeep, Johnny showed Lisa his process for filling his hollow ammo rounds—in this case, the crossbow bolt tips—with whatever magical concoction fit the purpose.

"Think you got it?"

"Sure."

"Here." He tossed a pair of thick work gloves across the table, then handed her one of the small vials of blue-white Crystal magic. "Grab some tips. I got another funnel here somewhere."

"How many of these are you trying to fill?" She pulled the gloves on, lifted a hollow bolt tip from the open box, and held it to the light.

"A couple of dozen. Maybe more. We'll empty half these vials and save the rest for a rainy day."

"Right. It always helps to have a half-Crystal's magic lying around for who knows what."

Johnny snorted and pried the small hatch in another bolt tip open.

They worked together to fill as many shootable Crystal tips as they could using half the vials from Wallace. As he snapped the hatch shut on another full, glowing projectile, a small alarm beeped from the vicinity of the police scanner.

"What's that?" Lisa asked as she poured liquified magic carefully into the funnel.

He set the bolt tip down, ripped his gloves off, and grinned. "'Bout damn time."

She closed the bolt tip and turned to watch him stride across the workshop.

The dwarf opened a small black box beside the police scanner, took out a thick black device the size of a cell phone, and chuckled. "There you are, you gooey bastard."

"What?"

Johnny wiggled the device at her, still grinning.

Lisa leaned away from him with a frown. "You look like a mad scientist right now."

"Not a scientist, darlin'. A bounty hunter about to close in on a target. Which, by the way, is now moving." He flashed the device at her and she caught a brief glimpse of a radar tracking screen and a small red dot that moved slowly up the side.

"You've been tracking it."

"Naw, that just started." He set the device down and stared at it as he picked up his half-empty double whiskey and took a large sip. "It was one of the first bolts I used on that tentacled beast. Wasn't on purpose, and I assumed it hadn't hit home when no signal came through." He snorted. "I ain't often wrong, darlin', but it's a damn good thing I was in this case."

"So the Logree's on the move and headed…"

"It looks like up the coast toward Naples." He wiggled his

eyebrows at her. "As soon as we fit these tips, we'll roll out and have us a little showdown. With ice this time."

Lisa pulled her phone out to check the time. "It's seven-thirty, Johnny. The sun sets in…what? An hour?"

"I have no problem seein' in the dark."

"I'm talking about Amanda. What if she comes home while we're gone?"

Johnny grunted and downed the last of his whiskey. "The hounds are with her. She's safe."

"But she won't know where we are."

"All right, fine. Christ." He stormed into the kitchen, rummaged in a drawer, and returned with a pen and a crumpled sheet of paper. "I'll write her a damn note."

The agent chuckled and drew a handful of untipped bolts from the long box to work on fitting them with the new Crystal-magic-infused tips. "All this gear and tech, and you're going old school with a handwritten note."

"What, you have a better idea?"

"No. I like it."

He scribbled his note for Amanda, swallowed when he finished, and read through it.

Went off to bag the big purple game. Don't forget to feed the boys. And yourself. We'll talk later. —J

With a sigh, he tossed the pen onto the table and left to tape the note onto the wall just inside the front door.

Five minutes later, he and Lisa zipped the two cases filled with bolts they'd fitted and he took his crossbow from the shelf. "Time to go huntin.'"

CHAPTER TWENTY-FOUR

With one hand on the throttle of the airboat as they skimmed the water along Florida's western coast, Johnny glanced at the tracking device in his other hand and nodded. "Kill the lights, will ya?"

"The lights?" Lisa stepped hesitantly across the deck.

"Right there on the mounts. Big black button."

Despite the sunset still reflecting off the water and filling the western sky, the work light on Johnny's airboat had given them a clear view of the coast as the daylight faded. That vanished when she found the power button and the bright lights shut off with a heavy thunk.

"We should be comin' up on it in another...two, three minutes."

"Or less." She pointed directly ahead.

About a mile away, an unnatural swirl rippled sideways up the coast and intersected the waves breaking along the shore. A thin, dark-purple tentacle rose from the water and dropped into the surf again with a barely visible splash.

"Well, look at that." Johnny twisted the throttle and increased their speed. *Good thing it's a calm night. The airboat wouldn't work so well on choppy water.*

"All right. Come here."

Lisa joined him at the stern and darted glances over her shoulder at the Logree hurtling along the coastline.

"Keep this control stick steady and the fan pointin' us right at it, yeah?"

"What are you gonna do?"

"I aim to catch the bastard." With a nod, he stepped past her toward the harpoon gun bolted to the starboard side of the deck. "Hold her steady, darlin'. I'll do the rest."

"Sure." She barely had to move the control stick. "Good thing you have a partner to steer the boat while you aim the gun. It seems like that'd be hard to do all on your own."

He frowned over his shoulder at her and snorted. "Naw. I would've rigged somethin' else up to do both. It's nice to have a second, though."

Johnny returned his attention to the scope on the harpoon gun and fiddled with the dial.

The agent focused on the Logree's wake moving quickly up the coastline, although it made the creature seem much smaller than it was. "Partner," she muttered with a small smile.

They gained on their quarry, and the bounty hunter swiveled the harpoon gun an inch to the left and down. "Hold on tight, darlin'."

"For what?"

He pulled the trigger, the gun fired with a muffled boom, and the harpoon sailed over the gentle waves. The cable at the end wobbled after the heavy projectile, then entered the water with a splash. A puff of purple mist rose from the waves, followed by a warbled cry drowned out by the roar of the crashing surf.

Johnny pulled his face away from the gun's scope and grinned. The cable drew taut and jerked the airboat forward with a groan as the Logree raced through the water and dragged them with it.

Lisa shouted and stumbled against the fan mount. He laughed and steadied himself against the mounted gun. "For that!"

The Logree swung away from the shore and turned tightly to double back toward the airboat while it towed it simultaneously farther out to sea.

"It's gonna ram into us," the agent shouted.

"No, it ain't." Johnny pulled the crossbow strap over his head and shoulder, then fitted a bolt into the barrel. The cable attached to the harpoon gun thrummed with tension, and it creaked as the Logree pulled them along and doubled back past the airboat. The angle made the boat tilt violently to the starboard side. "Turn the fan!"

"What?"

"Starboard!"

"Johnny, I don't—"

"Push the damn thing as far as you can away from you!"

She leaned forward against the slope of the listing deck and shoved the throttle control stick away from her with both hands. The heavy fan turned and blasted air at the water to push the tipping boat upright again. They leveled out and turned to face the Logree, which jerked them forward again as it increased its speed down the coastline and away from Naples.

The airboat lurched with a groan and skipped over the waves. Lisa stumbled against the fan base but didn't need to be told to pull the control stick toward her and level the fan.

Yeah, she's gettin' the hang of it now.

Johnny hooked his left leg and arm around the harpoon mount in case the Logree tried any other smartass moves and aimed his crossbow at the creature's wide wake ahead of them. The crossbow fired with a thump and a twang, and he immediately drew another bolt from the case at his back to re-load.

"Come on, you big bastard," he muttered and stared at the

water as the tentacled creature hauled them down the coastline. "You know what's holdin' you back."

A puff of purple mist and a spray of water as if from a spouting whale burst from the waves before the harpoon cable slackened. The airboat sloshed across the water and slowed to its regular speed.

"That's right. Come to Johnny."

"What's it doing?" Lisa asked and ignored the pain in her hand clenched tightly around the control stick.

"Makin' a stand." The dwarf fired another bolt into where he thought the Logree's domed body should be. *It's hard to tell with all those tentacles.*

The harpoon cable slackened completely and dropped with a clank against the hull. In the next moment, the creature's huge wake broke across the waves and raced toward them at frightening speed.

"Okay, so now you're gonna take it down." Lisa tried to step back, but her shoe knocked against the fan base and reminded her there was nowhere else to go.

"Yep." Johnny drew, reloaded, and fired again. A burst of blue-white light illuminated below the surface of the water and filtered quickly around the massive creature that simply plowed toward them as if it hadn't noticed. "Bingo."

"Johnny—"

"We're good."

"I don't think—"

"Not now, Lisa." He loaded another bolt and fired. Then another. "We're fixin' for a showdown."

"Shit."

The Logree raced toward them and spouted puffs of purple vapor above the waves. It pulled up fifteen feet from the airboat and sent a violent wave of seawater splashing onto the prow.

"Ha!" The bounty hunter shook the water out of his eyes, blew it off his mouth and beard, and unhooked himself from the harpoon mount to stride toward the prow. "Come on!"

Two huge tentacles elevated from the water, followed by a couple of inches of the Logree's glistening domed head. The appendages slapped the surface and two more rose to join them. These were much wider and studded along the underside with suckers Johnny expected them to open and drip their flammable goo at any minute.

"Just fuckin' try it." The tentacles reared and the suckers fluttered open, and he fired.

His Crystal-magic-laced bolt pierced one of the openings in the center and a flash of blue-white light raced across the tentacle and petered out quickly. The Logree bellowed and slapped the appendage onto the water to break the bolt, but the magic-imbued projectile had already done its part.

The creature's goo-spraying tentacles opened all their sucker-shaped valves, but only another puff of purple mist sputtered out, nothing else. The suckers squelched open and closed a few more times before the thick tentacles dropped beneath the water again.

"Good tip, Sevol." Grinning madly, Johnny raced toward the stern as the Logree raised half a dozen more appendages into the air and held them there. The airboat skimmed toward the creature. "Watch yourself."

"What?" Lisa stepped away from him quickly and almost slipped on the drenched deck. "What are you doing?"

He pushed the throttle away to steer them to the creature's right, then pulled it back past the center. "Hold it right there."

"Johnny!"

He slid across the deck toward his net gun invention bolted on the port side and swung the swiveling head toward his quarry as the airboat made a wide circle around eight black-purple tentacles undulating above the waves like flames. "Hold it, darlin'! We ain't done yet."

The dwarf fired the net gun with a bang, and a wad of twisted rope launched toward the Logree, fell around half the tentacles, and knocked the others down. The creature's limbs slipped through the holes in the net to resume their waving in the air.

After snapping another canister off from where it dangled on the side of the net gun mount, Johnny shoved it into the back of the gun and pulled on the swiveling mount again to take aim.

Two thin, surprisingly long tentacles rose at the side of the boat and snuck up over the side of the deck.

"Woah. Uh-uh!" Lisa reached out toward them and launched a yellow attack spell from her fingertips. Her aim was perfect, and they whipped away from the boat before they fell and submerged again. *It's not as good as a fireball, but it'll do. I'm not trying to blow all three of us out of the water.*

Four more wavering limbs sloshed out of the water and reached for the airboat that circled the creature relentlessly. Johnny fired the net gun again, oblivious to the close call with the Logree's longer tentacles, and caught the new ones in the second net.

"That's it." He darted starboard toward the harpoon gun and punched the button to turn on the mechanical reel. The cable wound through the mount and pulled taut again with a metallic groan and a clunk. He stopped the reel when the Logree and the airboat jerked toward each other.

The creature's netted tentacles shuddered, then dropped to the water with multiple wet slaps and a splash of salty spray.

The bounty hunter stared at the two inches of dark-purple domed flesh protruding from the surface as the creature bobbed just below. The Logree snorted and more water sloshed into his face, but it made no further effort to attack.

"Shit." Lisa breathed deeply and wiped seawater off her face. "Is it dead?"

Johnny stared at the tentacles that swayed slowly on the surface of the gentle waves—not like seaweed or drifting plants caught in the tide but as if the Logree had focused on treading water now instead. The net around its tentacles dipped below the water and reappeared, but the creature had stopped fighting altogether.

"Naw. It's restin' for a spell." He sniffed and locked the harpoon gun's swiveling head into place. "Reckon we wore it out —for a few minutes at least."

"A few minutes. That doesn't leave us with many options."

"Maybe longer. Who knows?" The dwarf hurried to the stern and reached for the throttle control stick. "You can let go now, darlin'."

"Oh. Right." The agent relinquished the control stick and stretched the cramp out of her hand. He took his place in front of the massive fan and steered the airboat south in the direction from which they'd come. "It's the first time I've seen someone shoot like that."

The dwarf glanced over his shoulder with a smirk as the harpoon cable tightened again. The netted Logree was hauled along behind them and created a wake in theirs without resistance. "I reckon it's the first time anyone's gone up against one of these."

"Well, you got it."

He looked directly ahead, his hand loosely around the control stick, and nodded. "Yes, we did."

Where she stood and wrung seawater from the hem of her soaked shirt, she stared at him with the hint of a smile. *It's "we" now. Johnny Walker might finally be coming around.* "So now we take it to your place, right? Tie it up and call it in?"

"Naw, not yet. I wanna get a good look at it before I hand it over to Nelson's goons." He raised an eyebrow at her. "You can leave that out of the report."

"Not a problem."

CHAPTER TWENTY-FIVE

They stopped along the river at a soggy mess of land in the swamp which Johnny said was good enough to study an Oriceran monster. He tied the airboat off, retrieved a pair of gloves from the black box hooked to the stern, and hopped off the deck with a splash. The harpoon cable grew taut in his hands as he followed it behind the boat and tugged the Logree toward him with every step. Lisa remained where she was and watched him, ready to draw her weapon if necessary.

"All right, now. It's time to see what we're workin' with." He waded farther into the swamp until the water reached the middle of his thighs. With his feet stabilized, he reached for the closest end of the net and pulled.

The creature snorted with another spray of water but didn't attempt to fight. With a grunt, the dwarf hauled it toward the swampy bank and kicked aside a floating log. He managed to drag the netted tentacles and only a quarter of the domed purple-black body onto the mud before he dropped the net and wiped the sweat and seawater off his forehead with a forearm covered in thick red hair.

"Damn. Hell of a big'un, ain'tcha?" One tentacle curled away from the nets and unfurled gently in front of his boot. "Sevol said you ain't as brainless as everyone thinks. Now would be your chance to prove him right."

Half a dozen eyes on the Logree's uncovered head blinked open. All six of the glowing orbs with slitted pupils centered on him, and the creature snorted with far less force this time.

"Yeah, I see you too." Johnny folded his arms and inclined his head. "Remember me?"

A large bubble emerged from its underbelly and popped stickily in the mud. "What do you want from me, dwarf?"

"Johnny?" the agent called from the airboat.

"Lisa."

"Did that thing just talk to you?"

"This *thing* has a name," the Logree replied in an unmistakably female voice, "if either of you had bothered to ask it."

"Huh." He chuckled. "You know, I remember tryin' to talk to you the last time we crossed paths."

The creature snorted. "That was different."

"Yep. Last time, you took my weapon instead of agreein' to a little chat. This time, I got you tied up and half out of the water."

"You were in my way. I was gentle."

"With me, sure." The bounty hunter sniffed and stood his ground as the outstretched tentacle at his boot flicked its glistening tip toward his face. *If that had fur, a tail, and four legs, I'd say it's lookin' at me like a hungry hound does when he's beggin'.* "But you weren't gentle with that market. Or the gas station. Or that resort in the Keys. I bet you didn't plan on bein' gentle with wherever you were headin' tonight. It looked very much like Naples."

"And you stopped me." The Logree sighed heavily, and it sounded surprisingly like relief. "Thank you."

Johnny gaped at it. "Say again?"

"I'm so tired."

"Lisa," the dwarf called. "Come on down here and say hello. It sounds like we did this one a favor without even knowin' it."

With a frown, she slid off the boat and squelched through the swampy mud to stand beside him. "Um…hello."

She cast him a sidelong glance, and he shrugged.

"I am called Una," the Logree said as her tentacles inched slowly and unthreateningly along the mud toward them. Her uncovered golden eyes all moving independently to study her captors at the same time. "And you are?"

The dwarf cleared his throat. "Johnny. Lisa."

"A pleasure."

"Yeah, see, that's the part that's trippin' me up. Most times, a creature I haul up on land don't thank me and introduce themselves."

Una sighed again. "I can only assume most of those creatures are not being forced to wreak havoc against their will."

The agent scratched the side of her face and lowered slowly into a crouch. "So all the explosions—the attacks over the last few weeks. You're saying someone else is making you do it?"

A small tentacle slithered across the mud toward her, and the Logree's domed head and body underwater swelled even larger with a deep breath. "He has the perfect leverage. My offspring."

"Shit." Johnny rubbed his mouth. "More goddamn child kidnappers."

"Who?" Lisa asked.

"I do not know. Six weeks ago, I heard my offspring calling to me from this planet. Terrified, alone, and lost." Her eyes closed slowly and she snorted again. "I crossed through the open gates to retrieve her."

Johnny frowned. "From Oriceran?"

"Yes."

"You heard your kid calling you from Earth and no one else heard it?"

"We do not often use our voices to reach each other, dwarf." The Logree sighed again and focused all six eyes not buried beneath her body on him. "She called to my being."

"Intelligent, well-mannered, and telepathic." He glanced at Lisa. "Sevol left that out."

The agent leaned closer toward the creature. "So someone has your offspring and is using her to blackmail you into destroying Florida property?"

"Yes. I have no other interest in this planet."

"And this asshole tells you where to go and what to blow up with your…goo?" he asked.

"The attacks are not random if that's what you're asking." Una's tentacles curled and uncurled, buried themselves in the mud, and slid out to coat her head and body with the dampness. "They are only made to look so."

"Like a mindless beast on a violent rampage up and down the coast," the bounty hunter muttered.

"Which you're not," Lisa added.

The Logree heaved another sigh. "Indeed I'm not."

Johnny lowered his head with a frown. "What can you tell us about the bastard who has your kid?"

"That his focus is on the more populated areas. Those like the first one I attacked."

"The resorts." The agent nodded.

"If that is what they are. I only know where I am to go next and that when I finish, if this monster keeps his word, my offspring will be returned to me." Una closed her eyes again and her body shuddered in the mud. "I have to believe he will."

"Do you know where he's keeping her?" Lisa asked.

"No. But she sends me bits and pieces. An image of a dark room. Snippets of conversation—things like 'wiping out the competition.' Her view from the inside of a tank."

"Jesus." Lisa stood and looked at Johnny. "We had this all wrong."

"Uh-huh. So did the department." He shook his head and grimaced. "The plan's changed."

"Now that I am caught, yes. But I fear for my offspring if I do not finish what I was sent to do tonight."

"Well, you ain't caught anymore." Johnny took his knife from his belt and whipped it open. Una's tentacles jerked away from him. "Not for you. For the nets."

He waded into the swamp again to cut the ropes and returned his knife to his belt as the Logree's appendages slithered out of their bonds. As he hauled the damaged nets onto the shore, he shook his head. "Sorry about the harpoon."

"I will heal if you remove it."

"Yep." He returned to the creature's side, and Una lifted herself out of the swamp and turned slowly to offer her glistening side with the harpoon embedded four inches into her flesh. "It ain't gonna be a tickle."

"Do it."

Lisa winced as he wrapped both hands around the steel barb and gave one mighty jerk. It pulled free with a wet pop, followed by a cascade of glowing violet liquid from the hole in Una's side before the wound sealed itself. A burst of purple mist preceded the last piece of flesh knitting together and in a moment, it was finished.

The creature sighed. "Much better."

"I bet that comes in handy."

"On the rare occasion when I am skewered by a hunter, yes."

Johnny snorted. "Well, you put up a hell of a fight. I'll give you that. Fightin' for your kid too. Where else did this guy tell you to strike?"

"I have no details of the others. Not yet. I was told there are four resorts. The one you stopped me from reaching would have been the second. They only give me one location at a time."

"And keep stringin' you along much like I hauled you out here." The dwarf tossed the harpoon onto the airboat with a clang. "Where do you meet with this shithead?"

"I can't return until I do what they expect." Her voice trembled with something close to terror.

"Well, you can't simply swim out of here and go blow up a Naples resort, either."

"Johnny—"

He looked sharply at Lisa. "Come on, darlin'. It might look like it, but this ain't a black-and-white situation."

"I don't want to," Una added. "But I can't return to them tonight with nothing to show for my efforts. Which you so fortunately interrupted because I had no desire to do so, but I don't know what else to do."

"Tonight, huh? Go meet with 'em anyway."

A shuddering hiss rose from her trembling body and her tentacles whipped with more force against the mud. "They'll kill my offspring."

"No, they won't. They'll wanna hear from you why it wasn't done." He spread his arms placatingly. "And I'll be there to tell them. I have a feeling these bastards are the same as those who tried to start trouble for me too today 'cause they knew I was chasin' you. You tell me where you're supposed to meet, and I promise you I'll get you your kid back. As long as you're not spinnin' a yarn and tryin' to strangle me with it."

"I don't understand."

Lisa nudged him with her elbow. "He means as long as you're telling us the truth."

Una stared unwaveringly at him. "You had me tied and pinned halfway on land, dwarf. Why would I lie to you?"

Johnny sniffed and scratched under his nose. "Yeah, good point." *The draksa did say these beings were intelligent.* "But I can't help you if I don't know where to be."

"The place is called the Flamingo for Visitors, or something like it."

"The Flamingo Visitors Center?" he asked.

"Yes. Two miles up the western coast from there. Midnight."

"Goddamn tourists." The bounty hunter nodded. "I know it. We won't leave you hangin', Una. Or...floatin', I reckon. But be ready for anything."

"That is easily done. You have been the most surprising aspect of this entire ordeal."

Lisa snorted a laugh and covered her mouth quickly.

"Yeah, I hear that often one way or another." He nodded. "I'm not sure how long that Crystal magic will last. I wish I'd known all this before I shot you up with it."

"Ah." The Logree's body trembled again and her tentacles curled and uncurled quickly as something like a laugh escaped her. "So that's what dampens my secretions."

"The purple goo? Yeah."

"By the time I see you again, dwarf, it will be restored. Logree are resilient."

"That might be an understatement," the agent said.

All three remained where they were and Una splashed herself with swamp water again. "I would appreciate some assistance off this bank."

"Oh. Right." Johnny waded toward her and scowled at her tentacles, but they moved out of his way as he approached her head. "I don't wanna poke your eyes out or nothin'."

"You can't."

He placed both hands on her glistening body-head, tried to avoid her eyes anyway, and pushed. The Logree's flesh pressed inward beneath his palms and she snorted.

"Sorry."

"A little more, I think."

"Here." Lisa waded toward them too, ignored her sopping wet pants, and stepped carefully to avoid losing another shoe in the swamp. She bent at the knees and pressed her shoulder against Una's face.

"One...two...three." The dwarf grunted and pushed against the creature with his shoulder this time in an effort to lift her somewhat.

Together, they unbeached the incendiary sea creature from Oriceran. Una's tentacles slapped into the water as she reoriented herself. She bobbed away from the bank and pushed herself up at least four feet to expose all twelve eyes. "I hope to see you in three hours, dwarf. And you, Lisa."

"We'll be there." Agent Breyer raised a hand for a slightly awkward wave, and the Logree swam away again downriver toward the gulf.

Johnny cleared his throat. "She remembers your name, but I'm simply 'dwarf,' huh?"

She gave him a sidelong glance and shrugged. "You're the one who shot her with a harpoon. And half a dozen crossbow bolts. And two—"

"Yeah, yeah. I get it." He gathered the severed pieces of his roped netting and hauled them onto the airboat. "It's time to head home and swap out supplies. We're goin' for the real fuckers behind this mess. On land."

Lisa hopped onto the airboat and steadied herself with more poise this time as he untied the craft and shoved it away from the bank. He joined her with a wet thud and started the huge propeller. "I can't believe no one at the department looked into this closely enough to see what was truly going on," she muttered

"You can't believe a group of suits sittin' in their workboxes got lazy and dropped this into our lap to let us take care of the problem?"

"I guess. But a kidnapped Oriceran used as bait to blackmail an even bigger monster? That's an important angle."

"'S long as it's true." He turned them slowly on the river before he twisted the throttle and they raced through the Everglades toward home.

"You don't believe her?"

"I'm takin' her word for it, darlin'. Like she said, she's got no reason to make up somethin' like that. Makes sense if those chickenshits who ran away screamin' from Ronnie's were sent by the same chickenshit holdin' a magical baby squid hostage."

"But you're not doing this only to get back at them for threatening you."

"Naw." He smirked and hooked his free thumb through his belt loop. "I'll get a certain satisfaction out of it. But I reckon I also have a soft spot for anyone doin' what they have to do to keep a kid safe. Even a kid with two dozen tentacles."

CHAPTER TWENTY-SIX

There was no sign of Amanda or the hounds when they returned to the cabin shortly after the last traces of twilight faded from the Everglades. Johnny tapped the note he'd left for the girl on the wall. "I reckon she'd have torn it off and ripped it up if she'd come home already."

"Or left it there."

He walked through the kitchen to the back of the house and called from the mudroom inside the back door. "The hounds ain't been fed, either. They wouldn't have let her get away with not feedin' 'em this late."

"So they haven't been back at all." Lisa opened the girl's bedroom door to peer inside, but that was empty too.

"I guess not." He strode through the kitchen and ran a hand through his hair. "I can't say I'm a fan of knowin' she's out after dark. But shifters can see in the—"

His cell phone buzzed in his pocket and he pulled it out to answer the call. "Ain't it past your bedtime, Arthur?"

The man chuckled on the other line. "Most nights, Johnny, yeah. But I got a young woman and two coonhounds here at my place keepin' me company."

"Is everyone okay?"

Lisa turned to him with a questioning look and he nodded.

"Oh, sure. We're all as right as rain. Well, at the very least, she's safe. And now you know where she is."

Johnny sniffed. "She's still pissed at me, huh?"

"Yeah, that's one way to put it. You want me to put her on?"

"Does she wanna be put on?"

The phone rustled as the man presumably pressed it against his chest, which didn't do anything to block out the sound of him asking Amanda if she wanted to talk to her guardian. He cleared his throat. "Uh… sorry, Johnny. I don't think she's feeling up to it."

"Did she say that?"

The man chuckled. "She said, 'Hell no,' to be honest. I thought I'd letcha down easy."

"All right. Thanks for keepin' an eye on her. And for the call."

"You bet."

The dwarf ran a hand through his hair, stepped into the hall, and peered absently through the door into Amanda's bedroom. "I got somewhere to be in a few hours, Arthur. Might not be here when she decides to come home. Can you tell her somethin' for me? I reckon she'll pull the stuffin' out of her ears if it's comin' from you."

"You might be right."

"Tell her after tonight, we're gonna sit down just the two of us and have a real talk 'bout what's goin' on."

"Anything else?"

"Naw, that should do it."

"All right. I'll keep you updated." Arthur ended the call, and Johnny shoved his phone into his pocket with a scowl.

"At least she's safe," Lisa said.

"Yep." With a heavy sigh, the bounty hunter stepped into his workshop and scanned the contents of his shelves. "And outta mind for now. I gotta focus on puttin' together the right gear.

You know, the kind for huntin' monsters on two legs who use baby creatures as leverage."

"It's not like we haven't done it before," Lisa said and joined him at the table.

"True. I wish we hadn't."

They loaded his weapons and a cache of explosives into the back of the Jeep and headed out through the Everglades at 11:15 pm. Johnny drove like a sane person—despite taking the side roads at a little over seventy miles an hour the whole way—and didn't have to dim his brights once with no other traffic this late at night. "These Logree-snatchers will be expectin' somethin' comin' in at 'em from the water. They won't bother to check what's headin' their way from the road."

"We're not simply gonna drive right into their little meetup, are we?"

He snorted. "Naw. That'd be fun, but I aim to listen in long enough to make sure that tentacled mama is who she says she is. Make sure we ain't had the wool pulled over our eyes."

"And if we did?"

The dwarf nodded toward the back of the Jeep. "What d'ya think the Crystal-laced shells were for, darlin'?"

"That's a last resort, Johnny."

"'Course it is. Better'n no resort."

Lisa stared at him and they both chuckled. "Pun not intended, right?"

"Naw, but it fits."

Johnny lifted a middle finger at the closed building boasting Everglade airboat tours when they passed, then drove another mile up the road. He pulled Sheila off onto the shoulder in the first place he knew the wet swampland wouldn't suck her down and carry her away at the height of the tide and they unloaded his gear from the back and began to strap it in place.

Lisa snorted when he struggled to secure three different

firearms over his head and shoulder and the barrels clacked noisily against each other. "Do you need a hand?"

"No." He paused, rolled his eyes, and removed one of the rifles. "But if it makes you feel better, you can carry this one."

"Oh, thank you." She gave him an exasperated glance, took the weapon, and turned it in her hands. "I'm not sure I'm familiar with this particular model."

"That's 'cause it ain't on the market, darlin'. Public or private." He pointed out the safety, chamber, and how to release the magazine. "Jam it against anythin' solid. It pops out and you have an empty magazine waitin' for a reload."

"I thought you made improved weapons." She smacked the magazine with the side of her fist and caught it as it ejected. "This seems more like a liability. Anyone or anything could hit it and no more ammo."

"That's a long-range weapon. Anyone or anything wouldn't get close enough to touch it. Only you."

"What caliber?"

The dwarf grinned at her and shut the swinging door of Sheila's trunk. "Boom 5. Technically 4.5, but I'm roundin' up."

"Right." Lisa reinserted the magazine carefully and strung the strap over her head and shoulder. "Because then you'd ruin your six-level Boom system."

"You're catchin' on quick, darlin'. Come on." He patted Sheila's side as he passed, turned quickly, and pointed at the agent. "If you have to take a shot with that, make sure you aim real good."

She responded with a quiet laugh. "I'm very sure aiming real good was covered in my training. And field experience."

"Just sayin'."

They moved quickly down the empty road toward Una's meeting location with sufficient starlight on a clear night in late May to light their path. When they reached a wide right-hand bend, the sound of angry voices carried with perfect clarity across the water. Johnny nudged Lisa's shoulder, then pointed at the reeds that grew along the winding road and blocked the dock at the end of the road from view.

She nodded and followed him quietly through the reeds. They moved slowly and their cautious footsteps through the two inches of water left at low tide made barely any noise above the drone of crickets and cicadas and the occasional splash of nocturnal wildlife around them. Stealth was aided by the fact that the men meeting Una at the dock were way too loud to hear anything coming toward them.

Stupid motherfuckers.

Johnny paused at the edge of the reeds and peered out at the dock. The kidnappers and their boss had brought bright floodlights connected to a humming generator in the back of one of their trucks. The lights were aimed at the water off the dock and illuminated Una's waving tentacles and her glistening purple-black flesh. Four unsubmerged eyes blinked heavily against the harsh light, but she'd kept her end of the bargain at least. She was there.

"See, I'm having a hard time understanding why you're here and that resort in Naples is still standing out there." A man's nasally voice carried from the dock above the sounds of his hired guns readjusting their stances and tightening their grasps on their weapons. The bounty hunter counted five of them.

I'm good with those odds.

Una snorted an agitated breath and a small puff of purple mist. "I already told you. I was intercepted."

"Well, who the fuck by?"

"I don't know. But I was shot and had to rest in order to heal."

Intelligent and crafty. None of that was a lie. She's forgotten my name by now and doesn't know who I am other than "dwarf."

The man shouting on the dock stepped forward through the floodlights and his shadow shortened in front of him and in crossed doubles on either side. "You expect me to believe some random boater gearing up for summer vacation shot you enough to stop you? Where's the wound? Where's the moaning and groaning about how much it hurts?"

The Logree slapped a tentacle on the water, although not hard enough that the splash reached the man interrogating her. "You have seen what I can do."

"Sure. Those disgusting noodly arms of yours are strong enough to remove a projectile. Maybe even a harpoon. And then you simply healed yourself without so much as a scar, is that it?"

Una's eyes blinked wearily against the floodlights. "You know exactly how it works. You have seen it many times."

The man reached behind him toward one of his thugs, who stepped forward and handed him a long metal rod. "I do. And I'm gonna see it again and again until you decide to tell me the goddamn truth."

"Please don't." She stared at the sparking tip of the electric rod in the man's hand. "That's completely unnecessary."

"For you, maybe." He stepped toward the edge of the dock, joined by two of his hired men wielding some kind of enhanced whips that threw crackling orange sparks.

Those two are magicals, even if he's not. Why the hell won't she fight back?

"Give me another day," she begged and her tentacles roiled out of the water like so many writhing snakes. "I will have it done. I promise."

"Oh, I know. But see, you didn't go back to Naples where you were supposed to be to finish the job. That should've happened tonight before you slithered back here to give me a bullshit report I don't like the sound of."

The sparking tip of the electric rod lit a circle of Una's flesh as it drew closer to her head. Her eyes widened. "Please."

"You know exactly what happens to that little grub of yours if you so much as raise a gooey appendage at me, don't you? *Don't you?*"

"Yes!" Una snorted in fear and anger and released a spray of water all around her.

"Good." The man shoved the prod tip against the Logree's flesh and her entire body flared with crackling white-blue lines as she flailed and splashed in the water.

Her scream sent a ripple of gooseflesh down Lisa's arms and back. "Johnny—"

"I know. Only one more minute."

The magicals with the orange-flashing whips attacked the thrashing creature and added more color to her illuminated body. But she still didn't try to escape.

"Stop! Stop it, please!" Una shrieked. "You're hurting her!"

"Johnny, her offspring," Lisa whispered in horror.

"He's torturin' both of 'em." *Damn creature could've said they feel each other too.*

The bounty hunter lurched forward through the reeds and slogged out of the low-tide muck onto the side of the road closest to the dock. He fired a shot at the closest floodlight, which shattered and winked out. The man and his two thugs with the whips ducked and whirled to face the dwarf's dark shadow moving toward them from the road.

CHAPTER TWENTY-SEVEN

"Who the fuck is that?" the man shouted. "You said this place was cleared."

"It was!"

Una sighed in the water and bobbed almost motionlessly while thin streams of purple smoke drifted from the top of her body. She submerged fully with a hiss and reappeared again a moment later.

"Y'all fuckers gettin' a kick out of fryin' a mama and her kid, huh?"

The man swung the electric rod toward Johnny and turned the voltage up. "Well, I'm a fan of calamari. Stop right there. Hands up."

"Naw, I like my hands where they are." From the corner of his eye, the dwarf saw the other three hired guns move down the dock toward the leader of this fucked-up operation. "Tell your boys to stand down and maybe I won't have to shoot that other lightbulb before I bash your face in."

The man sneered and stepped between the magicals with the whips. "Shut this idiot up."

The wizards—he knew that was what they were once they

turned the orange sparks on their whips into a constant roar of magical energy—darted toward the bounty hunter and snarled. He lowered his weapon and shot the first one through the kneecap. The wizard fell with a shriek, and the other one's whip cracked around the barrel of his rifle.

A small jolt ran up through the dwarf's arms. He growled and jerked his weapon toward him. The wizard stumbled forward, unwilling to release his whip, and Johnny drove his forehead into his face. His rifle butt cracked against the side of the wizard's head and he fell too. The orange sparks of his magic faded.

"Who's next, assholes?" The bounty hunter trudged across the road toward the truck and the two SUVs parked at the end of the dock. He yanked an explosive disk from his belt, pressed the button, and lobbed it at the three thugs who aimed their weapons at him.

One of them looked at the projectile that blinked with a tiny red light and kicked it into the swamp. It detonated halfway into the water and shredded reeds, and muddy water erupted all over them. "You're screwed now, ain'tcha?" He sneered unpleasantly.

"Not even close." Johnny raised his rifle again and a pistol's crack rose behind him.

Lisa's first shot struck one of the thug's hands and pinged off his weapon beneath it. "Aw, fuck!"

"Shit! He's not alone. Second shooter's in the fucking reeds!"

Her second shot barely missed the ducking men as they ran back toward the one remaining flood lamp. One of them grasped the cage around the bright light and swiveled it across the water toward Lisa's position.

The dwarf shot the other light and it shattered as the much larger report of a fired weapon rang out across the water. The second the floodlight went out, the truck holding the generator erupted in a furious blaze of fire and smoke. Metal shards and glass flew everywhere, peppering the mud around the reeds, and showered over the thugs and the man with the electric rod. The truck's cab lurched a foot in the air before it crunched down again and bounced on three full tires and a shredded fourth.

Grinning at the blazing fire that lit up the end of the road and the dock, Johnny trudged toward the men who shielded themselves from the explosion. "Boom 4.5, fuckers."

Lisa appeared beside him with the explosive rifle swinging against her back and drew her service weapon again. "Yeah, we can simply call it Boom 5."

One of the three remaining hired guns searched frantically for the weapon he'd dropped in the explosion.

"You should hold onto your valuables," the bounty hunter growled.

The man looked up with wide eyes and caught the butt of his assailant's rifle on the underside of his chin. He spun and fell without a sound as his eyes rolled back in his head. A second man recovered from the explosion and raised his rifle.

A wad of thick, dark-purple goo sprayed with impressive precision from one of Una's dripping tentacles. It splattered the man's face and he screamed and discarded his weapon to claw at the stinging flammable substance in his eyes and filling his mouth.

The third henchman was a real Einstein. He attacked Johnny with a roar instead of using the semi-automatic strapped across his shoulder. The bounty hunter dropped to one knee and ducked the meaty arms that swung toward him. He snatched an explosive disk from his belt and smacked it onto the man's lower back before he caught him by the back of the shirt, spun, and hauled him across shattered glass and metal to fling him over the side of the dock. The man fell with a splash, the disk detonated, and nothing more than an extra collection of bubbles rose to the surface.

The man's head breached and he gasped for air as he moaned.

"That one is still breathing," Una said.

"How observant of you." Johnny dusted his hands off and

watched the guy flail in the mud and drag himself out of the swamp. "He's lucky I threw him in the water. Otherwise, he'd be draggin' his top half up while the bottom half floated out with the tide."

The man slumped forward in the mud, gasping, and clutched his back. "My fucking ass, man. You broke my fucking ass."

The bounty hunter snorted. "You're one of the real smart ones, ain'tcha?"

He turned to locate the man who'd headed this operation and who now crawled across the glass-littered road toward a lost and abandoned rifle. His hand came down on the barrel, and Lisa's foot settled on his hand a second later.

"Don't even think about it."

The leader froze and looked slowly at Agent Breyer, whose face was blocked from view by the barrel of her service weapon aimed at the center of the man's head. "You won't shoot me. Do you have any idea of the kind of hell that'll come down on your head if you—"

Lisa thumbed the hammer back and inclined her head. "Do you?"

"All right." Johnny trudged toward them and sneered in the flickering light of the blazing truck. "Let's get a better look at this scumbag." He grasped the man by the lapels of his casual suit jacket and hauled him to his feet. "Naw. Still ugly as shit."

"You have no idea who you're fucking with." The man spat a glob of something unpleasant.

"So why don't you tell me. Wait. Hold on." He drove his fist into the leader's gut and elicited a sharp grunt and a gasp, then pulled him upright again by his jacket. "Okay. Now tell me."

Una splashed lightly in the water, still bobbing at the end of the dock. "That was wonderfully satisfying."

The bounty hunter sneered at his captive. "You're tellin' me."

"My—" The man wheezed and drew in another gasping breath. "My name is Terrance Glaston."

"Uh-huh. Now try tellin' me somethin' useful."

"Have you ever heard of High Tide Resorts?"

"Oh, yeah. I think I've heard the name," Lisa said, her service pistol still aimed at Terrance's head. "Up-and-coming tourism and travel conglomerate, right? Only been around a few years, huh?"

"I heard your hotels were shit," Johnny added. "That why you're tryin' to tear down all the others on the coast? Swoop in to buy up all the properties after they've been destroyed and prices plummet?"

The man sneered at him, still breathing heavily. "A smart move after an Oriceran piece of shit like that one leaves its mark with an uncontrollable rampage. Think of it as an economy boost."

"Yeah. The economy of your company's damn pockets. Who's your boss?"

"I'm chairman of the fucking board, you moron."

"Good for you." The dwarf clicked his tongue. "Not cool, Terrance. 'Specially when you're holdin' somethin' like a kid over that Logree's head to get the job done."

"It's a fucking animal," the man snarled. "Doesn't even belong on this planet. Who gives a shit?"

"Huh. Una, for one. And her kid. And me." He punched him in the gut again and Terrance dropped to his knees. The dwarf stooped to mutter in his ear, "Now you're gonna fix it."

The closest thug Johnny had knocked out with his rifle butt groaned and rolled onto his stomach. He stared at his employer, who wheezed on his knees with his jacket wadded in his captor's fist. Lisa trained her weapon on the hired help instead. The man blinked woozily through a trickle of blood that spilled down his forehead. "You got this, boss?"

"No, you fucking idiot." Terrance's shoulders sagged as he fought for breath. "Does it look like I fucking got this?"

The bleeding man swiped the blood from his forehead and struggled to push into a seated position.

"Watch it," the agent warned and stepped toward him. "Nice and easy."

The chairman grunted. "You're the bounty hunter, aren't you?"

"Well, not the only one." Johnny gave the man's jacket a little shake. "But probably the best."

Lisa glanced at him and cocked her head.

"Damnit, Raul." Terrance snarled at his one remaining henchman. "I told you to eliminate him."

"We were on him." Raul glared at Lisa's gun and blinked heavily again, most likely from a severe concussion. "We trailed him around Everglades City and would've had him in Marco Island if your idiot son hadn't gotten in the way at the fucking jewelry store."

"Oh, that wannabe jewelry thief was your son?" The dwarf grinned and gave his prisoner another shake. "Is that right?"

Terrance's teeth clacked together and he scowled before he muttered, "Shut your fucking mouth, Raul. I swear. It's like everyone west of Miami was born with half a brain."

"Naw, you're merely dippin' into the wrong pond, asshole." Johnny hauled the man to his feet again, shoved him away, jerked him forward again, and slapped his cheek. "You and me are gonna take a ride, Terrance. And Agent Breyer here's comin' with us, 'course."

Both men both widened their eyes at her.

"Yeah, that's right, shithead." He slapped the man's face again. "I have friends in the Bureau. And unless you wanna sit down for a little chitchat with about a dozen of 'em who ain't near as friendly or easy on the eyes as she is, you're gonna do everythin' I say."

Lisa raised an eyebrow at the bleeding thug who swayed at

the front of the dock but decided to ignore Johnny's summary of her character.

"Why the fuck would I do that?"

The bounty hunter sneered at Terrance and leaned forward until his face was inches from his. "Because I'm the one who tied up your idiot son. His words, not mine. But they ain't wrong."

The man on the ground sighed heavily and hung his head.

"So come on Terrance Asswad." He yanked the man's jacket toward the SUV least damaged by the exploding truck. "We're gonna get that Logree kid outta whatever cage you're keepin' it in. And you get to keep your kid out of a cage in county. How's that sound?"

Terrance snarled and scrambled across broken glass as Johnny hauled him toward the SUV.

Lisa stepped toward the woozy asshole seated on the ground and nodded toward the vehicle. "You too, genius."

"No, I'm...I'm good right here—"

She squeezed off a shot that went through the boards of the dock beside him and flurried splinters of wood over him. "I wasn't asking."

"Damn...okay, okay. Jesus Christ. Who gives a woman a gun anyway?"

The agent removed one hand from her weapon to grasp the back of the guy's collared shirt and help him roughly to his feet. She shoved him toward the vehicle and returned both hands to her pistol. "I still have my weapon. And I'm the one who scared you so badly you dropped yours."

The bounty hunter shoved Terrance roughly into the passenger seat of the SUV and called cheerfully, "Do I need to come shut someone up for ya, Agent Breyer?"

"We're good for now, Johnny. I think this one's used up all his brain cells."

"I will stay here," Una called after them with a low rumble and a spray of water. "And await the return of my offspring."

"As agreed." Johnny walked around the front of the vehicle to take his place behind the wheel. "This shouldn't take too long."

Lisa opened the back door, muscled Raul inside, and waited for the hunched man to scoot across so she could get in beside him. She shut the door and kept her pistol aimed at him, although he looked like he was about to drop again at any second. "Let's get going, then."

Johnny started the engine. "This is the part where you give me an address or goddamn directions, Terrance. Unless you want another slap first."

"Fine." The man grimaced and leaned forward to punch the address into the GPS. "You're wasting your time playing savior to those brainless invertebrates, dwarf."

"Brainless, huh? You had no idea that baby was sending everything it heard and saw from your little meetings back to its angry mama, did you?"

The chairman lowered his hand slowly from the dashboard and remained silent.

"Yeah, didn't think so. That invertebrate's a better parent than you ever were."

"You don't know what you're talking about."

"Oh, sure. But I seen your boy. He's in bad shape, Terrance, and might need an intervention."

The man jerked on the lapels of his suit jacket as Johnny followed the GPS prompts leading them to their destination. *It'd better be the goddamn right one.*

A thump and a loud snore rose from the back seat. Terrance turned to see the barrel of Lisa's service pistol trained on him now. She nodded toward Raul beside her. "Your buddy fell asleep. So now you get all my attention."

He turned quickly in his seat and released a shuddering breath.

Johnny snorted. "Lucky you."

CHAPTER TWENTY-EIGHT

The GPS took them to an industrial business complex on the southern edge of Miami. Lisa was more than happy to holster her pistol again after she'd trained it on Glaston for the hour it had taken them to get there.

They left Raul in the SUV.

Terrance led them to a huge room on the third floor and snapped commands at the four men keeping watch over the large aquarium tank at the back of the room. "Get that ready to move."

"Boss, we ain't even got past Naples—"

"I'm not paying you to tell me what we haven't done!" He pointed at the aquarium. "Get that fucking maggot ready to move!"

"Someone has a problem with name-callin'," the bounty hunter muttered. The men lurched from their chairs when they saw Lisa's pistol trained on Terrance's back. Two of them reached for their weapons, but the dwarf swung one of his rifles to aim it at them first. "I don't think so."

"Don't try to shoot him either," Terrance ordered as he strode toward a long table crammed with computer monitors. "I promise he's smarter and faster than all of you. That's not saying much, but if you prefer to not die with bullets in your bellies, stand down."

"Aw." Johnny swung his rifle toward Terrance. "Looks like it hurt to give even that much of a compliment."

"Fuck off," the chairman muttered. He snatched a radio off the computer table and muttered into it, "Get a speedboat ready to go at dock three. Fifteen minutes."

"Change of plans, boss?"

"I don't need to tell you what the goddamn plans are. Just do it!" Terrance slammed the radio down and turned. "There. Everything's in motion."

"Uh-huh. And you're sticking around for all of it until that watery purple kiddo is back in her mama's lovin' tentacles."

A quick splash came from the aquarium tank at the back of the room. "Johnny!"

"What the fuck?" He turned to scowl at the tank.

"Johnny, you're here! You came!" The shrill, tinny voice of Una's offspring filled the room and two small, light-purple tentacles draped over the edge of the tank as the baby Logree's head bobbed above the surface. So maybe Una had remembered his name after all.

"Uh…yeah. You hang tight."

Lisa stepped toward him and shifted her gaze from the tank to a glowering Terrance. "Telepathy, Johnny."

"Yeah, I know. It's still damn weird."

Two of the hired men secured the tank with an airtight lid, lifted it between them, and shuffled toward the door and the elevators in the hallway beyond.

"Does that give her enough air?" the dwarf asked.

"They live at the bottom of the fucking ocean, moron."

He stalked toward the man, who straightened and raised his chin belligerently. With a smirk, Johnny swung a fist at his face. Terrance flinched, but the bounty hunter stopped himself before he made contact and sniggered. "Two for flinching."

With a grim smile, he slapped the man twice on the cheek and shoved him toward the door. "Let's go."

As dumb as Terrance Glaston's hired brutes were, they were surprisingly efficient in preparing the speedboat and loading Una's offspring's tank onboard before Johnny, Lisa, and the High Tide Resorts' chairman of the board stepped up. One of the thugs tried to come with them, and the agent leveled her gun at him and shook her head. "Private cruise, buddy."

"Don't do anything until I get back," his boss muttered. "Check in with the others."

The bounty hunter steered the speedboat away from the dock and in moments, they cruised along the coast toward Una, who waited for them on the other side of Florida's southern coast. Terrance's men stood dumbly on the dock and watched their boss leave as a hostage. Johnny chuckled and shook his head. "Morons."

When they approached the hidden dock off the road from the Flamingo Visitors Center—which was easy enough to locate with the still-burning truck illuminating the area like a makeshift lighthouse—Una was where they'd left her. She backed away when Johnny pulled the speedboat up to the dock and tied it off.

"You did it."

"Ain't no good if I don't keep my word now, am I?" He unlatched the lid of the tank and tried to tip it to release the baby into the water. The creature squeaked with joy and scrambled out and almost knocked him over in the process.

The Logree emitted a huge cloud of purple mist and splashed and rumbled as her child darted toward her through the water. In the next moment, the baby Oriceran was completely hidden by her mother's thick knot of coiling tentacles.

"Thank you."

"Uh-huh." The dwarf folded his arms and nodded.

"Are you going back to Oriceran?" Lisa asked.

"We will find our way together and we will not return."

He snorted. "Yeah, I don't blame ya. Good luck."

Una dipped below the surface and dragged her offspring lovingly with her. As they headed out into the gulf, one of the Logree's giant tentacles emerged and unleashed another spray of thick purple goo at the speedboat. The slime sprayed over Terrance's clothes and the speedboat's seat.

The agent chuckled. "Hell of a way to say goodbye."

"Look at that." Johnny nodded at the retreating creature. "Look like she's wavin' to you?"

The chairman swiped the purple goo off his jacket and flung chunks of it into the marsh. "Disgusting."

"Yeah, and you know exactly what that shit's for, don'tcha? You'd best stay away from lighters until after you wash that stink off ya. I'd say that's the smell of failure, by the way." The bounty hunter stepped off the boat and offered Lisa a hand onto the dock. She holstered her weapon and they both stared at the disgruntled board chairman who sneered at them.

"You think you're so smart."

"Well, yeah. Your big resort and rental-property takeover plan was as dumb as shit." Johnny hefted one of the rifles strapped across his chest and aimed it at the water—for now. "And you're a pain in my ass. Make any other moves like this, and you know who I'm comin' for first."

Lisa leaned toward him and muttered, "We need to take him in for—"

He drew his knife, whipped the blade out, and sliced through the rope he'd tied to the dock. The speedboat bobbed away on the low tide that had begun to rise slowly again through the swamps.

"What are you doing?" she hissed.

The bounty hunter sniffed and jerked his chin at the man. "Hope that boat has GPS."

Terrance glared at them and grasped the controls of the speedboat before he turned it again to make the long solo trip to Miami in the middle of the night.

"Honestly, I expected you to shoot him or at least throw him overboard or something."

Johnny looked at Lisa and raised an eyebrow. "That's addin' insult to injury, darlin'."

She stared at the rapidly receding outline of the speedboat and shook her head. "I know that's generally your style, but what we should have added is a set of cuffs and an indictment for kidnapping, arson, blackmail, and illegal racketeering. At the very least."

"I already slapped him enough times for one night. He'll remember that. And knowin' I have his son's face locked away up here is all the hurt I need to bring him to make a point." He tapped his temple. "That asshole ain't gonna push the line when his kid's on it."

"Johnny, it's our job to push the line."

"Then push it." He headed down the road for the mile-long walk to Sheila. "You already know where he's operatin'."

Lisa cocked her head, then turned to follow the bounty hunter across the dock. "If he's dumb enough to stay there."

She followed with a mixed feelings of frustration and amusement and when they reached the Jeep and slid in, he started the engine in silence. As they drove quickly down the empty road toward the cabin, the dwarf tugged on his beard and grunted. "Feel like grabbin' a drink?"

"At almost three in the morning?"

"Trust me, many places are still servin' booze right now. You simply gotta know where to look."

"It's tempting." Lisa stuck her hand out the window and trailed her fingers through the warm, muggy breeze. "We should go back to your place and check on Amanda."

"Yeah...if she's up. I don't know if I can handle all that." He pulled his phone out and found a text from Arthur.

Kid wanted to stay here for the night. Hope you're okay with it. Still safe. Hounds too.

"Huh." Johnny dropped his phone into the cup holder. "Never mind. She's crashin' at Arthur's."

"Oh. She'll come around, Johnny."

"I know."

"It takes patience and understanding—"

"You can stop now." He rolled his eyes. "I didn't ask for a pep talk."

"Sure." Lisa dropped her head back against the headrest and turned to look at him. "How about that drink, then?"

"Kid's not at the house…"

She laughed. "I mean only for a drink, Johnny."

He cleared his throat. "I wasn't thinkin' anythin' else, darlin'."

"And then I'll probably ask for a pillow and a blanket and sleep on the couch."

"Fine plan."

"Okay."

"Uh-huh." He sniffed and stretched his fingers over the steering wheel. "Feel free to let me know if you change your mind."

With a grin, she swept her hair out of her face. "About what exactly?"

"The drink."

"Yeah, okay. I'll let you know."

CHAPTER TWENTY-NINE

The next morning, Johnny woke in his bed—alone—and scowled at the sunlight streaming through his bedroom window. He went to the bathroom first, then stepped into the hallway and stared at the fluffed pillow and neatly folded blanket on the couch.

Huh. Don't usually see a sneak-off in the mornin' when the friendliest a woman gets the night before is a toast and a glass of whiskey.

With a shrug, he scratched under his armpit and moved to the front window beside the door to check out front. Lisa's rental car was gone too. *Naw, she has her own life, Johnny. Like most folks, it's better for her if she don't have you twisted all up in it.*

He went into the kitchen to fill a glass of water from the sink and his phone buzzed in the back pocket of yesterday's Levi's. It was Arthur and with a smirk, he answered the call. "Kid drivin' you out the door yet?"

"Yeah, Johnny... Any other time and that would've been funny."

The dwarf's smile faded instantly. "What happened?"

"Amanda's gone, man."

"What do you mean gone?

"I mean *gone* gone, Johnny. The hounds with her." He sighed

MARTHA CARR & MICHAEL ANDERLE

heavily, accompanied by the banging of either kitchen cabinets or a lot of doors. "Look, she was here all night. I made sure of it. I stepped out to go grab some breakfast biscuits at the station down the road. Came back, and all three of 'em were gone. I didn't wanna bother you with it first thing, man, but it's been 'bout half an hour. Took me at least that long to get breakfast and drive back."

"Shit." The dwarf rubbed his mouth. "Thanks for the call."

"Yeah."

"If you see her or hear even a whisper about a girl—"

"And Johnny Walker's coonhounds? Yeah, you'll be the first fella I call."

"All right." He ended the call and grimaced at the kitchen counter. *What's that fool girl doin' runnin' off like that without a word? She could've given the old man a damn heart attack.*

He pressed his hands onto the counter as his phone rang again. This time, it was an unknown number.

Johnny hated unknown numbers. "Fuck it."

He accepted the call anyway. "Who are you?"

"Johnny?" Amanda said with a fearful yet relieved sob. "Johnny, I...I'm so sorry. I didn't have a choice."

"All right, kid. Calm down." He ran a hand through his hair and paced across the kitchen. "Are you all right?"

"I...don't know. I don't think I'm hurt but I don't think I'm okay, either. I need your help."

"What happened?"

"I was in a fight. With...it seemed like there were so many of them, but now I only...they're all over—" The girl swallowed thickly and choked back another sob.

"Amanda, you listen to me, understand? Take a breath. Slow down. First thing. Did anyone hurt you?"

"I don't think so. I—maybe I'm in shock or something?"

"Where are you?"

"I have no idea. Everything looks the same around here."

The bang of a door opening and closing came over the line, followed by Rex's voice. "Shit, pup. You came all the way inside for a phone?"

"Who you talkin' to, huh?"

"It's Johnny," she whispered.

"Johnny!" Rex barked.

"Johnny! Hey! Can you hear us?"

I can fucking hear the hounds over the phone. The bounty hunter shook his surprise away and cleared his throat. "Do the hounds know where y'all are?"

"Guys, where are we?"

"Down by Odie's, Johnny!" Luther barked twice. "Three houses down from his old pig barn. You know, the one with all the treats."

"I've been trying to keep him away from those mushrooms, Johnny. Haven't had a lotta luck so far—"

"Girl, you wait right where you are, ya hear me?"

"Yeah."

"Don't leave the property but get outta the goddamn house. I'm comin'."

"Okay—wait. Johnny."

The dwarf paused, gritted his teeth, and squinted at the countertop when her voice broke.

"Are you mad?"

The dwarf cleared his throat. "If anything happens to you before I get there, kid, I will be."

He ended the call and wiped his mouth and beard. *Some dumb motherfuckers picked a fight with the wrong kid. My kid.*

With a low growl, he stalked toward his bedroom, shoved his socked feet into his boots, and marched out of the house toward Sheila.

Furious, he raced toward the property beyond Odie Madison's pig barn in a haze. Fortunately, the road was mostly straight, but he wouldn't have slowed even if he had to drive through rush-hour traffic across the Jersey Turnpike. *And I've already done that a time or two.*

Sheila's tires skidded across the dirt drive of the empty property from which Amanda had called him. The front door of the sky-blue-painted ranch house on stilts hung wide open, and no one came out to greet him or threaten him with the usual around these parts—shotgun, crossbow, guard dogs, or electric fence.

Johnny slid out of the Jeep and paused.

Six bodies lay in the dirt drive between the house and the adjacent wood-and-tool shed. The whole strip of dirt was drenched with blood, most of it already having been sucked up by the dry earth and lightened as it baked under the sun. It seemed every one of the full-grown men in their thirties was missing at least one of their limbs—a severed hand here, a boot tossed there with the foot still inside it, or half an ear. One unlucky bastard's head was barely still attached to his neck by a thin strip of gory sinews.

Guns were visible among the bodies, but he barely paid attention to those. *She got in a fight, huh? I hope to shit she didn't start it but she sure as fuck finished it, didn't she?*

In silence, he drew his knife from his belt and flicked it open as he walked slowly toward the mess of bodies while his gaze scanned the house, the shed, the overhanging trees, and the swamp behind all of it. "If anyone's sneakin' 'round corners," he called as quietly as he could despite his boiling anger, "I ain't here to make trouble. It looks like this place has had enough of that as it is."

A thump and scrabble sounded from the shed, followed by a warning yip.

"Johnny!" Luther bounded around the corner of the building and skidded to a stop. "That was fast."

"You're here. Oh, man, Johnny. You wouldn't believe what—"

"Where is she?"

"The shed. She's in the shed. Come on." The dogs trotted

around the simple structure, although their tails had lowered almost straight out behind them and didn't wag.

"She's okay, Johnny."

"Yeah, physically. Pup put up a hell of a fight, that's for sure."

Johnny stepped around the back of the shed and tried not to let any reaction at all slide onto his face when he found Amanda.

The young shifter was huddled in the corner against a stack of firewood, her knees pulled up to her chest and her arms wrapped tightly around them. She was covered in blood and as naked as a jaybird.

Goddammit. The dwarf closed his knife and shoved it into his belt before he stepped inside. "Hey, kid."

She was trembling, and when she looked slowly at him, tears spilled down her cheeks. "I didn't do anything, Johnny."

"I know. It's all right."

"They came out of nowhere, and I… They wouldn't listen. They had guns and one of them threw a rock at Luther."

Johnny glanced at the smaller hound, who sat on his haunches to scratch behind an ear.

"Not worth mentioning, Johnny. I'm fine. Took a chunk out of the bastard's thigh, so I'd say we're even."

Johnny nodded. "You were defendin' yourself."

"Yeah…"

"And the boys."

"Hey, we defended her too," Rex added with a low whine. "It was technically a team effort."

Luther stopped scratching and stood to sniff the coils of rope hanging almost to the floor. "Yeah, but she did most of it."

He snapped his fingers and both hounds sat. "Ya'll did good. All of you. I don't wanna hear another word until we're home and you're cleaned up and a little less shell-shocked. Understand?"

"Yeah, Johnny." Rex licked his muzzle. "Not another word. Got it."

"Johnny, it was nuts—" Luther crouched low when his brother nipped at his neck in warning. "Okay, okay. Shutting up."

Johnny glanced around the shed, snatched an old picnic blanket hanging from a hook on the wall, and draped it over Amanda's shoulders. "Come on, girl. Let's get you home."

To spare her from the sight of what she'd done, he made sure to take her around the opposite side of the shed. They traveled home in silence punctuated only by the odd sniff from the girl and the dogs' pants.

After a shower, a fresh change of clothes, and a cup of hot tea —into which Johnny added the tiniest splash of whiskey because he couldn't think of a better way to help the kid out of her shock —Amanda managed to tell the rest of the story in more detail. Of course, the hounds put in their two cents as well.

She'd decided to go for a short run on her own that morning after Arthur left to get breakfast. Rex and Luther had stayed with her every step of the way—their pack of three, two hounds and a young gray wolf.

"Then a group of people just...attacked me. Guns and other stuff."

"Locals?" Johnny asked.

"No way, Johnny," Rex panted. "Not shifters. Not rednecks."

"Not even from the Everglades," Luther added.

Amanda shook her head. "They were something else. I assumed they wanted to hunt a wolf or something. Maybe they thought Rex and Luther were strays. I don't know."

Not likely with those collars.

"So I shifted to show them, Johnny. To tell them who I was. They said they already knew who I was." The girl frowned and drank more whiskey-laced tea but didn't comment on the extra flavor.

"They called her your 'little bitch,' Johnny."

The dwarf glanced sharply at Rex, who lowered his head slightly.

"Their words. Not mine."

"Said you crossed a line in Miami," Luther added, "and now they were crossing it back. Drew guns on her anyway."

"Yeah, and then the pup...did the rest."

"That sonofabitch." Johnny rubbed his mouth and tugged his beard angrily.

"What's in Miami?" Amanda asked.

"Don't you mind that, darlin'. It's got nothin' to do with you."

"Then why did they say it?" She set the tea down and stared at him.

"'Cause someone's tryin' to get at me."

"I wasn't trying to get into trouble, Johnny. Promise."

"I know. You handled it and you did everything you had to do. I'm proud of you." He squeezed her shoulder briefly. "And now, I'm gonna do what I have to do. Don't you worry about any of it, understand?"

She nodded slowly and pulled her knees up to her chest on the couch.

The dwarf strode through the house, more enraged than he'd been earlier. *That High Tide Resorts motherfucker. He couldn't leave it settled last night and admit that he's as stupid as his fuckin' hired goons. No, he had to send more of the bastards after a goddamn kid and make it my fault.*

He's fucking with the wrong dwarf. Wrong shifter too.

The front door was thrust open and Lisa stepped inside with a to-go coffee caddy in one hand and a paper bag of breakfast in the other. "It took longer than I thought, but I assumed coffee would be a big help after last night. You don't have a coffee maker, so—"

"Hey, lady!" Luther called from the living room, which of course went unheard by Agent Breyer.

"Oh, shit, Johnny." Rex laughed and his tail thumped on the rug. "After last night, huh? You bring her home to—"

"Johnny?" Lisa's smile faded as she stepped inside and kicked the door shut behind her with the heel of her shoe. "What's wrong?"

His teeth gritted, the dwarf stared at the hallway floor and pointed behind him.

She saw Amanda in the living room and frowned. "She's home. That's supposed to be a good thing, right?"

"Lisa!" The girl leapt off the couch and raced toward her and she barely had enough time to move the coffee caddy to the side to avoid a hot coffee spill over both of them when she wrapped her arms around her.

"Hey, kiddo. What's going on?"

"Terrance fucking Glaston needs to back the fuck off is what's wrong," Johnny grumbled. "I aim to deliver that message in person."

As he stepped into the workshop to select a pistol and load his explosive disks, Luther and Rex each barked once and trotted toward the door.

"Someone else here, Johnny."

"Sounds like your least favorite fed."

Johnny grunted. *That could be any of 'em.*

"Oh…it's the balding one."

Rex growled and shook his head vigorously. "The one who tastes like ass."

"Ha. Good one."

The screen door opened and shut, followed by a brisk knock. "Johnny. It's Nelson. I have something you want to see, so open up."

"This is not a good fucking time," the dwarf muttered as he thrust an extra magazine into his back pocket in case. *I ain't goin' into this one expectin' to use it, but Terrance ain't exactly playin' by the rules anymore. I might have to join him.*

"Johnny?" Tommy Nelson called.

Rex and Luther barked once.

"For chrissakes, Johnny. At least put your dogs out this time."

"We can go around back, Johnny," Luther suggested.

"Yeah, and chase him off that way. He's so dumb, he won't know where we came from."

He was too pissed-off and too intent on showing Terrance Glaston that Johnny Walker didn't fuck around. *Not when he sends six fuckers after my kid. The only one I got now.*

Lisa pried herself gently out of Amanda's hold to answer the door for agent Nelson and darted Johnny a confused frown that went completely unnoticed. "Hey, Tommy."

"Oh. Agent Breyer." The man cleared his throat. "Johnny here?"

"Yeah, but he's… I mean…" With a shrug, she closed the door behind him as he walked down the hallway and darted wary glances at the hounds.

"Give the word, Johnny."

"We'll send him packin' for ya."

"Johnny?" The agent stepped into the workshop where the bounty hunter slipped one black explosive disk after the other onto his belt. His eyes widened. "I came as soon as I could—"

"This is not a good time, Nelson."

"You're not exactly gonna like what I have to say, but I thought you'd be even more pissed off if you found out that I'd sat on it for a few days before I brought it to you."

"Not now." Johnny growled his annoyance. "Whatever it is can wait." He finished strapping his belt and pulled his phone out to text Arthur and at least let the man know that Amanda was safe and home in one piece. Physically, at least.

"You were right." Tommy stepped toward the worktable and slapped a huge, heavy green file folder onto the wooden surface. "The department cleaned Dawn's file before you saw it. Before either of us saw it. It looks like their agenda for hiding what they did only went so far as the clerk's bribe limit. Which, by the way, was much higher than I expected."

The bounty hunter froze. *This asshole must have bad timin' in his goddamn blood.*

Slowly, he turned to study the folder. "That's her file?"

"That's the one."

"All of it?"

"As far as I can tell." The agent folded his arms. "A fair amount is still redacted, but there's a hell of a lot more than either one of us was shown fifteen years ago."

"Fuck!" He took one step toward the folder, growled, then spun and stormed into the kitchen.

"It's not that much of a surprise, is it?" Tommy followed him. "You're the one who suspected it in the first place. Otherwise, this would've stayed buried."

Johnny snatched up his bottle of Johnny Walker Black Label with one hand and jabbed a thick finger at Agent Nelson with the other. "Any other day, Nelson."

"What?"

"I got shit to do. Business to take care of. And you bring me this fucking cherry on the bullshit Sunday."

"I…" The man's eyes widened when the dwarf lifted the bottle to his mouth and took a massive sip. "That was the deal, Johnny. Your deal. I thought you wanted to see—"

"Not now." He thrust the corked lid onto the bottle and walked through the kitchen, past agent Nelson, and forced himself to not look at the fifteen-year-old file on his daughter's murder. He whistled sharply, and both hounds jumped away from sniffing the visitor's shoes. "It's time to pay a shit-for-brains businessman a little visit."

"What?" Tommy gestured in bewilderment. "Johnny, I just got here. You can't leave without at least—"

"I don't give a fuck whether or not you're still here when I get back, Nelson. But try to follow me, and you won't leave Florida in one piece or twenty." Johnny jerked the door open and the hounds bounded out after him.

"So what do you want me to do with the file?" The door slammed shut again. Tommy sighed and turned to look at Lisa. "What crawled up his ass? Hey, kid."

Amanda raised her chin in the semblance of a greeting but stared at the hefty file on Johnny's worktable.

Lisa extended the to-go caddy toward Agent Nelson with a weak smile. "Coffee?"

CHAPTER THIRTY

Johnny knocked forcefully on the front door of a two-story Victorian in Marco Island. *Three weeks ago, I was startin' my days with a good hunt and complete privacy. Now, it's this fucking shit.*

A muffled thump came from inside before the door unlocked and opened. Wallace stood in boxer briefs and fuzzy sky-blue slippers and gaped sleepily at the bounty hunter on his front doorstep. "What the hell are you doin' at my house, Johnny?"

"What'd you do with the failed thief I tied up in your shop yesterday?"

The gnome yawned and tried to rub the sleep out of his eyes. "You mean the one you tied up with the chain from a designer handbag?" He snorted. "Not your best work, but I guess you get points for creativity."

"I told you to put it on my bill. What happened to him?"

Wallace frowned and rubbed his balding head vigorously. "The second I saw his eyes, I knew what he was tryin' to do and why. We roughed him up a little. That's all. Had a couple of my boys give him a clear warning and we let him go."

"Not without a contingency, though, right?"

"Come on, Johnny," he replied with a smirk. "We've known

each other too long for you to ask a stupid question like that. And I can see you want it. Come on in. I'll fetch it for you."

"I'm good right here, Wallace. But I'd appreciate whatever you have."

"Yeah, okay. And I'm gonna close the door to keep the bugs out." The gnome studied him for a long moment, then shut the door and shuffled through his house again in his slippers.

The three minutes it took for him to return felt like three hours. But the door opened again, and the jeweler-cum-magical-scientist handed Johnny a small gray device. "I know yours is better but this gets the job done."

"Where'd you put the tracker?"

"In his skin." The gnome grinned. "With a good ol'-fashioned bitch slap."

"Thanks." The bounty hunter shook the tracking monitor at his friend and nodded. "I'll bring it back."

"Well, if you don't, I'll add it to your bill with the rest."

With a brusque wave of thanks, he scrambled into his Jeep and stared at the device. Rex and Luther panted and their tails thumped against the back seat.

"What'd he give you, Johnny?"

"You need us to sniff the bastard out?"

"Wait, can we trail somebody all the way to Miami?"

"We'll get to Miami in a while." Johnny reversed Sheila out of Wallace's driveway and headed toward the other side of Marco Island. "I gotta pick up a squirmy little package first."

"Ooh, like some kinda rodent?"

"The smelly ones are always the most fun to chase."

The dwarf's grin was closer to a madman's determined sneer, but Johnny Walker wasn't crazy. He was simply done playing nice. "Somethin' like that."

Ten minutes later, they pulled into a run-down property with overgrown weeds and a sagging chain-link fence around the front yard. The gate hung crookedly on its hinges, and it flew off completely to thump onto the dirt yard covered in patches of dry grass when Johnny kicked it open.

"Whose ass are we kicking today, Johnny?" Luther asked.

"Ha. Or biting. We can bite too."

"Same as the hog, boys." Johnny drew his knife and flipped it open as he stalked across the yard toward the sunken, rotting steps of the front porch. "We're takin' this one in live."

"You're gonna feed a guy to that dragon?" Luther asked.

"Draksa, numbnuts." Rex snorted. "Dragons aren't real."

He glanced at his hounds and didn't bother to correct the misconception. "We're here to send a message. And then we'll head to Miami."

"Yeah, yeah. No problem, Johnny."

"We're great at messages."

The bounty hunter readied himself to break the front door down if he had to, but it was unlocked and already slightly open. He kicked that too and it thunked against the inside wall with a puff of dust.

The thick curtains in front of every window were closed. Low yellow-brown lights cast a sickly pallor in the dusty, smoke-filled entryway. Random articles of clothing were scattered across the floor between empty beer cans and food wrappers. Johnny's boots left footprints in the layer of dust along the floor. *Yeah. He's usin', all right.*

"Hey, Johnny!" Rex called from the next room. "I think I found something. Someone? I don't know."

Luther sniffed the dark pile on the couch. "Ugh. Is he dead?"

He clomped through the house and stopped at the sight of the wanna-be jewelry thief—Terrance Glaston's idiot son—passed out on the couch with a still-smoking cigarette dangling precariously from his loose lips. A syringe, spoon, and lighter were among the other prized pieces of trash on the coffee table in front of him.

The dwarf closed his knife and returned it to his belt. *This'll be easy.*

Johnny leaned toward him and plucked the cigarette from his lips. The drug-addled young man took a sharp breath and mumbled something unintelligible before he sank deeper into the couch as his visitor crushed the cigarette beneath his boot.

He snapped his fingers. "Time to wake up, asshole."

"Yeah." Rex barked. "Get your shit together, man."

Luther barked too but didn't have anything else to add.

The druggie startled, felt for the cigarette that was no longer between his lips, and frowned. Johnny smacked the side of his head and that did the job.

His eyes snapped open, his pupils barely visible pinpricks even under the low light. "Shit!"

He lurched off the couch and stumbled against the coffee table. The dwarf caught the back of his shirt and hauled him onto the filthy couch again.

"Hey, hey, hey!" Terrance's son raised both hands and his eyelids drooped despite his panic. "I didn't take anything, man. I swear. Didn't hit another shop."

"But you got your fix."

"Man…" He looked away and almost fell sideways onto the armrest. "My old man's got money. Okay? You happy now? I finally took it."

"Yeah. That makes this even better." Johnny gave his cheek two brisk pats—not quite smacks, but close enough—and leaned down to look him in the eyes. "Your old man's fucking with the wrong dwarf. Make sure he knows that."

The young man sighed and started to nod off again.

"If you even remember any of this." Rolling his eyes, Johnny grabbed the man's shirt collar again, hauled him to his feet, and dragged him through the neglected house.

"Woah, Johnny." Luther sniffed at the drug paraphernalia on the coffee table. "I don't know what this is, but it smells like—"

Rex nipped at his brother's face with a snarl. "It smells like you need to stay away from everything in here. What's wrong with you?"

"Hey. I like to sniff. You know what it is?"

"Let's go." Johnny snapped his fingers and both hounds scrabbled after him across the dirty, dusty floors and his stumbling hostage. Before they left, he snatched an empty cardboard box from inside the front door and didn't bother to close the house behind him.

Terrance Glaston slammed his cell phone on the computer table. *These assholes have no idea how close we were.*

"What'd they say, boss?" Raul stood two feet behind the High Tide Resorts board chairman, his arms folded and a stupid-looking bandage covering the gash in his forehead.

"It doesn't matter what they said," he all but spat. "We lost our fucking angle."

"Yeah, but the dwarf has a whole new one to deal with now, doesn't he?" The huge, infuriatingly stupid hired gun guffawed at his not very funny play on words.

"Shut up." He snapped his fingers and idiot's laughter lapsed into a low chuckle. "Where is Jerome, anyway? He and his guys should've been back from the armpit of Florida by now."

"It's a long drive," Raul suggested with a shrug.

"It's not that long." *Not nearly as long as driving a speed boat around the coast in the middle of the night.* "Call him. Find out where the hell he—"

An explosion wracked the south end of the building, muffled by the layers of cement and plaster, but it still sent a shudder through the room on the third floor.

"What the fuck was that?" Terrance bolted to his feet and

whirled toward another of his men who sat with his feet propped on the table holding the security monitors. "Kevin!"

"Shit, boss." Kevin withdrew his mud-splattered boots from the surface and wheeled back in his chair. "You wanna take a look at this."

The chairman stormed toward him and peered at the single screen that displayed the backlash of the same explosion. Flames flickered along the edge of the frame, but directly in the center, a scuffed, bright red Jeep raced out of the parking lot outside. In a moment, it was gone.

"Motherfucker." He headed toward the door to the elevators—fortunately on the north side of the building—and shouted over his shoulder. "Get everyone downstairs! Armed. Whoever's trying to fuck with us might get sloppy. We won't take any more chances."

Raul called it in on the radio, and the hired guns the other High Tide Resorts' board members knew nothing about left their stations on multiple levels of the building to join their boss in the south parking lot.

When Terrance reached the ground floor and shoved the exit door open, the heat from the explosion almost made him withdraw again. His expression grim, he forced himself out and led the way for the brainless oafs with guns behind him, then stopped at the sound of a muffled groan on his left.

He looked down to where the young man sat propped against the brick wall, his ankles bound and wrists tied behind his back. A dirty black shirt had been stuffed into his mouth and secured around his head as a gag, and a torn piece of cardboard rested on his chest.

"Jesus Christ, Richie." He knelt in front of his son, who's eyes widened and drooped closed again, although he seemed to want to open them as they twitched repeatedly. With a muttered oath, he studied the piece of cardboard.

The words were written across it in thick black Sharpie. *I do drugs and make my daddy real angry.*

A small folded piece of paper was stuck to the bottom of the cardboard with what looked like a glob of mud. He lifted the flap and read the shorter message. *First warning. I don't do seconds.*

"Goddammit!" Terrance leapt to his feet and shook his finger at his son. "You...you— Raul!"

"Yeah." The huge man swung a pistol across the parking lot, the weapon like a toy in his massive hand.

"Get Richie inside."

"That asshole could still be here, boss—"

"Forget about the bounty hunter. We'll take other avenues. And no, I won't tell you which ones. It'd go right over your head anyway." He glanced at his son, who'd nodded off again with his chin wrinkled against the top of the piece of cardboard. "And get this idiot inside and wash him. I can't even look at him like that."

The rest of his men filtered through the area to make sure it was clear, and he waited for all of them—including his highly disappointing grown offspring—to go inside before he returned to the open back door. He glanced around the parking lot again, seething.

That damn bounty hunter's everywhere. Someone should throw him in the swamp for good.

CHAPTER THIRTY-ONE

Johnny shoved his front door open two hours later, grinning like an idiot as the hounds bayed and raced toward the swamp. *Nothin' like a little cleanup to make the world right again. Time to clean up at home, too.*

"All right, kid." He headed toward the living room and dusted his hands off. "I hope you're still here, 'cause I reckon this is the best time we're gonna get to sit down and have us a little—"

He stopped when he saw Amanda, Lisa, and Tommy Nelson all seated in his living room. The dwarf's smile faded immediately into a scowl. "You're still here."

"Imagine that, huh?"

The dwarf glanced at Lisa, who shrugged and sniffed at the FBI liaison. "Why'd you stay?"

"Honestly, Johnny, it was out of pure curiosity this time. You left without a word." Tommy gestured toward the door. "Then Agent Breyer and Amanda had the chance to fill me in on the last twenty-four hours, and I guess I wanted to make sure you're doing okay."

"You didn't check up on me for fifteen years, Nelson. And now you give a shit about how I'm doin'?" He snorted. "Piss off."

"And I wanted to make sure you got that file." The man stood and followed him down the hallway.

"You saw me lookin' at it. I got it."

"Right." He glanced at Lisa seated on the couch with her arm around Amanda and smoothed the front of his black suit jacket. "Then I guess that's it."

"I guess so." Johnny strode into the kitchen.

Agent Nelson cleared his throat and headed out the door. Thirty seconds later, the hounds barked madly and their voices moved from the back of the house to the front.

"That's right, Tommy boy!" Rex shouted. "You better run!"

"You're so afraid, you're like a scared little man running to his car. Ha-ha!"

Normally, the bounty hunter would have smiled at the sound of Nelson's curses before he slammed the door of his black SUV shut and the vehicle raced away. Right now, he didn't. Instead, he clutched the edge of his worktable and stared at the bulging file of his daughter's case like it was a bomb he had no idea how to diffuse.

And it'll go off sooner or later. Ain't nothin' I can do 'bout that.

Lisa stopped at the entrance to the workshop and leaned against the doorway, her arms folded. "Is everything taken care of?"

"Yep." He glared at the file.

"Anything I should know about?"

"Nothin' worth repeatin', but here." He took Wallace's tracking device from his pocket and tossed it at her.

She caught it deftly and turned it in her hands. "What's this?"

"Ain't a pair of cuffs, but it'll lead you to that indictment for… whatever charges you wanna stick on Terrance Glaston. You ask me, bad parentin' should be illegal too."

Lisa fought back a smile and pocketed the tracker. "I agree." She glanced at Amanda, who'd stretched on the couch with her head on the armrest. "I'm gonna head to the hotel, Johnny, and start a formal report on this Logree case. Let the department know everything that's worth telling them and advise them of Glaston's location. He won't get out of this scot-free but I have no problem leaving out the rest. Then we'll wait for the next case to come in."

Johnny turned to look at her and cocked his head. "Naw, darlin'. You shouldn't have to wait around for me to take a job I only kinda want."

"Oh, that's what these are, huh?" Lisa fought back a smile. "You only kinda want these cases."

He sniffed and didn't say anything else.

"You know, I might hang around for a few other things if I had a reason to."

He studied her for a long moment. *Any other time, that one-liner would be an open invitation I might take.* "Well. Your reasons are your own, darlin'. Your car. Ain't no one forcin' you to stay in the swamp."

She stared at him and her coy smile faded into one of understanding instead. "Right. I'm getting this 'Johnny needs his space' vibe, so I'll get out of your hair. You let me know about whatever case finds itself in your lap next, okay?"

"Uh-huh."

The agent glanced pointedly at the stuffed file folder on his worktable. "And if you still want to take me up on my offer with that one."

"'Preciate it."

"Yeah, I know." She headed down the hall and the door shut quietly behind her.

The dwarf grunted and stared at the file again. *I ain't in the right mindset for this one. I can't fuckin' do it today.*

He returned to the living room, fully intending to slump onto the couch and put his feet up.

Amanda stretched with a pre-teen sigh. "Ugh. I thought they'd never leave."

Johnny snorted. "Kid after my own heart, ain'tcha?"

"Maybe a little." She sat and leaned against the armrest on the far side of the couch, silently offering him the other side.

The bounty hunter sat and rubbed his mouth. "It's been a weird couple of days, huh?"

"Kind of. Yeah."

"I reckon things will be a little quieter 'round here. At least until the next case comes up." *Or the next time a redneck shifter tries to step foot on my property lookin' to recruit.*

As if she'd read his mind, the girl looked away from him with a grimace. "I did go see that pack yesterday."

"Oh…" He closed his eyes. "Confession time, is it?"

"I want to tell you what happened, okay? I told them I don't need a pack and I don't want one."

His eyes snapped open and he stared at the coffee table. *That's not what I expected.* "I reckon they didn't take that one too well."

"It could have been worse." She shrugged and picked at a loose thread on the couch cushion's seam. "They laughed at me and told me to get lost. Which I did. Well, not literally. But I left."

"Fine distinction."

"Yeah, well, I don't want anything to do with shifters like that if they're gonna keep treating me like a kid."

Johnny snorted. "You are a kid."

"I mean a stupid kid. Like I have no idea what I want or what I think or what I'm doing."

"Uh-huh." He folded his arms and studied her. "Well, you ain't anywhere close to stupid. Don't let anyone tell you otherwise."

"Duh."

They both laughed and he steeled himself for what he expected to be another tense conversation. *It needs to happen.* "Listen, kid. We still have a few bugs to work out with this whole livin' situation in the swamps. Now, maybe I wasn't specific enough the first time—"

"I'll do better." Amanda nodded quickly and gazed at him with wide, eager eyes. "Promise. I'll listen. I'll pay attention and follow the rules. This morning was..." She swallowed thickly. "I don't want that to happen again. Yeah, anyone coming after me with guns trying to get to you is seriously an asshole."

He sniggered but nodded for her to continue.

"And they would have killed me. So... I feel bad about it, but not really."

"Yeah, I know the feelin'."

"But I don't want to leave. I truly don't, Johnny. I like it here."

"All right."

They sat in silence for a moment before she turned quickly toward him. "I should get a cell phone."

Johnny laughed gruffly. "You mean I should get you a cell phone."

"Well, yeah."

"Naw. All that's a whole different kinda trouble I ain't fixin' to deal with it."

"Think about it, though. If I'd had a cell phone this morning, maybe I could have called you before things got weird with those...guys with guns."

He frowned at her. "You just said you didn't want that to happen again."

"I don't. But if it did—"

"Yeah, yeah. Tryin' to stay two steps ahead of the game, huh?"

She grinned and pointed at him. "Exactly. And all the other kids at my school in New York had cell phones. I don't know why we didn't, but it's stupid to not do the one thing that would let us talk to each other no matter where we are, right?"

"You callin' me stupid, kid?"

Amanda gave him a one-shouldered shrug. "Only if you don't get me a cell phone."

"Yeah, keep talkin' to me like that. See how far it gets ya."

"Please?"

The dwarf pushed off the couch. "I'm takin' a shower."

"Will you at least think about it?"

"Maybe."

"It's not like you're giving me one of your grenades or anything—"

The bathroom door shut behind him, followed by the sound of running water. Staring at the door, Amanda rolled her eyes and lay back on the couch. *He's gonna get me a phone.*

CHAPTER THIRTY-TWO

One week later

Johnny walked down the spiral staircase in the old church and half-watched two kids who couldn't have been older than ten race past him up the stairs. The other half of him focused on finishing his last text to Amanda after she'd asked if she could take the airboat out for a spin.

Don't forget to tie it up when you're done.

He slipped his phone into his pocket and headed down the hall once he'd reached the basement. *Okay, fine. Gettin' the kid a phone was a good idea.*

"You know where we're going, Johnny?" Rex asked and sniffed along the floor beside the wall as the folks talking in the hallway backed away from the dwarf and his hounds.

"Hey, mister." A woman wrapped tightly in a baggy shawl stared at the coonhounds and shook her finger at him. "No dogs allowed down here. Those are the rules."

Luther whipped his head up to sniff at the edge of her shawl, which she jerked away from him with a humph of disapproval. He sneezed and shook his head. "Yeesh. You'd think if they had rules about dogs, Johnny, they'd have rules about showering."

"Not allowed!" she shouted.

A door opened quickly on the right up ahead, and a man with shaggy gray hair in an oversized sweater stepped into the hall. "It's all right, Kiki. They're guests for the day. Dogs and all."

The woman frowned at Johnny, then sidled down the hall and jerked her shawl even tighter around her.

"You the doc?" Johnny asked as he approached the man. *Looks more like a hippie on the run than a doctor.*

"Leahy." The man nodded and shook his hand with a small, tight smile. "Thank you for coming out on such short notice."

"Well, you caught my attention, Doc. That's sayin' somethin'."

"So I've heard." Leahy eyed the hounds. "Those dogs housebroken?"

"They do fine. And they stay with me."

"Of course. Come on in." The gray-haired man held the door open and gestured for him to step inside.

"Johnny, there's some serious smell coming out of that room," Rex muttered.

"Yeah, were you supposed to be at a solo meeting?"

He snapped his fingers and both hounds fell in line behind him to enter the office. The doc shut the door behind him and pointed across the cluttered room scattered with books and loose papers. "Please have a seat, Mr. Walker, and I'll make a few introductions."

"Naw, just Johnny." The dwarf headed toward the third metal folding chair in front of the cluttered yellow desk in the back.

Standing behind the other chairs were Doc Leahy's two other guests. The first was a huge, muscular man in a duster and boots, his hair closely cropped and his expressionless face covered in layers of what looked like oddly shaped scars. The second was a Jasper Elf with dark hair cut just above her shoulders. Both of them studied him with appraising glances, and the woman raised an eyebrow at the hounds sniffing around the sunken couch at the side of the room.

"This is James Brownstone," Doc Leahy said and gestured toward the large man as he took his place behind his desk.

"Woah." Johnny studied him as he paused at the third chair. "I'm guessin' you ain't the kinda fella hears, 'Hey there, handsome' all that much, huh?"

The muscular man nodded brusquely at the knife hanging from Johnny's belt. "I'm guessing you're the kinda guy who carries a blade like that around tryin' to compensate for something."

"Yeah. Like a bigger knife."

"Tell him what you brought in the car, Johnny," Rex muttered.

"Bozo has no idea who he's messing with," Luther added.

The dwarf snapped his fingers again, narrowed his eyes at the man, and raised an index finger. Both hounds sat and shut up.

The Jasper Elf folded her arms over her dark jacket and frowned. "The doc called a meeting, not a pissing contest. You guys can compare knife sizes later."

Doc Leahy cleared his throat, and all three of them turned to look at him. "Leira Berens. And Johnny Walker. Now you know each other and I want to thank you all for agreeing to meet me here. Have a seat."

His guests all sat at once, and Johnny sniffed. *Already off to a fine start.*

"So I'll get straight to the point." The doc nodded at Leira and sat behind the desk. "We have something of a minor problem in LA. Beneath it, to be more precise—a fairly large community of wayward minors living beneath the city, all of them magicals. A few prefer to keep to themselves, staying under the radar and out of trouble. But the majority of these kids have a knack for causing trouble. Now they're not the worst we've seen around here, but I can't help thinking that if we could find some way to provide them with a little direction—more of a purpose beyond scrounging beneath the city for their survival—we'd be doing both them and LA's streets an invaluable favor."

"I don't see why you called us in for a couple of kids," Brownstone muttered.

"It's rather more than a couple, Mr. Brownstone. At the last count I received—and it was only an estimate, mind you—there were close to a hundred."

"I reckon you already know what I do," Johnny added and squinted at him. "But I ain't seein' the connection either."

Doc Leahy gave Leira a knowing glance, then nodded. "I called the department's Level-Six bounty hunters together because I'm hoping the three of you can help."

The dwarf snorted. "In my experience, doc, magical kids runnin' 'round on their own with no supervision ain't exactly keen on bein' rounded up and brought in as a bounty."

The other two visitors both gave him calculating glances.

"There's no bounty on their heads, Mr—" Doc Leahy inclined his head. "Johnny. I merely hope to open an avenue to offer these kids a little more...structured guidance, if you will."

"Why not send them to my grandmother's school?" Leira suggested.

"Ah. The School of Necessary Magic is an excellent institution, yes. But as I'm sure you can imagine, these young magicals beneath the city don't exactly have the kind of background and life experience to qualify them for enrollment. They're smart enough, yes, but rough around the edges. With a certain aversion to authority, if you catch my drift."

Like us. Johnny cast the other two bounty hunters a sidelong glance.

"It's understandable," Doc Leahy continued, "but not exactly suitable for an already established school. Not to mention the fact that the School of Necessary Magic most likely can't support an influx of a hundred magical kids all needing a little...extra attention."

"Why are we here, doc?" The Jasper Elf folded her arms.

"All three of you have had experience raising children," the man said and slid his hands onto the desk. "And I've heard a thing or two about the Bounty Hunter Department running a little short these days on available bounty hunters."

"Who told you that?" Johnny asked.

"My sources. Which have also expressed to me that these kids, generally speaking, have what it takes to follow in a bounty hunter's footsteps. With the right discipline, of course. And that's where I believe the three of you would be particularly useful."

The office fell silent.

Damn, Doc.

Johnny scratched the side of his face. "You ain't gonna come on out and say it, are you?"

Leahy raised his eyebrows. "Say what?"

"You want us to start a damn Quantico for magical kids with no roots and turn 'em into baby bounty hunters."

Brownstone grunted. Leira turned wide eyes onto the doc.

He gestured with a wide smile. "It's an excellent suggestion, Johnny."

A knock came at the door, which then opened to reveal a thin man in overalls who peeked into the room. "Sorry to interrupt, Doc. We have a live one just came in. You mind takin' a look?"

"Sure. Thanks, Leo." The man stood and nodded at the bounty hunters in his office. "Excuse me. Never a dull moment here, but I shouldn't be too long."

When he left and closed the door behind him, Johnny, Leira, and James stared at different points of the desk, and the room filled with a thick silence.

The dwarf's phone buzzed and he pulled it out to see another text from Amanda.

Can I take the big gun with me?

He snorted and texted back quickly.

No.

"Are we holding you up from some other important meeting?" Brownstone asked.

Johnny slid his phone into his pocket. "It's my kid—ward, actually. But she might as well be mine."

"That's a big undertaking," Leira commented.

"One way to put it, yeah." He sniffed. "Both of y'all got kids too, huh?"

They both responded with noncommittal nods.

Yeah, and I reckon kids of other Level-Six bounty hunters ain't exactly the type to listen and follow rules left and right, either.

"What's her name?" Leira asked.

"Amanda. Smart kid. Shifter. Little rough around the edges too, like the doc was sayin'. But she's gettin' better. I just ain't got the time to give her what she needs right now. Beyond the necessaries, mind."

Brownstone raised and lowered his eyebrows. "Sounds like she'd fit right in with these LA hoodlums underground."

He snorted. "Yeah, she'd have a time. Call it all in good fun."

"That was an interesting way to put it." Leira shrugged. "Quantico for magical kids."

"But to be bounty hunters?" Johnny shook his head. "That road ain't for everyone, and from the looks of ya, y'all know exactly what I'm sayin'."

The large man leaned back in the folding metal chair, which groaned beneath his weight. "It worked fine for us."

"It might be the only thing that works for us," Leira added.

"Y'all are serious?" He glanced from one to the other. "You gonna entertain this hippie doc's idea?"

The woman smiled. "It's not the worst suggestion he's made."

"I'm sure the feds would take your ward if you wanted her off your hands," the other man muttered.

He narrowed his eyes at him. *Mr. Funny Guy over here, huh?* "I didn't say I wanted her off my hands. And I don't trust the feds half as far as I can throw 'em."

The others both smirked and nodded.

They know exactly what I mean.

"But if you had a say in a new school…" Leira shrugged. "Bounty hunter school or whatever, would you feel safer placing Amanda there?"

The dwarf frowned and rubbed his mouth. "Depends on how far away from home she was."

"And where's home for you?"

"The Everglades." Merely saying it brought a tiny smile to his lips. "Home to the kid now too."

"Huh." Brownstone cocked his head and searched the stuffed shelves of Doc Leahy's office. "Considerable open land in the middle of nowhere down there."

"Sure is." He nodded slowly. "I own a good deal of it."

The other bounty hunters studied him with renewed interest. "Big enough to build a training base and keep it out of the public eye?" Leira asked.

"Forget the public eye," the man added. "It'd have to be big enough and hidden enough to keep the department's greedy little hands out of it."

Johnny smirked. *He likes the Bureau as much as I do.*

"Sure. More than enough room for a hundred kids, a few bounty hunter drill sergeants, and completely off the radar."

Brownstone nodded. "I've never been to the Everglades."

"Best place on two worlds," he said.

Leira looked thoughtful. "It sounds like a horde of magical kids might feel the same way. Including your Amanda."

"Yep." Johnny sniffed and glanced from one to the other. "So we're entertainin' this, then?"

"With a few extra bugs to work out," she said with a crooked smile. "But sure."

Brownstone shrugged. "Sounds simple to me. Exactly the way I like it."

One day, they're going to learn to leave this dwarf alone. Apparently it's not today. Join Johnny, Lisa, Amanda and the coonhounds on their next adventure in *ALL DWARF'ED UP!*

The story continues in book 3, *All Dwarf'ed Up*, coming in December.

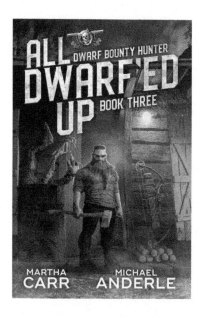

Pre-order today to have your copy delivered at midnight on December 6, 2020!

Get sneak peeks, exclusive giveaways, behind the scenes content, and more. PLUS you'll be notified of special **one day only fan pricing** on new releases.

Sign up today to get free stories.

Visit: https://marthacarr.com/read-free-stories/

There's a unique writer's challenge that happens every November known as NaNoWriMo or National Novel Writing Month. Writers attempt to write a fifty thousand word novel from the first of the month and stop on the last day. The popular novel, *Water for Elephants* was the product of a NaNoWriMo challenge and was even turned into a movie.

I remember when I thought that writing a novel in a month was impossible. Now, I do it every month and then some. The turnaround turned out to be a product of using some good software to help with an outline and changing my mindset.

That last part was really key.

It's so easy to look around at what others are doing, or not doing and decide based on that alone what I'll be able to do.

That's called contempt ahead of information. I make up my mind, and worse, make decisions based on observation rather than actual data. I could even make it look like I was collecting info by surveying friends' opinions and arguing with myself, but none of those were sources.

It's amazing how often I've had arguments with myself and

come to a conclusion without noticing I was the only one in the conversation.

Accurate information from several angles would require asking questions of professionals, trying a few ideas and struggling through what doesn't work to get to the other side. It turns out that it also takes courage because I can't know how things will work out. No control mixed with a good dose of trust.

Boy, was that not my specialty in the past.

I was so tied to a particular outcome and so afraid it might not happen that I barreled forward without doing the groundwork. A good idea might have actually worked if I'd taken the time and done the footwork and had some patience.

Fortunately, I wore myself out and became willing to try a different way. I stopped trying to control everything and started listening. Turns out a lot of people thought I was capable of writing a book in a month and for some reason I listened and gave it a try. That was the start of the Leira Chronicles just three years ago.

Yeah, it surprised me too. It also made me wonder what else I could do if I just let go of deciding what I could do before I even tried. Turns out listening as if my mind could be changed could really add up to positive change and a lot of books. And even better, a bigger life.

Another weird twist – it took just as much courage to walk into that bigger life. More adventures to follow.

First, thank you for not only reading this book but these *Author Notes* as well!

The year is almost done. For us here in America, the final day of voting is tomorrow (Nov 3), and then we get to deal with the fallout.

Hopefully there won't be any more political phone calls. The ONLY person I know who lives in the state of Florida is Steve Campbell. However, I get calls from Florida (not from Steve) daily to as many as five? Seven?

All I know is TOO MANY.

I've voted. I'm done. I got a call just five minutes ago from Florida, and without thinking too hard, I picked it up.

My mistake.

On the other end was silence. I thought I could hang up, but then a pensive voice called, "Hello?"

<Inward cursing.>

"Yes, hello? This is Mike, how can I help you?" Slight pause on my side then, "If this is a political call, I have already voted, thank you."

"Uh…thank you?"

"Bye!"

I'm not really sure what the person was responding to. The question of whether this was a politically based call or saying thank you for voting. Either way, I was off the phone and getting prepped to write this author note, and now I had a subject.

Presently, I live right outside of Las Vegas, Nevada, almost the length of our country away from Florida, and I have no idea which side or for what agenda the phone call was being made.

I'm just glad to be free, both living in a free country and presently free of any obligation to talk to a soul about voting because I'm done.

This is the first time I can ever remember voting early. Just for the ability to tell political phone callers, "My vote has been cast," and then hang up means I think I'll vote early again next time.

I hope YOUR end of 2020 is fantastic and enjoyable!

There is an old commercial series where the punchline is "We'll leave the lights on for ya." (Motel 6).

Here at LMBPN, just know if you need to get away from life for a few hours, "We will publish another book this week (or six) for ya."

;-)

Ad Aeternitatem,

Michael Anderle

Solve a murder, save her mother, and stop the apocalypse?

What would you do when elves ask you to investigate a prince's murder and you didn't even know elves, or magic, was real?

Meet Leira Berens, Austin homicide detective who's good at what she does – track down the bad guys and lock them away.

Which is why the elves want her to solve this murder – fast. It's not just about tracking down the killer and bringing them to justice. It's about saving the world!

If you're looking for a heroine who prefers fighting to flirting, check out The Leira Chronicles today!

<u>AVAILABLE ON AMAZON AND IN KINDLE UNLIMITED!</u>

CONNECT WITH THE AUTHORS

Martha Carr Social
Website:
http://www.marthacarr.com
Facebook:
https://www.facebook.com/groups/MarthaCarrFans/

Michael Anderle Social
Website:
http://www.lmbpn.com
Email List:
http://lmbpn.com/email/
Facebook:
https://www.facebook.com/LMBPNPublishing

ALSO BY MARTHA CARR

Other series in the Oriceran Universe:

THE LEIRA CHRONICLES

THE FAIRHAVEN CHRONICLES

MIDWEST MAGIC CHRONICLES

SOUL STONE MAGE

THE KACY CHRONICLES

THE DANIEL CODEX SERIES

I FEAR NO EVIL

SCHOOL OF NECESSARY MAGIC

THE UNBELIEVABLE MR. BROWNSTONE

SCHOOL OF NECESSARY MAGIC: RAINE CAMPBELL

ALISON BROWNSTONE

FEDERAL AGENTS OF MAGIC

SCIONS OF MAGIC

Series in The Terranavis Universe:

The Adventures of Maggie Parker Series

The Witches of Pressler Street

The Adventures of Finnegan Dragonbender

OTHER BOOKS BY JUDITH BERENS

OTHER BOOKS BY MARTHA CARR

JOIN MARTHA CARR'S FAN GROUP ON FACEBOOK!

Made in the USA
Monee, IL
24 February 2022

91753027R00174